Also by John Schork:

Destiny in the Pacific

The Flames of Deliverance

The Jack Stewart Trilogy:

The King's Commander
A Journey of Honor
The Falkenberg Riddle

The Winds of Battle
The Journey of James Addington

John Schork

The Deadly Sky

First edition: February 2013
This book is an original publication of
Jupiter Pixel Publishing, Jupiter, Florida

CONTENTS

The Death of the Ball Turret Gunner

From my mother's sleep I fell into the State,
And I hunched in its belly till my wet fur froze.
Six miles from earth, loosed from its dream of life,
I woke to black flak and the nightmare fighters.
When I died they washed me out of the turret with a
hose.

-- Randall Jarrell

The Eighth Air Force suffered half of all USAAF casualties during the Second World War in all theaters of operations. Over 26,000 airmen were killed in the battle for Europe.

From 1939 to 1945, the German Luftwaffe lost over 320,000 men, killed or missing in all theaters of the war.

Prologue

RAF Paddington
Suffolk, East Anglia
June, 1943

Standing on the windswept concrete parking ramp, the pilot stared at what remained of the aircraft's nose compartment. The Plexiglas had been shattered by German cannon shells over Mannheim. Inside the wrecked fuselage, two army medics worked to remove the bodies of the bombardier and navigator. A small group of ground crew and several fliers watched quietly as the first body was lowered to the ground.

Sean McGowan had landed the damaged B-17 ten minutes earlier, completing the crew's twenty fifth mission. They would now rotate home. Everyone except First Lieutenant Jimmy Duggin and Captain Max Atterberry. The crew had been together for almost a year in training and flying the first combat missions of the Eighth Air Force. Now McGowan stared at his friend's bodies, covered with blankets, hiding the hideous wounds that exploding cannon shells had inflicted on the two young men. He had seen too much death over the last two years, but this was different. Jimmy and Max had been as close as brothers, now they were gone, torn bodies about to be loaded into "the meat wagon," their names removed from rosters and soon forgotten. Someone would pack up their trunks and he would write the letters home. And that was it. He felt anger, deep anger and a sense of futility.

Major Sean McGowan was twenty-nine years old, but the last six months had aged him and the strain in his face was evident in the pale blue eyes and grim set of his mouth.

"Come on skipper."

He turned to see his co-pilot, Dean Hall.

"We can't do anything here, we need to go to debriefing."

Looking up at the aircraft he saw blood dripping from one of the cannon holes.

"Screw the debrief, I need a drink."

Chapter One

"There they are," a man called, shielding his eyes from the glare of the afternoon English sun.

Across the grass, which stretched from the control tower to the nearest runway, men turned to search the sky almost in unison. At first, no one said anything, and then they began to count the small black dots that were now clearly aircraft.

"General, we can see them."

Major General Ira Eaker looked up from a message board.

"Thank you, Sean."

The general and his senior aide, Major Sean McGowan, walked out onto the second-story deck of the control tower at RAF Paddington. McGowan was a tall, well-built man with close cropped brown hair who looked natural in a flight jacket.

The steel railing was lined by men with raised binoculars. That morning, thirty B-17F bombers had departed their base in East Anglia to bomb the railroad marshaling yard in Stuttgart, Germany. The only question on the mind of every man at Paddington now was how many would return?

The Eighth Army Air Force had been conducting offensive operations against the continent since mid-1942, over a year ago. Flying against the Luftwaffe in daylight, often without fighter escort, the squadrons of the Eighth had suffered terrible losses. General Eaker and his staff continued to struggle with the viability of daylight bombing. Whether they would be able to complete their attack plan or arrive at the same conclusion as the Royal Air Force, that only bomber raids at night were survivable, had not been decided. But high-altitude bombing at night was notoriously inaccurate. What was the correct priority, accurate bombing or survival of your aircrews? It wasn't a decision that was coming easily to the Americans.

Sean McGowan counted to himself as the aircraft closed on Paddington. He could see at least twenty, with more certainly following. As Eaker's senior aide, McGowan accompanied the general to the briefing early this morning. It had been a bittersweet journey for him. While he'd been able to see his closest friend, Major Todd Smith, a squadron commander in the 23rd Bomb Group, he was attending the briefing as a "ground pounder" or "staff puke," not a combat aviator.

Todd had been gracious and welcoming, but it had been clear to Sean that the pressure of preparing for a combat mission had prompted a quick handshake and ..."Better get going, see you later."

The first bombers were now approaching the field boundary, their big radial engines filling the air with a roar that never failed to draw the attention of the surrounding countryside. However, the people watching the olive-drab aircraft return had spent their day going about their routine business, not fighting for their lives in the skies over Europe.

At 2,500 feet overhead the field, the lead aircraft began a slow left turn to enter the landing circuit. Sean could see the orange tips of the group's vertical stabilizers, each emblazoned with a large "E." Following in order, the fortresses turned down wind, each pulling power and beginning a decent to 800 feet while lowering flaps and landing gear.

Across the ramp, two red fire trucks moved from their hard stands out to positions near the runway. Mechanics and plane captains headed toward their individual parking areas on foot and in jeeps to receive the aircraft.

"Damn," Eaker said as he watched a bright red flare arc from the lead aircraft, now on final for landing. "Bloch's got wounded aboard". Immediately an olive-drab ambulance started its engine and moved out toward the runway.

Sean watched the wing commander, Colonel Paul Bloch, touch down, small puffs of smoke appearing behind each main mount of his B-17. Putting himself in the cockpit, he unconsciously thought through slowing down the bomber as he had so many times during the past. He remembered the natural relaxation he always felt when clearing the runway, mission complete and bringing his crew home safe again. However, his thoughts returned to his last mission.

A another flare rose high above the second bomber indicating more wounded. Sean looked at Eaker, who now stood alone, everyone on the deck respecting his privacy. The general's hands were gripping the upper steel rail, his eyes riveted on the bombers as a flare streaked up from the third aircraft.

"Damn."

"Sir?"

Sean turned to see a sergeant, who saluted and reported.

"Seven missing, sir. One landed at Exmouth on two engines."

"Thank you," he said stiffly, returning the man's salute.

Sighing, he moved to the general's side.

"Initial report, sir. One aircraft landed at Exmouth. There are still seven missing."

Eaker said nothing, just nodded.

The number burned into Sean. Seven aircraft missing. Seventy men possibly not returning. Seventy men the Eighth Air Force couldn't afford to lose, seventy men who would never make it to twenty five missions and go home. Seven bombers missing from thirty dispatched. The Army Air Force couldn't continue to take losses like that or the Eighth would run out of aircraft or mutiny.

One bomber after another, the procession continued, over half of the forts signaling wounded on board. On deck, the squeal of brakes echoed over the tarmac and exhaust from the idling engines blew across the field as aircraft taxied in to shut down. Around the operations area of Paddington, a flurry of activity was now taking place on the aircraft as propellers wound to a stop.

An ambulance sped away from the leader's aircraft, a siren signaling the urgency of their run. Sean thought it ironic that the siren meant someone might live, while an ambulance quietly returning from an aircraft often meant it carried only bodies.

Borrowing a set of binoculars, Sean searched the final group of four aircraft approaching the field. He spotted Todd's aircraft as the big fort began its left turn to downwind and Sean could see the number three engine was feathered, smoke trailing from the nacelle. He searched with the binoculars as the aircraft descended to pattern altitude. The starboard wing appeared to have major damage inboard of the engine, probably inflicted by Luftwaffe cannon shells. The B-17 was a tough bird, but if the main spar in the wing breaks, the wing comes off, simple as that. There was nothing he could do to help his friend. It was in God's hand's now.

"I'll want to get the initial debrief sheets before we go into the wrap up, Sean."

McGowan said, "Yes, sir."

6

The general moved toward the stairs on his way to the briefing hut.

Realizing his aide was watching the pattern, he said, "I'll meet you there."

Sean turned to watch Todd roll onto his final approach, the inevitable flare shooting upward from the aft fuselage.

McGowan had been there before himself, trying to land a crippled aircraft with wounded men aboard, the entire mission coming down to one desperate attempt to get the big bomber on deck without crashing.

The main landing gear appeared down and locked. Come on, he thought, just set her down. Watching the final moments before touchdown, he knew that power was coming off as Todd flared the big bomber, setting the landing attitude. Too much, Sean thought, watch the sink rate, his mind screamed, knowing Todd was losing the battle.

As the fortress slammed down, Sean watched in horror as the starboard landing gear folded, the right wing slamming hard into the concrete. In an instant the number four propeller tore itself apart on the runway.

Slewing right, the damaged wing began to separate from the fuselage as the aircraft slid down the runway, bright flames erupting from the stricken bomber. The wail of the crash alarm was joined by the scream of the fire truck sirens as they both began to roll toward the stricken bomber.

Sliding to a stop, the flames rolled forward over the cockpit for a moment, and then the air was shattered by a massive explosion as the aircraft was violently torn apart in one sickening instant.

Chapter Two

"General, I have a personal request."

Eaker turned from the window overlooking his headquarters courtyard to face McGowan.

"Sir, I'm requesting a return to operational flying."

The older man walked over to his desk and sat down.

"What brought this on?"

He's probably expecting me to tell him Todd Smith's death, he thought. But it's more than that.

"Sir, if we're at war, I belong in the air."

"Have you been looking in the mirror and feeling guilty?" the general asked.

"Something like that, general."

"I understand, rest assured of that, major. I've had too much mirror time lately myself, and I don't like who I see."

"Sir?" Sean and the general had developed a close and informal relationship, the aide's seniority and his experience being very different from most junior staff officers.

"We lost a hundred and sixty two men yesterday, dead or missing. The Brits think we're crazy to continue daylight bombing. But every day I sign the op order, and more men go out and die. I understand command, but that doesn't make it any easier. Now

8

you want to go back out there. You and I both know the odds."

Sean saw the fatigue in Eaker's eyes. Was he trying to desert one of the best men and officers whom he'd ever known, just when the general needed all the support he could?

"Yes, sir."

"You know, Sean, I'd trade places with you right now if I could. Let me go out and worry about one crew or one squadron and forget the bigger problem."

"Yes, sir."

"But that's not to be, and so I'll have to get some reward from watching you go back to war."

"Sir?"

Before we left Paddington, Paul Bloch told me he needed an experienced squadron commander to replace Major Smith. I had already decided it would be you."

"All right, everyone out."

The engine of the two and a half ton truck stopped as men in rumpled class "A" uniforms began to jump down from the covered bed.

"Grab your duffel bags and follow me," a tall, skinny sergeant called to the soldiers who were grabbing olive-drab canvas bags from a smaller truck.

"Where's the chow hall," a deep voice called from the group.

"Chow hall secured twenty minutes ago, let's go."

"That's not what I asked, sergeant. I asked where the chow hall was. And it's common courtesy to introduce yourself."

The skinny man pushed through the group, the expression on his face a mixture of surprise and anger. He began to speak then stopped abruptly. Standing in front of him was a huge master sergeant who looked like he had just stepped off a recruiting poster.

Master Sergeant Billy Hass stood six four and weighed in at 220 pounds, with not an ounce of fat on his frame. The dimple in his army issue tie was exactly centered on his collar. While the rest of the men looked like they had slept in their uniforms, his greens appeared crisply pressed, the creases of his trousers ending above highly polished shoes.

"S…sorry, sarge…I mean master sergeant. But they really are closed."

"And your name is?"

"Oh, sorry, Wilson, Sergeant Tommy Wilson, master sergeant."

"Sergeant Wilson, my name is Hass, Master Sergeant Hass. Now, our gear will remain here until we get these men fed. By the time we're done at the mess hall, you should have the billeting all worked out, don't you think?"

"Uh, yes, sir."

Hass glared at any man who dared to call him "sir."

"I mean, yes, master sergeant."

"Now, where's the mess hall?"

Colonel Paul Bloch laughed when his supply officer told him about a pushy master sergeant who had turned out the duty cook and had a late noon mean prepared for a group of newly arrived aircrew. The disruption to the afternoon routine would impact the cleaning and preparation for the evening meal. If the group commander wanted to provide good food for his men, they must obey the rules set down for scheduled meal hours.

"Murph, the pushy master sergeant you are talking about is Billy Hass. He's a legend in the air corps." Bloch chuckled again and said to himself, "I wondered how he would announce his arrival." He turned back to the red-faced major. "Don't get your tie in a knot, Murph. You're not going to change Billy Hass and in my experience, he's right most of the time. Go fight a battle you can win."

Bloch had requested Master Sergeant Hass's assignment to the 23rd Bomb Group for a very specific reason. His group was struggling from a lack of leadership in the senior non-commissioned officer ranks. A fluke of assignment loaded him up with a number of weak first and technical sergeants. That lack of leadership had been reflected in the poor operational readiness of his aircraft and the below average performance in the air.

He had known Hass since they had both served together at Rockwell in the mid-1930's. Bloch had been a squadron executive officer and Hass a young sergeant who had just put on his stripes. They had formed a mutual respect for each other, and the squadron had benefited from the "enlightened" leadership of the feisty sergeant. Now he hoped the 23rd Heavy Bomb Group would fare the same.

"Philby, go find Master Sergeant Hass and ask him to see me when he gets settled."

"Find an empty bunk and get your gear stored."

Sergeant Wilson had collected the group of newly arrived soldiers after a short but substantial meal hastily arranged by Staff Sergeant Chenoweth at the urging of Master Sergeant Hass. Chenoweth had been around the air corps long enough to have heard of Hass.

The men were standing at the door of a single-story wooden building that had clearly been recently erected, with little care shown for either the aesthetics or functionality.

"Master sergeant, your billet is down about three blocks."

Hass turned to Wilson and glared.

11

"Why would that be, sergeant?"

"Well, the senior NCO's have taken over one of the original buildings. It's pretty cushy."

"Before we go anywhere, sergeant, I want to take a look at where these men will be billeted."

Thirty minutes later, Hass and Wilson arrived at the two-story brick barracks that were adorned with a sign which said, "Senior Non-Commissioned Officer's Quarters, 23rd Bomb Group." Wilson was confused. Master Sergeant Hass had left all of his gear at the junior enlisted barracks.

"Who's the top dog around here, Wilson."

"That would be Master Sergeant Higgins. He's the senior enlisted maintenance supervisor."

"Where would I find him?" Common sense told Hass that the head maintainer would be down at the flight line right after the noon meal.

"I believe he's in the barracks."

"Then show me the way, sergeant."

Master Sergeant Lucius Higgins was pouring a cup of coffee from the small percolator that he returned to the hot plate. A rough looking man, he was heavy in the midsection, his uniform shirt partially unbuttoned to accommodate his bulging stomach.

"What's this?" The chunky man turned as the door opened.

"Are you Master Sergeant Higgins?"

The man's eyes narrowed as he took in Hass standing in the doorway.

"If you took the time to read the sign, you might be able to figure that out, Mack."

Hass walked up and stopped six inches in front of Higgins. Without taking his eyes from Higgins, he said. "Close the door, Sergeant Wilson."

The sergeant quickly shut the door as he backed out of the room.

"My name is Hass. I just came from the pig sty that someone around here is trying to call enlisted billeting. When is the last time you inspected that building?"

"And just who in the fuck do you think you are?"

"I'm a master sergeant who happens to give a damn about the health and welfare of his men. And if you're the senior NCO of this bomb group, you should be horsewhipped for letting your men live under those conditions."

Hass's vehemence took Higgins by surprise, and his only response was to glare back at his accuser.

There was a knock on the door.

"Enter," Hass bellowed.

A corporal stood at the door looking curious.

"Are you Master Sergeant Hass?"

"I am."

"Colonel Bloch would like to see you when you get settled, master sergeant."

Higgins's eyes widened, but he remained quiet.

Hass looked at Higgins's unbuttoned shirt and protruding gut, then said, "Now is as good a time as any."

"Damn it, Fortino, you want to spend this entire war in the stockade?"

Private Anthony Michael Fortino opened his eyes slowly. One side of his face was bruised, and several cuts showed through the stubble on his jaw. A wiry kid, he was short, only five foot eight but strong as an ox. His size had resulted in his assignment as a belly turret gunner.

"Yeah, I think I do. Ain't no German fighters in the stockade."

"Get on your feet, asshole, the lieutenant wants to see you."

Lieutenant Peter Allen, the assistant group adjutant looked up after reading the incident report filed by the military police after a fight outside the enlisted club the night before.

"So what happened?"

"Sir, Auferio and me were just having a few beers and these two jerks from the armory made some smart remarks about 'wops' which pissed me off."

"So you end up throwing punches?"

"No sir, the big fat one swung first. I was just defending myself."

"According to this report, the other two got the worst of it."

"I'm from Jersey, lieutenant. We learn how to fight early."

"Well you're lucky that a sergeant from transportation saw the first punch, so you're off the hook for now. But I don't want to see you in trouble again, understand?

"Yes, sir."

"Fortino, you're one of the best gunners in the group, the only one with two confirmed kills. You could be a sergeant if you'd just keep your nose clean."

The young flier stared back at the lieutenant, then said, "I don't wanna be a sergeant. Just fly my missions and go home."

Allen shook his head.

"Just fly my missions and go home, SIR!"

Fucking ground pounder, he thought. I hate these assholes.

"Just fly my missions and go home, sir."

"Dismissed, private."

Master Sergeant Hass came to attention and saluted.

"Reporting as ordered, sir."

Paul Bloch had already come around the desk and extended his hand. The wing commander was a stocky man with a pleasant face and thinning hair.

"Welcome to Paddington, master sergeant, sit down."

"Thanks, skipper."

Bloch poured a cup of coffee into a white ceramic mug and handed it to Hass.

"Black?"

"That's fine."

Sitting down behind his desk, the group commander smiled at Hass.

"You sure pissed off my supply officer."

"Nothing compared to some fat master sergeant I ran into in the barrack."

"Higgins?"

Hass nodded.

"Told him the junior enlisted barracks was a shit hole and he didn't seem to take my criticism well."

Bloch's expression changed.

"That's why you're here, Billy. I have some of the weakest senior NCO's I've ever run across. They're not trying to screw things up, they just don't know how to get things done. I need you to take over as top dog and get them squared away."

"You've been here for what, six weeks? What's the problem?"

"I've got two average squadron commanders. My best one was just killed trying to bring in a damaged fort. You met the senior maintenance supervisor. Aircraft availability is mediocre at best. We have the highest mission abort rate in theater, and a lot of those are repeat gripes. Airborne we're getting to the targets, but our bombing is weak.

15

"The group commander before you, Scoggins? What's the story on him?"

"He worked them up stateside and brought the group overseas. I didn't know him, heard he was all right. A German cannon shell got him over Wilhelmshaven."

"So they need a little ass kicking and back slapping," Hass said finishing his coffee."

"And that's why I asked for you. There's no doubt that you can do both." Bloch paused and took a sip of his coffee. "But there's something you need to know. I'm bringing in a replacement squadron commander who might be a problem for you."

Hass looked up, his expression curious.

"Sean McGowan."

The master sergeant's expression turned to hostility as he leaned forward and said, "You know what I think of him."

"That was a long time ago. He's still one of the most experienced Fort pilots in theater. He's also a hell of a leader and I don't have to tell you that, either."

"So I just forget about my brother?"

"For the good of the group, yes, damn it. I don't need you to kiss and make up, but I need both of you to do what I know you can do with people and aircraft."

Hass sat for a long minute then stood up.

"All right, I'll do it, your rules, but I have one condition."

Paul Bloch knew that master sergeants don't normally lay down conditions to full colonels, but Billy Hass was his friend.

"If I can."

"I stay on flying status."

Paul Bloch had expected that Hass, a fully qualified flight engineer, would take over the ground effort while McGowan would be his key man in the air. In addition, the master sergeant had completed twenty

16

missions with the 507th at Archbury. What Bloch didn't need was for his newest master sergeant to get shot down on a combat mission, leaving him right back where he started. However, he owed Billy Hass more than just loyalty. The big man had saved their lives on a training mission over Arizona in a B-12.

"Done. Just don't get your ass shot down."

"And I need Larry Weller in here as the maintenance chief."

"I'll see what I can do. Anything else?"

A slight smile broke on Billy's face.

"I'll be sure to let you know."

MEMORANDUM FROM THE GROUP COMMANDER

3 August, 1943

Effective immediately, each barracks on station will have two senior NCO's assigned and billeted as NCO's in charge of quarters.

/s/ Paul Bloch, Colonel, USAAF

Chapter Three

Damn, this thing even smells new, Sean thought as he taxied toward the duty runway. Freshly delivered from the states, B-17F serial number 43-0938 seemed like a frisky horse waiting to start a race. Sean had noticed that the only marking so far on the bomber was the orange tip on the vertical stab and a large black "E" superimposed over the orange. He remembered seeing the same markings on the day that Todd had died, but pushed the memory out of his mind. That was in the past and meant to be forgotten or at least put somewhere you couldn't think about it.

Sitting beside McGowan in the co-pilot's seat was Captain Mike Sullivan, the 407th Heavy Bombardment Squadron's most experienced combat aviator. While it was just a formality, Paul Bloch had to certify that Sean was competent to handle the B-17. Sullivan had been assigned the task of checking out the new commanding officer in the Fortress. Mike Sullivan not only had over 1600 hours in the B-17, but he also had completed twenty two combat missions with the 23rd. Both men expected the flight to be a routine flight check and the atmosphere in the cockpit was relaxed.

"Tower's pretty sharp, they keep the pattern under control and take charge if there's a problem."

Sean glanced over to the three-story concrete structure where the tower controllers watched the goings and comings at Paddington. Today the field was practically deserted, the group having departed on a mission almost three hours prior. McGowan wanted to get his up check so he could fly on tomorrow's mission.

"How does Bloch assign mission leads?"

"The old man leads from the front. He flies on probably three-quarters of the missions. If he's in the air, he has the squadron commanders lead each squadron element. When he's not leading, the group lead rotates between the squadron CO's."

Sean had crossed paths with Paul Bloch in the pre-war years, but never served with him. He knew he had the reputation as a no nonsense leader and solid aviator. Their meeting this morning had been short and to the point.

"You're here because I need a strong leader to replace Todd Smith in the 407th. Tom Russell is in command of the 409th and John Hodges has the 410th. Both are both solid aviators, but frankly they lack experience. In time they'll both be good. But I need stronger leadership right now, on the ground and in the air. If the 23rd Bomb Group's going to carry its load in this war, I need you to help me whip them into shape. Effective immediately, you're the commanding officer of the 407th Heavy Bombardment Squadron. But as far as I'm concerned you're my assistant wing commander. You and I will alternate leading the group until it reaches what I think is acceptable performance. You with me?"

McGowan looked across the desk and nodded.

"Yes, sir."

"Also you need to know I just had Master Sergeant Hass assigned here from Archbury. We've got some issues with maintenance reliability and I asked him to fix it."

Sean's thoughts flashed to Robin Hass and that terrible day four years ago. It was something that McGowan would carry with him for the rest of his life. He had made a decision and a man died. That was the way of war, but it had been peace time.

"I know there's bad blood between you two, but I need both of you to help me get this group where it needs to go."
"Yes, sir."

He turned the Fortress into the hold short area and brought her to a stop.
With a second nature from his hours in the B-17, Sean checked the sliding windows closed, adjusted the throttle friction, noted the cowl flaps open.
"All set?"
Mike Sullivan nodded and keyed the radio, "Tower, Ripsaw 938 holding short for takeoff."
Immediate clearance came back and Sean taxied onto the runway, lining up with the centerline.
"Tail wheel locked, light out, gyros?"
Sean set the directional gyro to correspond with the magnetic compass. "Gyros set." He paused for a moment and looked at Sullivan. "Ripsaw? What a great squadron call sign."
The copilot smiled, "Used to be cupcake, but Todd Smith changed it."
Pushing the throttles forward, Sean said, "Good for him. Rolling at time 34."
Slowly, then with increasing speed, the light loaded B-17 accelerated to 115 knots and Sean eased the control wheel back, the bomber smoothly lifting off.
Every time was still a thrill, Sean thought. "Gear up."
Mike tapped the brakes to stop the wheels from rolling and called, "Gear coming up."

Two tech sergeants stood guard at each entrance to the aircrew briefing hall. The chairs had been full earlier that morning with sleepy aviators listening to the specific mission requirements for the raid.

Now the first three rows were occupied by all the senior NCO's of the group. Standing in front of the group was Master Sergeant Billy Hass. His hands were clasped behind his back and it almost appeared he was at parade rest. Billy had been standing in that spot for the last ten minutes as the sergeants had trickled in and sat down. He hadn't addressed anyone nor even seemed to notice they were there.

"Lock the doors," he said loudly, gaining the silence of the audience who had been quietly talking among each other.

"My name is Billy Hass. I called this meeting to make sure we all understand what the plan is around here."

A few low murmurs came from the seats, but Hass ignored them.

"I've been here for two days and it's clear to me that there isn't a plan right now. If there was a plan, then there wouldn't be so many things that are fucked up in the group and on the base."

Now the murmurs became louder, some of the men shifting in their seats.

"And if you don't think this operation is fucked up, then you're too stupid to be sitting in this room. Anyone in that category can leave right now."

He scanned the group that sat motionless, not a word spoken among them.

"It takes a lot to make a bomb group work. But more importantly, it takes a hell of a lot of hard work to make a bomb group combat effective. Right now, the

22

23rd is marginally combat effective. And that's not good enough."

Murmurs rose from the seated men.

"That's right. This group has the highest inflight abort rate in the Eighth Air Force. Every B-17 that drops out of a formation weakens the defensive firepower of the group. In case you haven't put two and two together that means people die. Well I'm here to tell you that we're done with maintenance aborts. I don't give a damn if the wrench turners live on the birds. And you're going to be there to supervise them. I want gripes fixed and fixed right the first time. Maintenance manuals are meant to be read and followed. No short cuts and no excuses. Master Sergeant Larry Weller will be here tomorrow to take over as maintenance chief. His word is law."

A voice from the back called, "If he's the maintenance chief, what's your job?"

"I'm the son of a bitch who's going to kick your ass if you don't start doing things the right way. I'm also going to fly on every mission, and if I see a maintenance failure, you best hope the Germans bag my ass, 'cause I'll be coming back looking for the supervisor who screwed up. Any questions?"

The sergeants sat, not moving or making a sound.

"I didn't think so......Dismissed!"

McGowan finished his post flight inspection, noting that the starboard main mount had a nasty slice and making a mental to write up the discrepancy back in the line shack. It had felt good to get airborne again and judging by the lack of comments by Mike Sullivan, he hadn't been as rusty as he thought. Most of the cockpit chatter had been about the group's performance on combat missions. Sully had some thoughts, but McGowan would decide for himself, starting tomorrow. He turned to walk to the line shack and immediately saw a large figure walking toward him. It had been a long time since he had seen Billy Hass.

"Good afternoon, major," Hass said as he came to a stop and saluted.

Sean returned the salute.

"Good afternoon, master sergeant."

The two men looked at each other, neither offering the other his hand.

Hass's face was impassive, his eyes showing no emotion at all.

"We've got some problems to fix," McGowan offered after a long moment.

"Agreed."

"Is there going to be a problem between us?"

Hass hesitated then said, "I told Colonel Bloch I would do what was needed to make this group work." His voice offered no indication of cooperation.

"I guess that means no."

"I didn't ask for this job, Major. But I'll give Paul Bloch everything I can. That includes working with you, as much as I hate your guts........sir."

"At least we understand each other," McGowan said, "The colonel told me you were staying on flight status."

Hass nodded. "I want to see the maintenance job up close."

"Come on," McGowan said, starting for the line shack.

The two men walked across the tarmac, the sun providing a hint of warmth.

"You were the best bombardier I ever saw in the old days," McGowan finally said. "And I'm not trying to blow smoke up your ass, you know how to drop bombs. The story is that this group couldn't put a turd in the toilet if they were squatting over it. That's got to change and you can help me do that."

24

"I haven't dropped a bomb in over two years."

"You've forgotten more about the Norden bombsight than most of the bombardiers in the Eighth Air Force will ever know. And don't give me that false modesty horse shit either. You're a good bombardier, maybe one of the best."

Hass had been an enlisted bombardier who worked on the development of the Norden bombsight during the late 30's as it was perfected and integrated into the B-17's auto-pilot system.

"I used to be. So what are you thinking?"

"We train the hell out of the bombardiers, and then make them accountable in the air."

Hass stopped and turned to Sean.

"What makes you think that a bunch of junior officers are going to listen to a sergeant when it comes to flying?"

"I don't think that will be a problem.

Hass looked at McGowan, his blue eyes hard, the set of his jaw like steel. "Where are you going with this?"

McGowan said, "Changing the attitude of a bomb group, once it's established, is not an easy thing, you know that."

Hass nodded but said nothing. He had seen it all during his years in the service, great outfits and shitty outfits. But once a unit established itself, one way or the other, they seldom changed.

"These guys are comfortable going through the motions, on the ground and in the air. We've got to change that. And it won't be pleasant. I need someone they can hate as much as me."

At that comment, the master sergeant nodded slightly, "I don't disagree."

Sean stopped at the door to the line shack and turned to Billy Hass.

"And I want you to fly with me."

25

The words stunned Billy Hass. It had been only four years since his kid brother Robin had died, killed by a malfunctioning parachute after bailing out of a B-17 piloted by McGowan. The post maintenance flight had been hurried and no one had caught an unsecured fuel line on the number one engine. While it wasn't Sean's direct fault that Robin had died, if he hadn't been pushing to complete the flight, perhaps someone would have caught the line that came loose in flight, turning the port wing into a mass of flames and driving the crew to bail out. He hated the son of a bitch and that would never change.

Billy pushed the memories out of his mind.

"Why?"

"I want to train master bombers."

Hass knew the concept, the master bomber dropped and all other aircraft in the squadron or box pickled in unison.

"You fly in my ship and we lead until we find other crews that can do the job."

Hass stopped and looked at McGowan.

"Okay, I'll fly with you. Maybe I'll be there when you get it."

McGowan saw the hate in Hass's eyes.

"Maybe."

MEMORANDUM FROM THE GROUP COMMANDER

14 August, 1943

Effective immediately, Master Sergeant Billy Hass is designated the Group Bombardier for the 23rd Bomb Group.

/s/ Paul Bloch, Colonel, USAAF

Chapter Four

Sean McGowan had always been a risk taker. In fact, he had been the pilot voted most likely to kill himself doing something stupid by his flight class. However, the advantage to pilots who do push the envelope and survive is that they become better aviators and more capable of rising to any challenge. In fact six of his classmates had died at Randolph Field and McGowan had graduated number one.

For that reason, Major McGowan now sat in the left seat of B-17 serial number 43-0498 as the mission commander for the 23rd Bomb Group, leading two hundred and forty American airmen against Germany.

Level at 22,000 feet, he was the formation lead of the group's twenty four B-17's as they flew west toward the Dutch coast. The strike today was small by most measures, three groups, totaling eighty six Forts which now were packed into three miles of airspace enroute to hit the dock facilities at Wilhelmshaven.

In the only concession to conventionality, Sean's right seat was occupied by Paul Bloch, who would qualify McGowan as a group lead after the mission was complete. Bloch was more nervous about Billy Hass down in the nose compartment, preparing to give the signal on which all twenty-four of his bombers would drop. But he also knew Billy and if anyone could hit the target, it was the big master sergeant.

"Pilot, navigator, the crossing the Dutch coast in ten minutes."

Sean scanned his instruments, everything normal.

"Pilot to crew, test your guns."

Without acknowledgment, short bursts were heard and felt as each man charged with operating the ten Browning .50 caliber air-cooled machine guns tested his weapon. Around the formation, tracers could be seen coming from the other fortresses as each aircraft duplicated the ritual. By the time the formation crossed the coast, every gun would be ready and each crew member watching for German fighters that could appear at any moment.

Behind the cockpit, Technical Sergeant Don Parr tested the two twin .50's that he controlled from the power operated top turret. Parr was also the flight engineer, but once in enemy territory he spent his time in the upper turret.

Sergeants Fred Thompson and Larry Kucinich, the waist gunners, made one last check of their Browning's, ignoring the jerky movements at their feet from the ball turret as Private Tony Fortino settled in for the long cramped ride suspended under the B-17's belly.

Aft of the bomb bay, Tommy Moore, the radio operator, let go a quick burst from his single .50 at the rear of the radio compartment. The youngest member of the crew, he had just turned 19, having enlisted the day after his 17th birthday. Turning back to his radio set, he continued to adjust the band for the best reception on the strike frequency.

Alone in the tail section, Hubert Loggins, the tail gunner, yawned and surveyed the aircraft maintaining formation on their B-17. It seemed funny to him that in all those planes, the pilot or copilot was watching him and would be for the entire flight. He casually raised his hand in the universal "fuck you" symbol. He hated officers.

Billy Hass took a deep breath and looked at the intelligence photographs one more time. The targets for today's mission were the docks and warehouses on the eastern end of the harbor. If he was going to demonstrate his bombing ability to the group, what better target than a large dock and industrial area that would be easy to find? Of course if he missed them, his credibility would be forever gone. He thought back on how many missions he had flown as the bombardier in the old days and knew that he would not let Paul Bloch down.

"Last mission to Wilhelmshaven the enemy fighters hit us about twenty miles east of here," Bloch called over to Sean. Only critical enemy fighter calls were allowed on the intercom, and in the fortress cockpit, it was easy to hear your companion.

"109's?"

"Mostly, although we've been seeing some 190's over the last several weeks."

Sean had seen the statistics at headquarters and the Focke Wulf 190 appeared to be flown by some of the most experienced enemy fighter pilots.

"Their controllers are damned good and with those long-range radars, they're able to beat us up most of the way to and from the target."

Long range fighters were going to even the score if Ira Eaker was right, Sean thought. It would be nice to see some friendly fighters out the windscreen

The German air defense sector radio suddenly broadcast:

"Red Wolf, Red Wolf, your steer, zero two four, repeat, zero two four. Large group, enemy aircraft, forty kilometers, estimated course of your target zero seven zero."

Lieutenant Colonel Rudolf Steinfeld looked over his right wing as number three and four stabilized.

"Roger, Red Wolf acknowledge heading zero two four."

Adjusting his course slightly, Steinfeld quickly scanned his instruments, making sure oil pressure remained within limits. The FW-190 was a wonderful aircraft, but temperamental compared to the trusty Messerschmitt-109. He thought briefly of the old workhorse he had flown in France and North Africa in the early years of the war. Now he was the old workhorse, flying in a newer aircraft.

Steinfeld was one of the "old gang," having joined the Luftwaffe in 1937 right out of university. Officially the tallest man ever accepted for fighters, Steinfeld had proved he could outfly even his instructors. Looking back now, those times seemed very different to him. The challenge of learning to fly the Me-109 coupled with the knowledge that war was coming had made every day exciting. Despite what the politicians of Germany had told the world, the military had known what was coming and had made every preparation for it. Now, six years later, Rudolf Steinfeld found himself the wing commander of Jagdgeschwader 95 at the advanced age of twenty nine. With eighty four aerial victories, he also was the only surviving member of his original flight school class.

Looking back in his left mirror, he saw Major Karl Ulrich's second division of four fighters assuming their combat spread position. With that hard-headed Bavarian covering his back, Rudolf knew he didn't have to worry about getting jumped. Reaching 27,000 feet, he throttled back to cruise and pulled out his small chart from the side screen. Doing some quick dead reckoning, he decided that the enemy aircraft must be heading for Wilhelmshaven.

"Red wolf, red wolf, your steer now zero two eight, acknowledge."

"Red wolf, copy zero two eight."

Making a slight adjustment, he knew with his airspeed now indicating 280 knots, the enemy aircraft should be ten miles ahead. Rudolf looked over his left shoulder and made a slicing motion with his right hand. Luther Steinke, his wingman, acknowledged the signal and passed it along to number three. "Ready to attack."

"Eight minutes to the initial point," came the call from the navigator to the cockpit.

Sean looked at the current heading, noting that the final bomb run would require an easy turn to the port of about fifteen degrees.

"Bandits, right one o'clock high, two groups of fighters."

Paul Bloch had seen them first and knew immediately that these fighters were setting up for a frontal attack. While the Flying Fortress's defensive weapons were designed to cover completely around the bomber, an aircraft coming in level from twelve o'clock would mask many of the .50 caliber guns.

"Heads up in the nose, one section coming right at us, level."

Billy Hass trained the single barrel forward and looked for the Germans. If they were making a head on attack, he would only have a brief chance to fire as the fighters roared past at a combined speed of over 400 knots.

Steve O'Loughlin, the navigator called out, "Just right of the nose," as the four fighters appeared in a line abreast, tracers indicating that the Germans were already in their firing run. "Christ."

Billy sighted the machine gun on the second fighter from the right and squeezed the firing handle. The smell of cordite filled the nose compartment as he tracked the blur that was the fighter scream by the right side of the aircraft.

"It's those fucking orange-tailed bastards," O'Loughlin yelled as he pivoted his machine gun hard left.

"Whaddaya mean?" Hass called back, continuing to scan the sky.

"Bad news. Those guys are good. We've run into them before."

Steinfeld fired a short burst, his aim toward the cockpit area of the lead fortress. Kill the pilots and the aircraft will go down, a simple but effective rule he had always used. The airframe vibrated as the guns fired, a stream of 1200 rounds a minute arcing toward the American B-17.

Five seconds later the fortress flashed by Steinfeld's left wing as he rolled inverted and pulled aircraft's aircraft's nose hard into a near vertical dive. His flight of four would now have split into two pairs of 190's, the wingmen covering their leaders.

No fighters, Steinfeld thought as the g-forces smashed him back into the seat pad, his mind already setting up the re-attack on the enemy formation. Pitching to the rear, he reversed his heading, straining hard to scan for Luther coming off the attack

Private Tony Fortino caught the German fighter flashing past as he drove the ball turret hard to his right and down, but the aircraft had opened the distance too quickly for a shot. His fingers poised over the firing handles, he began to scan to the right as a second fighter flew into his gunsight and he fired by reflex.

"Christ," Sean blurted out as he involuntarily jerked his head to the right as debris flew off the port side of the cockpit. The sudden realization that the cockpit had been hit by the first fighter jarred him back to reality. The fortress's guns continued to hammer as four more fighters attacked from the right.

"Bandits coming in at 3 o'clock level," Bloch called on the intercom.

Checking engine instruments, Sean heard the top turret cranking around and gunfire erupted from behind him.

"Got the son of a bitch," Fortino yelled as the port wing of the FW-190 snapped off at the wing root, the fighter tearing itself apart and beginning the long fall to earth.

"Three bandits coming in from two o'clock high," Parr called, the urgency in his voice overcoming his attempt at detached professionalism. The new wave of German fighters had used the sun to mask their approach and now tracers were floating toward the bombers.

McGowan tore his eyes away from the instrument panel, comfortable that the four big radial engines were undamaged. Above and behind his head, the flow of outside air screaming through the torn metal skin drowned out Bloch, who was now yelling.

"We should be approaching the IP, the fighters will break off soon," Bloch yelled as he scanned the instruments. "You're bleeding."

Billy Hass turned away from his gun, knowing that they had to get to the business of dropping bombs and quickly.

"IP four minutes ahead," O'Loughlin passed on the intercom after checking his chart.

Ahead through the scattered cloud layers, the Jade Estuary lay like a great navigation beacon.

Cannon shells tore through the thin aluminum skin as two FW's screamed by the bomber, making a north to south firing run out of the sun.

"Thomson's hit!" came a frantic call from Kucinich in the waist.

"Radio, check him out," Bloch passed on the intercom.

Pulling hard to the right, Rudolf's mind registered the debris as Luther's 190 tore itself apart. Forget it, he told himself quickly, nothing to do now but look for another attack, scan for any enemy fighters and keep checking your back....stay in the fight. Scanning the sky, he slowed his breathing and turned north. Climbing hard, Steinfeld reached 23,000 feet and reversed back toward the bomber formation. He would bring down the leader, he told himself, for Luther.

"Approaching the IP, stand by to mark left to a course of zero six six," O'Loughlin called.

Sean ignored Bloch and smoothly rolled the fortress to ten degrees of left back, watching for the first movement of the compass card.

"You okay?" Bloch yelled across the cockpit.

"Yeah," McGowan answered as the big bombers turned toward the bomb run heading.

"Target on the nose at six miles," O'Loughlin transmitted.

Hass scanned forward of the bomb sight, the harbor now clearly visible through a thinly scattered cloud layer. He checked the intervelometer for the last time. 200 milliseconds would elapse between releases once he pushed the pickle.

35

"PDI centered," McGowan called on the intercom, the big bomber now tracking the course indicator from the Norden Bombsight.

"Bomb bay doors open," Hass called back as he locked the control lever.

In front of the formation ugly black bursts erupted as the anti-aircraft gunners below began to open fire with the batteries of 88mm guns that surrounded the harbor.

"Damn," Steinfeld said to himself, realizing his best attack would be on the second box of B-17's down and to his right. The enemy bombers had distinctive orange tails, and the letter "E" painted on them. He wouldn't forget who had killed Luther.

The Wilhelmshaven flak batteries had now opened fire and it was time to attack and retire. He checked his gun switch and pulled right, shoving in hard right rudder to slice the fighter down toward the bombers. Coming in from the American's two o'clock, he knew it would be a fast deflection shot, but years in the cockpit had made the shot second nature. This time he concentrated his fire on the left side of the cockpit, seeing pieces of metal fly off the bird as he raced past and dove for lower altitude.

Behind him, "Ace of Spades," B-17 42-0218 slowly nosed over, both pilots dead in the mangled cockpit. In the aircraft, frantic cries by the flight engineer to bail out resulted in three parachutes opening above the bomber as she tightened her death spiral toward the German countryside.

Watching the dock area slide under the cross hairs, Hass checked the instruments one more time and pushed the pickle. Immediately he called "Bombs away."

The aircraft reacted to the rapid loss of 4,000 pounds of weight, the wings oscillating slightly as Sean adjusted the nose trim.

"Mark left to 335 degrees magnetic," the navigator commanded, starting the off target turn.

Behind the leader, twenty three loads of general purpose bombs were following the leader's toward the target. In the space of six seconds, multiple sticks of five hundred pound bombs ripped across the storage and wharf areas of the eastern harbor, a direct hit.

The 23rd Heavy Bombardment Group, call sign "Thunder," had lived up to its name.

Chapter Five

As his engine wound down, Rudolf Steinfeld sat in the cockpit looking across the wide aerodrome. While his mind recorded several discrepancies he would report to his crew chief, he watched other fighters landing from the mission. The orange tails made them easy to spot and he realized that he had been counting. All of his aircraft were home except Luther. Around him, the frenzy of re-arming and refueling began, all of the ground crews slipping into a well-practiced routine. He saw Feldwebel Hartz looking at the aircraft as they taxied into the parking area. Hartz had been Luther's crew chief for the past six months.

Rudolf took off his flying helmet and ran his fingers through his hair. Taking a breath, he tossed the leather cap down to his crew chief Fritz Werner and jumped down to the ground.

"I'll be back," he told Werner and walked toward Hartz.

It must have been the look on Steinfeld's face, but all he had to do was shake his head and he saw the recognition in the young airmen's face.

"Oberstleutnant, he's not coming back?"

"I'm sorry, Hartz, no."

"Yes, sir," the young man replied, there was nothing else to say.

"Would you help Werner get my aircraft ready to go?"

Hartz nodded and jogged off toward the parked FW.

"Shit," Rudolf said to himself and began to walk to the line shack.

"Hey," Karl Ulrich called from behind.

Rudolf waited for his friend to reach him.

"What happened?"

Steinfeld resumed his walk with Ulrich in step beside him.

"Luther. First pass. He must have taken a full burst from the leader's lower turret, his wing snapped off."

"Damn it. He was a good pilot."

"You and I both know that doesn't mean a damn thing if it's your time."

"I know, but I liked the kid."

Rudolf thought of the young man, Luther Steinke. Barely twenty years old. Put it out of your mind, he told himself, there's nothing you could have done. It was just his time.

The two men continued toward the hangar in silence. Both knew they had cheated the odds for too long.

Sean stood back as two medics pulled Thomson's body, wrapped in a bloody blanket, out of the aft hatch. The two men gingerly laid the sergeant down on an olive-drab stretcher, throwing another blanket over him.

"Give me a hand," one of the medics said as he reached down to lift the stretcher. Larry Kucinich and Don Parr grabbed the handles and helped the medics lift Thomson into the ambulance. The door slammed and the two medics got in the front.

Sean stood with Bloch as the ambulance drove away, the siren silent.

"Come on," the wing commander said with a sigh, "We need to get to debrief."

A sedan drove up, the driver getting out and saluting Bloch.

"Hop in."

Sean nodded and followed the colonel.

Behind them Master Sergeant Hass and Lieutenant Steve O'Loughlin walked around the ship, looking at the battle damage from the mission.

"Never even knew that happened," the navigator said, noting several bullets holes not more than two feet aft of his station.

Hass looked up and saw the torn metal over the pilot's window. McGowan, always the lucky son of a bitch, he thought, but everyone's luck eventually runs out.

As the sun neared setting, Jagdgeschwader 95, the Orange-Tailed Shrikes, straggled back from their third mission of the day. Crew chiefs directed the aviators to their parking spots, shutting down the engines as each FW-190 pulled to a stop. With the coming of darkness, the pace had now slowed, knowing that the wing likely would stand down until the morning. The mechanics would have a chance to try and fix the many problems that came from a day of violent combat flying. Defending the Reich took a heavy toll on the aircraft as well as the men who flew them.

Rubbing his eyes, then the rest of his face, Rudolf Steinfeld took a moment to relax. As the last engine shut down, the quiet suddenly seemed very special to him. Another day of battle, he thought. A good pilot had died and I destroyed an enemy bomber.   He suddenly realized all he wanted to do was have a drink and take off his boots. Nothing more was needed to make him happy.

Christened "*Jezebel*," B-17 serial number 43-0498 lifted off the runway at Paddington on its eighth combat mission in the last twelve days. A maximum effort by the Eighth Air Force had kept aircrews and maintenance personnel on a day and night effort to make every sortie assigned. If there was a blessing in the frenzy of missions and debriefs, Major Sean McGowan was no longer the "new guy." Paul Bloch had made a decision that he would have McGowan lead the group or his squadron on every available mission. Sean liked it that way and the wing commander heard no complaints from his new squadron commander.

The crew of *Jezebel* had solidified with most of the men from the first mission, the dead Thomson replaced by Sergeant Harry Baumstark, a lanky kid from North Dakota, known as a superb gunner. Billy Hass remained as the assigned bombardier after Paul Bloch selected two other bombardiers as "Group Master Bombers."

Now sitting in the co-pilot's seat was Squadron Leader John Forster of the Royal Australian Air Force. Assigned to the 23rd from 460 Squadron at RAF Binnbrook, he had been flying combat since the beginning of the war. Flying Halifax bombers initially, most recently his squadron had transitioned to Lancasters. The RAAF was trying to decide whether to use the B-17 or B-24 as they built up their airborne striking capability in the Pacific. John Forster, a 24 year old from Hobart, Tasmania, would have a key input to that decision and his time with the 23rd might determine if the B-17 would be the choice of the RAAF.

The assignment of a full time copilot to the crew allowed Paul Bloch to move from squadron to squadron when he led the group on bombing missions. In the last two weeks the group's bombing record had been superb but the airborne abort rate was still higher than acceptable. With the arrival of Master Sergeant Larry Weller, the entire ground maintenance effort was quickly being re-calibrated. The 23rd Bomb Group was beginning to reach its stride.

"Gear up and locked," John Forster called as they passed 1000 feet, now climbing at 350 feet per minute.

McGowan turned left toward the Splasher beacon that would guide them to the rendezvous circle which was twenty miles southwest of Paddington. The blue sky was broken only by thin wisps of high clouds, which would allow the group to join up with a minimum of excitement. While every aircraft knew the pattern and followed navigation aids, trying to bring three squadrons of heavy bombers together in marginal weather tested the patience of the most experienced crews. Midair collisions were infrequent but normally catastrophic when two fully loaded aircraft collided.

"Passing ten thousand, everyone on oxygen," Sean called over the intercom. He hated wearing the uncomfortable mask, but at high altitudes there was no option, there wasn't enough oxygen to support life. Between the freezing cold temperatures at altitude and lack of oxygen, it didn't take much to put a man's life in danger. Heated and fleece lined flying clothes made the long missions tolerable, but certainly not comfortable.

Twenty minutes later the copilot called, "Three's in position."

"Huggie, how're they doing back there?" Sean asked the tail gunner.

"All aircraft are in position, looks like no aborts, skipper." Loggins watched the bombers settle in formation and remembered how McGowan had taken him aside after the second mission. "Huggie, you're my eyes back there and I'm counting on you. You see something that's not right, let me know." No one had ever called him "Huggie," in his life. But McGowan had made it sound so natural that he immediately felt good. Now the entire crew was calling him Huggie and he enjoyed it. Maybe the new skipper wasn't an asshole like all the rest of those officers.

Good man, Sean thought, he'll do just fine back there.

Today the group was part of a larger strike against several manufacturing sites just south of Dortmund. The 23rd's target was a chemical plant and they would be dropping both general purpose and incendiary bombs.

Sean checked his watch. One more turn in the rendezvous circle and it would be time for the 23rd Bomb Group to strike out for Germany.

"So how's this compare to a Lancaster?" Sean asked his copilot.

"Bit of a sports car by my book. The Lanc is a beast of an aircraft. She carries a good load and will take a heavy beating, but can't hold a candle to a fort for pure flying."

"You don't fly with a copilot, right?"

"Flight engineer in the right seat. Cuts down on the number of pilots you need. We were a bit short if you remember back a few years."

Sean knew that the Commonwealth air forces had lost a large number of pilots during the Battle of France and the Battle of Britain.

"The 'few.' I remember."

"Hard times change the way you do business."

In the distance the 507th Group, which had the lead, was crossing the coastline.

"Switchbox lead, Switchbox One. We've lost our number four engine, returning to base."

Damn, McGowan thought, we don't need another abort. But he was not going to second guess the aircraft commander. He would find out what happened after the mission.

John Forster leaned over and tapped one of the engine gauges.

"Oil pressure on number one has been dropping over the last five minutes."

Glancing down at the bank of instruments, McGowan focused on the problem. It was right at the lower acceptable limit for the big radial engine. Anything lower and he would have to shut it down.

Billy Hass heard both the radio exchange and Forster's comment on their engine. Coincidence? He wondered.

One hour later, *Jezebel's* number one engine lost oil pressure and had to be shut down, just as a swarm of thirty Bf-109's attacked the 23rd.

"One's feathered," Sean called as the propeller was hydraulically driven to the neutral position. He adjusted the power on the remaining engines to maintain airspeed.

"Bandits, one o'clock high, here they come."

Jezebel's airframe shuddered as her defensive guns came alive, the top turret elevating to track the attacking fighters. Parr knew their fortress was the target, he could continue firing without having to traverse the gun. The German fighters were coming right at them. He knew that the enemy aircraft had chosen an attack angle that protected them from the waist and belly guns of *Jezebel*. He could only hope that the other forts in their box saw the attackers and would throw their firepower at the line of Messerschmitts.

Fighters flashed by the Fortresses, their sleek forms seeming to race by motionless targets. From each of the bombers, streams of machine gun fire crisscrossed the sky, with no apparent effect.

"Call your targets, damn it, you're not talking," Parr yelled between bursts, encouraging the gunners to hand off tracking to another gunner, increasing the odds of a hit.

"Two crossing right to left under the belly."

Without hesitation, Fortino moved the ball turret to the three o'clock level position and tried to acquire the attackers, the guns opening up as he saw the two 109's diving below *Jezebel*, apparently attacking the 411th's number two box. He knew he'd scored hits, but the fighters continued their attack on the other group.

"Shit!" he yelled to himself, slewing the turret around to guard against forward attacks from below.

The firing runs by the Germans were spirited but scored few hits and all aircraft continued toward the initial point.

"Dodged a few bullets on that one, mate."

Sean nodded as he scanned the sky which now appeared totally devoid of fighters.

"They'll be back," he called on the intercom.

In the nose compartment, Billy Hass picked up a set of binoculars that he always carried and scanned forward, trying to pick out key navigation points as they approached the Ruhr River.

Behind him, Steve O'Loughlin bent over his chart and measured with a set of dividers.

"Twenty miles to the IP, skipper."

"Rog."

"Bloody hell, losing oil pressure on number three," Forster called out, leaning down toward the instrument panel.

A quick inspection of the oil pressure gauge told the story. They were losing their second engine. The formation was seven minutes from the target. By all rights, Sean should hand over the lead, drop their bombs to lighten the aircraft and head for the nearest English base.

"Shutting down number three," Sean said, pulling the throttle back in preparation for feathering. In one minute the engine had been shut down and the props were now aligned with the wind stream.

"I'm keeping the lead, we're too close to the target to switch."

Forster knew he was right. A lead change at that point would almost guarantee a poor bombing run. Just don't think about it, he told himself, just don't think about it.

"Right."

Ahead of the group, ugly black flak bursts filled the sky over Dortmund.

Jezebel touched down at Paddington one hour after the rest of the group. Transferring the lead to Tom Russell, Sean had detached from the formation, gone low and nursed the ship back home. He had made a conscious decision to try for home base and avoid having the aircraft struck at some outlying field waiting for maintenance. With all guns and other systems doing well, he thought it was a risk worth taking. He knew that Paul Bloch might disagree, but he was willing to take that chance.

A thorough post-flight revealed a total lack of battle damage on either of the feathered engines. By the time the mechs were removing the engine panels, Larry Weller was on the elevated work stand next to Billy Hass.

"Take a look, master sergeant," said Technical Sergeant Holloway after he had inspected the aft engine access panel.

"I'm gonna have someone's ass," Weller said, he jaws clenched tight. "Go open the other engine."

Hass caught up with McGowan coming out of debrief.

"The oil return lines on both engines had worked loose at the sump."

"How the hell does that happen," McGowan asked as John Forster walked up to them.

"You service the engine and then don't secure the fitting."

"We lost both engines from a maintenance screw up?"

Hass nodded. "That's about it. Weller and I have it for action. It won't happen again."

McGowan could tell by the tone of his voice it wouldn't.

Later in the officer's club the pilot and copilot of *Jezebel* sat across from each other, half consumed beers in front of them.

"Two days off ops according to schedules," John said.

"A good chance to catch up on sleep and paperwork."

"Criminy, don't you ever take any time off?"

Sean was taken aback. It hadn't really occurred to him. Since he had come to Europe, he had either been flying combat or working for General Eaker, which was a seven day a week job.

"What are you going to do?"

Forster smiled. "I'll be off to London to spend two glorious days with a lovely young woman who completely adores me."

McGowan laughed, "And who wouldn't?"

"I'll have you know that Miss Rose is a discerning young woman who insists on keeping company with only the most eligible men in Britain."

Finishing his beer, McGowan said, "You know, I should see London at some point."

"You've never been to London?" Forster asked incredulously?

"On official business, sure. The general had to go there several times. I've just never gone out on the town."

His ruddy face breaking into a wide grin, Squadron Leader Forster said, "We'll fix that in short order, my American friend, have no fear."

Chapter Six

It seemed to Sean that every other person on the London streets was wearing a uniform. What surprised him was the assortment of services and countries that were represented. John had helped him with the uniforms he didn't recognize, one being Polish, the other Dutch.

"Course you Americans have all the money, so the girls are all hunting for a Yank."

"So why did this beautiful English lass end up with an Aussie?"

"Good taste, of course."

The Leftwich Hotel once was a bright spot in this part of London. Now the four-story stone-faced building looked old and tired. Gone was the doorman, probably called up for service or maybe the Home Guard. In his place, sandbags covered the lower part of the entryway, with crisscrossed tape on the exposed windows. While the horror of 1940 was behind them, the British knew the threat was still there for German air raids.

As they entered the lobby, McGowan could sense the grandeur of the old hotel, the dark wood and marble still shining in the subdued light.

"They should be in here," John said, pulling off his cap and walking into the large public room.

Following his friend, Sean took a moment for his eyes to adjust and looked around at the patrons. Full for an early afternoon, he guessed that the eternal cycle of leaves and passes would keep places like this busy for the duration.

"There they are," Forster said, pushing past three American soldiers, all holding glasses of beer.

Two young women sat in a side booth, one on each side of the table.

"Hello, ladies. Aubrey, Jamie, this is Sean McGowan. He's a Yank, but don't hold that against him."

Sean smiled.

"Sean, I have the pleasure of presenting Miss Aubrey Rose and Miss Jamie Taylor-Paige."

"Hello," was all Sean could think of to say.

John motioned to the bartender, then said, "Sit down, I'll get the drinks."

Sliding in next to Jamie, Sean saw Aubrey watching John as he walked away. Her smile was infectious and John had been right, she was lovely. In the horror of a war, love could still blossom.

"First time to London, John told me," Aubrey said.

"Well yes and no. I've been here on business but never just to see the town."

"Really?"

He turned to look at Jamie who appeared unaware or unimpressed by the arrival of the men.

"Quite true."

Aubrey smiled. "Well then, we'll have to show you the sights of our fair city, remembering she is a bit battered right now."

John returned with four glasses of beer, held carefully balanced until he set them on the table.

"There we go, just what the doctor ordered."

Sean passed a glass to Jamie.

She was his age, he guessed. Her shoulder length hair was light brown and framed a lovely but sober face.

"Is this okay?" he asked her.

"Actually, it's about all there is with the rationing now," she said. "But it will do quite well, thank you."

Sean felt a chill from the woman, maybe he had it wrong, but it seemed she would just as soon be somewhere else.

"Aubrey and Jamie went to school together before the war. A girl's school named Exmouth in Kensington," John offered, trying to spark the conversation.

"Girls only?" Sean commented.

Aubrey smiled, "Horrid idea actually, but it's the way it's done over here.

John had told Sean that they both now worked at the Air Ministry and had been since the war began.

"You both work in London?" he asked.

"We do, at the Air Ministry."

"What do you do there?"

"We're really not allowed to discuss that," Jamie said, her tone almost hostile.

Outside the wail of a siren cut into the early evening.

"Christ," John said.

"An air raid?" Sean asked.

Aubrey's expression changed to one of concern as she looked at Jamie.

"It will be fine," Aubrey said.

Sean saw that Jamie was gripping her glass so hard that it shook.

"John, why don't you take Sean out to the shelter on Sherwood?"

Looking at John, Sean tried to figure out what was happening.

As if he read minds, John said quietly, "Jamie has trouble in shelters."

"I say we stay here and finish our beers," Sean said, taking a drink and grinning at John.

"Right. I agree. Ladies?"

Aubrey searched Jamie's face, then said, "A good idea. Besides, most raids now are on the docks."

"Okay with you?" Sean asked Jamie, turning to her.

She nodded her head, but remained silent.

"Besides, this seems like a very comfortable place to be," Sean said, as he put his arm around Jamie. He could feel the tenseness of her body and he applied just the slightest pressure on her arm.

"I agree," Forster said, putting his arm around Aubrey.

Sean could feel Jamie's tenseness subside as she leaned into his shoulder.

The small talk for the next forty-five minutes did little to cover the tension as they heard sirens and muffled explosions in the distance. Thankfully, none of the impacts were close to the pub and the all-clear siren told them it had been a small raid.

"That's better," Aubrey said, "Time for another pint."

"You drop bombs, don't you?" Jamie asked McGowan.

He turned to look at her, was that a smart remark, what was this woman thinking?

"I do, but then you know that."

"Have you ever been in a raid on the ground?" she asked, her tone sounding sincere.

"No, I never have and I think you probably have been through too many."

She turned to him, there was just a hint of a smile on her face.

"One is too many, major."

Later that night, John told him that Jamie had been in a shelter that partially collapsed early in the war, trapping her for almost a full day. She had been terrified of enclosed places ever since.

"Herr oberst, the general is waiting in your office."

Striding in from his second mission of the day, Rudolf snapped back at his orderly, "Which general?"

"Galland, sir."

His irritation disappeared. He liked and respected Adolph Galland, now head of the Luftwaffe's fighter command. A true warrior, the general had led the effort in France during the early part of the war, racking up over 90 kills. Now promoted to lieutenant general, he was charged with the defense of the Reich, and forbidden to fly in combat.

The general stood at the window, turning as Steinfeld entered, a cup of coffee in his hand.

"Steinfeld, this coffee tastes like horse piss. I would have thought you could do better!"

Rudolf extended his hand, grinning at Galland.

"Too busy shooting down bombers. It's good to see you, general."

"And you, Rudi. Too few of the old guard left anymore."

The two men sat down at a wooden table.

"What brings you here, an inspection?"

"In a way. I needed to get away from those bastards in Berlin."

Galland's face showed anger, but he quickly moved on.

"You and I are going to break the rules."

Steinfeld realized where this was going.

"I need to 'evaluate the current situation,' if you know what I mean."

"It would be my pleasure."

Galland smiled broadly, slapping Rudolf on the back.

"Then tonight we will drink some good wine and tomorrow we shall shoot down American bombers!"

The late September weather front which swept in off the North Sea produced multi-layered clouds from the English Channel all the way to the Budapest, wrapping the continent in areas of reduced visibility and precipitation. Following several close calls, the 23rd Bomb Group departed south from Splasher Beacon "R" enroute to their target in Frankfurt. Their position was "tail end Charlie" with four other bomb groups ahead of them in the stream.

In the nose compartment of *Jezebel*, Billy Hass watched the ground disappear as they climbed to the enroute altitude of 19,000 feet. Despite all that had been going on, he still marveled to watch the earth through a Plexiglass bubble miles below. Sometime it felt as if he was alone above the clouds, the entire world spread out before him. An opportunity for calm reflection before the mayhem of battle began.

It had been an eventful three days for the command structure of the 23rd. Master Sergeant Floyd Higgins left the station, reassigned to a motor pool in Northern Scotland. The maintenance supervisor who signed off on the faulty engine maintenance was busted back to staff sergeant and assigned to perimeter security. There was now a comprehensive list of all maintenance tasks that required a quality check following completion and Weller had started up a new group whose sole function it was to spot check all maintenance activity. The question in Hass's mind was how would the group take getting slapped down a bit?

"Your aircraft," Sean called, lifting one hand off the wheel.

"My aircraft," John replied, placing both hands on his wheel and taking control of *Jezebel*.

This would be done several times an hour to keep the fatigue of flying formation in the difficult weather from wearing down the pilot in command.

McGowan took off his mask briefly, rubbing his face and stretching his neck forward and back, then left and right. He wasn't tired, but knew that staying fresh might make the difference when the shit hit the fan. He let his thoughts stray to Jamie Taylor-Paige. She had been very quiet after they left the pub, but at the same time she seemed to enjoy Sean's company. A quick dinner and they had to drop the girls off at the townhouse they shared in Mayfair to get back to Paddington. When they had said good night, she kissed him quickly on the cheek as she quietly said, "Thank you."

He found himself having to force his thoughts back to the present, checking engine instruments, altitude, airspeed and warning lights. All conditions normal. She was quite lovely. Once she had smiled at him and her face had betrayed a much different woman than the one he had been with all evening. Perhaps the war affected her more than most. It was always hard to tell how people would react.

General Galland was violating the orders of Adolph Hitler and Hermann Goering by flying on a combat mission. The fighter ace really didn't care, but he wasn't being blatant. Now flying on Steinfeld's wing, he knew that as long as his pilots were flying combat, he would continue to defy the politicians. He did like the FW-190. All of his combat kills had been in the Messerschmitt, but he appreciated the maneuverability of the Shrike. Perhaps today he would get his first FW kill.

55

If all the generals had the spirit and courage of Galland, we would win this war in six months, Steinfeld thought as he leveled the flight of four at 20,000 feet. He wished the weather was better for the general, but an old war horse like him would take all of it in stride. He was more concerned about two of his newer pilots. It was clear that they had not received the amount of instrument flight training that previously had been considered mandatory. He understood the need to fill the holes in operational squadrons as more and more pilots were being lost but at what eventual cost? He knew that if these young pilots could stay alive for three to six months, they might survive. But for the near term, they were on borrowed time. All he could do was assign them to his most experienced division leads and hope they caught on quickly.

Scanning the forward quadrant, he picked up the first specks against the cloud cover. He knew the enemy formation would shortly break out enough to plan his attack. Adding power, he began a climb, at the same time he looked back at the general and pointed forward nodding. Galland waved back, he understood completely. The hunt was on.

"How far to target, nav?"

O'Loughlin quickly confirmed what he already knew and called back to McGowan, "Sixty five miles to Frankfurt, skipper. Fifty miles to the initial point."

"Roger. Good lookout doctrine, the krauts are out there somewhere."

Hass scanned forward of *Jezebel*. The clouds made the group in front of them stand out and he could see what looked like two full squadrons of that group. He thought about the visual cues for his target, a large factory complex at the northwest corner of Frankfurt. Today's aiming point was the headquarters building located in the center of the factory. Funny how you never thought about the people, only the target or the aimpoint or the bomb fall line. He would be concerned with drift and cross-trail during the attack, but not how many people might die from their bombs. That's just the way it was.

Steinfeld saw the attack developing as he continued his climb to three thousand feet higher than the lead box of B-17's. He would bring his fighters around a large cloud formation and be on the enemy before they knew what was happening. He pushed his division out into combat spread and checked his armament one last time, the glow of his gunsight bright against the clouds. Beginning his turn toward the bombers, he mentally tracked where they should be and then increased the "g" to pull his nose around. Flashing past the edge of the cloud formation, Rudolf saw the forts only a mile on his nose, their orange tails standing out against the clouds.

"Bandits, four o'clock high," came the call from Don Parr in the top turret.

"Right waist, got 'em."

Immediately the B-17's .50 caliber machine guns opened fire.

"Second wave, right behind," Parr called as he paused to track the small dots now growing in size rapidly. Green tracers laced across the sky as the first group of fighters opened fire on *Jezebel's* box.

In the nose compartment, both men, hands on their machine guns, searched in vain for a target. The urgency seemed to rise as the other guns continued to fire.

"Second wave's heading for the low squadron, belly head's up."

Fortino slammed the ball turret hand control grips hard left, leading the twin .50's ahead of two enemy fighters who were diving at the lower forts. As he had in the past, he let the angles develop and then when it felt right he squeezed the firing levers while following the two ships. Suddenly a sharp flame appeared at the starboard wing root of the second fighter, black smoke trailing the German, who turned away from his leader, the canopy separating from the stricken fighter. The last glance by Fortino caught the small dot of an aviator leaping clear of the FW as the flames enveloped the entire aft part of the fuselage.

"Hot damn!"

From a disciplined flight of eight, the fighters now free-lanced as they conducted follow-on attacks before the Americans reached the Frankfurt flak belt. As he knew he would, Rudolf saw Galland right in position as he reversed back toward the bombers. He picked the left wingman of the leader and began to fire at the maximum range for his guns. Years of practice now resulted in multiple hits on the fortress. He saw hits on both port engines and also under the cockpit and top turret. He continued firing, the fury of the attack taking over, driving him to press the attack. Cannon hits tore into the soft skin the enemy aircraft and he knew the damage would be fatal.

As Steinfeld broke to the right, the general poured more fire into the stricken fortress as smoke and flames broke out on the port wing.

"*My Gal's* hit," Huggie called, "She's on fire and losing altitude.

"Watch for chutes," McGowan said, his voice emotionless.

Inside *My Gal*, the cannon and machine gun fire had killed the top turret gunner, radio operator and pilot. In the cockpit, First Lieutenant Mike Gallagher desperately fought to keep the bomber under control as the fuselage began to vibrate badly. He knew it was over, the fear they all had was finally happening. Ignoring his friend and pilot who lay slumped against the left side of the fuselage, he keyed the intercom.

"That's it for us, everyone get out – bail out, bail out, bail out. Acknowledge."

"Tail, roger."

"Waist gunners, check in. Kelly, Forsythe, did you copy?"

The two gunners had already disconnected and were staring at the ball turret. A 20mm cannon shell had shattered the Plexiglas and tore the gunner apart, all they saw was blood and pieces of clothing.

"Nav, roger, we're gone."

The pressure on the control wheel was becoming almost more than the copilot could handle. Slowly the aircraft began a turn to the left as it continued to lose altitude.

"Is everyone out?" Gallagher screamed into the intercom as he pushed full right rudder trying to bring the aircraft back to level.

"Two chutes," Huggie called. "There's another one and another!"

As each crew member of *Jezebel* continued to fight their own battle with the Germans, they all listened.

"One more! That's five, come on you guys, jump"

A violent twist and the outer wing of My Gal separated from the aircraft amid a flash of fuel and smoke. In the spinning cockpit, Gallagher was thrown hard against the starboard bulkhead, the control stick now useless. Gasping for breath as the "g" forces pulled on his body, he tried to reach his lap belt to release himself from the seat. His hands seemed to weigh fifty pounds and he fought to find the release.

Outside the world spun faster and faster through the windscreen as the doomed bomber spiraled toward the German countryside. The young pilot from New York City knew he couldn't get out of the cockpit. In a state of shock he looked at the altimeter, spinning wildly down.

My Gal, a B-17F, serial number 41-9383-0, impacted six miles south of Erfstadt. Two men who were in the local forest looking for lost cattle heard the sharp violent explosion echo off the pines. By the time the police arrived, most of the fires had gone out, helped by a driving rainstorm which blew through the valley an hour after the crash. The explosion and intensity of the fire destroyed most of the aircraft and Luftwaffe technicians who surveyed the sight a day later determined there was nothing of value to recover.

First Lieutenant Michael Steven Gallagher was reported missing in action along with the rest of the crew.

"It was those orange tails again, the letter "E"," Rudolf told the debriefing officer. Tell Hauptman Dieter to find out who they are and where they're based"

"Yes, sir. And you claim one B-17 downed south of Cologne?"

Rudolf nodded. "Probably twenty kilometers." While he and Galland had downed the bomber, the general could not claim the victory, but he and Rudolf knew.

"Add that an unidentified aircraft contributed to the kill."

That afternoon he and the general shared a glass of wine to celebrate.

"You lost one?"

"Yes, sir. Trauble, he's been with us for two months."

They both sat for a moment, thoughts going to so many of their comrades who had been lost in the skies over Europe and Africa.

Galland raised his glass.

"To Trauble," he said.

"Trauble."

There was a knock at the door.

"Enter."

Hauptman Hans Dieter, the senior wing intelligence officer, walked in and came to attention.

"The information you wanted, herr oberst. The enemy bombers you sighted were from the 23rd Heavy Bombardment Group based in Paddington."

"Anything special about this group?"

"No, sir. In fact they are remarkably ordinary. The group arrived in England earlier this year and have been flying missions as part of the Eighth Air Force's Combat Wing One."

Steinfeld snapped, "We've lost two pilots to that group, Dieter. I want you to follow them closely."

Hans Dieter nodded curtly.

"As you wish, herr oberst."

The wing commander knew that Dieter would find out. A natural intelligence officer, he had contacts throughout both the military and civilian intelligence networks. Sometimes Steinfeld thought that Dieter knew more about what was happening in the war than Berlin. He was glad the young man was attached to Jagdgeschwader 95.

A slight breeze hinted that fall was soon to arrive in London, but for today the end of September brought sunny skies with only a patchwork of clouds over the city. They had walked for almost an hour, the mid-day crowds thin for a Sunday.

"Hyde Park," Jamie said as they crossed Carriage Drive.

"I've heard of it, looks like a big place."

"I'll show you," she said, smiling and taking his hand.

McGowan was happy to be with Jamie but walking in a park wasn't something he normally looked forward to doing.

They made their way down a tree-lined walkway that connected with a very wide walk which bordered a beautiful lake.

"I love coming here, no matter the time of the year. It make you forget the city."

He found himself actually enjoying the walk. Perhaps he was getting to be an old man.

"So what's the lake called?"

"It's The Serpentine Lake and it runs down to, as you might expect, The Serpentine Bridge, which you can see."

"This is nice," he said as they walked slowly down the lake toward the bridge.

Jamie released his hand and slipped her arm inside his.

Reaching the bridge, the two crossed to the midway point and stopped to look down the lake.

"There you have The Long Water, which runs down to the fountains in the Italian gardens."

"But it's the same body of water, how can it have two names?"

She looked up at him, her face impish.

"To confuse foreigners, like you, Major McGowan."

He laughed.

"I've been confused ever since I met you Jamie Taylor-Paige."

Her face looked momentarily sober.

"Is that good or bad?"

"Very good," he said and kissed her.

Chapter Seven

A cold November wind whistled outside the wing commander's office window, low clouds scudding across the quiet airfield.

"I guess it's a strange problem to have, sir."

Paul Bloch sat at his desk, feet up and hands interlocked behind his head.

"Any ideas?" McGowan asked.

"So we have one of the best gunners in the Eighth Air Force who's also one of the biggest screw ups on the ground. And now we have to deal with a recommendation for the Silver Star that will bring this guy to the notice of the press. And you're making the recommendation."

"Yes, sir, that's about it."

"Balls."

"You wanna see me, skipper?

"Fortino, come in."

The young man stepped into Sean McGowan's office to see Master Sergeant Hass standing by the window.

"Have a seat."

Looking cautious, he sat down opposite Sean.

"Fortino, you're probably the best natural gunner in the group, maybe in the entire Eighth Air Force."

"Yes, sir."

"But you have a problem."

Fortino made no response, but his eyes flashed anger. McGowan continued, "The adjutant told me you just wanted to fly your missions and go home."

"Yes, sir, that's right, New Jersey."

"But Master Sergeant Hass and I have a problem with that."

"Sir?"

"It's not enough," Hass broke in. "You've been sliding by since you got here. Knocking down four German fighters gave you some cover, but no more."

A stunned look swept across his face.

"I don't know what you mean, master sergeant."

"What he means is that you are being meritoriously promoted to staff sergeant, effective immediately."

'"From this moment forward you will conduct yourself in a manner that befits a staff sergeant in the Army Air Forces," added Hass. "If you need any incentive to follow that path, rest assured I will provide it. Do we understand each other, Staff Sergeant Fortino?"

Fortino walked back slowly to the olive-drab Quonset hut where he was billeted. He went over to his rack and sat down quietly.

"You in trouble?" Corporal Anthony Auferio asked, looking up from a copy of Star and Stripes.

"Not exactly," Fortino said softly, almost to himself.

"Huh?"

The smell of coffee and bacon pervaded the crowded mess hall, the tables packed with aircrew and maintenance technicians getting ready for the morning's mission. A constant buzz of conversation filled the room where many men had already lit their first cigarette of the day.

"How can you eat that crap?"

Staff Sergeant Larry Kucinich looked up from his plate of powdered eggs and corned beef hash. A liberal amount of ketchup covered the watery eggs and greasy hash.

"Just my routine, Harry."

Sergeant Baumstark sat with only a cup of coffee in front of him, a Lucky Strike smoking in the ashtray next to it.

"How 'bout you, Huggie?"

At the end of the wooden table, Sergeant Loggins munched contentedly on a sugar doughnut. The crew now all called him Huggie, in the air and on the ground.

"All I need's a doughnut, just a little something in my stomach until I can suck on some oxygen."

The effect of too many beers from the night before was often offset by the use of 100% oxygen in the aircraft. Huggie was known for liking his beer more than most and often had his oxygen mask on well before the mandatory 10,000 feet.

"Hey, there's Fortino," Huggie said quickly.

The enlisted crew had been told of the meritorious promotion the night before. Master Sergeant Hass made it clear he wanted the crew to support Fortino as he tried to keep his stripes.

"Hey, Tony, over here," Baumstark called.

Approaching the table with a metal mess tray, Fortino seemed subdued, far different from his normal swaggering bravado.

"Hey," he said, sliding in beside Kucinich.

"Way to go on the promotion, kid."

The group all offered their congratulations.

Fortino looked uncomfortable and he scooped some eggs into his mouth, "Thanks."

"Hey, rumor has it we get a milk run today," Baumstark said.

"There's Parr, maybe he's heard."

Technical Sergeant Don Parr roomed with one of the men from the operations department and often got the scoop before anyone else in the crew.

"Hey Don, over here."

Parr had a sober look on his face, and only carried a ceramic mug of coffee. Sitting down next to Fortino he leaned over and said quietly, "Way to go, sergeant."

"So what's the scoop?" Kucinich asked.

Huggie leaned over to Parr. "Milk run, right?"

"Marshaling yards at Kassel."

"Shit."

They all knew that Kassel lay inside the heart of the Luftwaffe's defensive ring that protected critical German industrial sites.

"Let's go. It's almost briefing time."

"Shit."

In the "Current Operations" section of the Air Ministry, Jamie Taylor-Paige reviewed the day's operational schedule provided by Eighth Air Force headquarters. Two large raids were scheduled. The first was a mission to attack the submarine pens at Lorient, France. The second would send 160 B-17's against the railroad marshaling yards near Kassel, Germany.

Her eyes searched the page, even as she told herself not to. Where would the 23rd be flying today, a short raid on the French coast or into the teeth of the German air defense network? It has been so much easier before when she had been able to tell herself they were just numbers. Now she felt herself being pulled back into the nightmare all over again. Two years ago she would pour over the daily operational orders to see if Ted would be flying that day. No longer were the units on the orders impersonal numbers. But there was a man connected to those numbers, a man she loved. Her thoughts returned to that terrible day when six Lancasters didn't return from a night bombing mission against Cologne. As if in a nightmare, she had confirmed that three of the lost bombers were from his squadron, shot down over Germany in the dark and deadly skies where young men died each night. But that night it had been Ted.

"Any idea?"

Jamie looked up as Aubrey approached her desk.

"Railroad marshaling yards at Kassel," Jamie said quietly.

"Cripes," Aubrey said as she sat down next to her friend.

"I know," Jamie said, both of the women well aware of the depth of the German defenses in central Germany. "Have you talked with John?"

Aubrey shook her head, "Not since the day before yesterday."

"Did he mention Sean?"

"No, why?"

Sitting back in her chair, she crossed her arms and closed her eyes.

"I don't know what to do?"

Aubrey pulled up a chair and sat down.

"This doesn't sound good."

Tears appeared in Jamie's eyes.

"I didn't think it could happen, I just didn't."

A look of alarm came over Aubrey.

"Bloody hell, are you preggers?"

"No!"

"Then what the hell are you going on about?"

Jamie shook her head.

"I think I'm in love with him."

Normally ready with a quick retort to anything, Aubrey said nothing. She remembered what losing Ted had done to her friend.

Aubrey put her hand on Jamie's shoulder as she stood up.

"I know."

Walking back to her desk, Aubrey felt the uneasiness of knowing that John Forster was going up today into the violent battle being waged over the continent. She knew the odds and the statistics on survival of Commonwealth aircrews, and it didn't give her any comfort. Now Jamie was being pulled into that world of worry again.

Jamie stood up from her desk and walked to the window. Outside the cloudy skies matched her mood.

" I can't do this," she said to herself.

"Okay, let's get going," Billy Hass called to the remaining crew that hadn't climbed aboard *Jezebel*. Across the ramp, engines began to cough into life. The cold wind blowing the acrid exhaust fumes across the parking area.

Hass ran up to the forward fuselage boarding hatch and swung himself up and into the aircraft.

Near the tail, Harry Baumstark dropped his cigarette on the ground and crushed it with his boot. "Come on," he said to Larry Kucinich as he walked to the aft hatch and climbed up.

Grabbing the hatch coaming with his right hand, the Kucinich leaned over from the waist and vomited his breakfast on the concrete. Pausing for a moment to catch his breath, he climbed up and pulled the hatch closed.

"Shit, did you see that?" a newly reported ground crewman asked Sergeant McCluskey, *Jezebel's* crew chief.

The heavyset sergeant laughed, "That's the way he starts every mission. Hell if he didn't puke, I'd worry. Now get ready for engine start and keep your head on a swivel. Got it?"

"Yeah, sarge."

"Looks like we have a full house, skipper," Huggie called from the tail turret.

Sean smiled, no aborts and they had been airborne almost an hour trying to rendezvous in what he liked to call "varsity shitty weather."

"Outbound heading, nav?"

Steve O'Loughlin came right back, "One nine five magnetic, skipper."

John Forster dialed the indicator on the compass to 195 as the formation began to push toward the continent. Today the 23rd was leading the entire formation.

Paul Bloch sat on a jury-rigged seat behind the pilot and copilot, his headset hooked into a large mixer box freshly installed on the starboard bulkhead. Today he was the airborne mission commander for the First Combat Wing. His job was to monitor the entire situation, communicate if needed with headquarters and direct any operational changes that were required to complete the mission. Making a final note on his clipboard, he leaned forward to Sean.

"Only missing two aircraft from the entire gaggle."

Sean nodded, knowing the bomber stream was rolling out behind them. He steadied on course over the English countryside, which was now disappearing in ragged clouds.

Kassel was going to be a tough nut. A major transportation hub for central Germany, the city and rail yards were ringed by some of the worst flak on the continent. Long range search radars would pick up the American formation as it crossed the channel and they could expect fighter attacks as soon as they neared the German border. The flight plan called for three hours to target and they were well within fighter intercept range for two hours going in and two coming out.

"Cleared to test your guns," John called on the intercom, "Remember to conserve ammunition today. When you're out, you're out. And that makes the krauts very happy."

Kneeling at the aft station, Huggie looked on each side of himself at the storage bins for the belts of .50 caliber ammunition. As much as there was, it didn't take long to use it up. He ran his hands over the smooth brass rounds and felt good that he could fight back at those bastards. Credited with one kill and one probable, Huggie knew he was a good gunner. In fact it was probably the only thing he'd ever been any good at in his whole life. Growing up dirt poor on a ranch in Ohio, he'd quit school in the sixth grade and gone to work in a local garage in Warrenton. With the exception of a summer liaison with a girl at the nearby church camp, his life had been uniformly boring. Until 1942 he'd never been more than thirty miles from the farm. If they could see me now, he thought.

"Weather's looking worse than briefed," Sean said over his shoulder to Bloch.

"Yeah," was the terse response. In his mind, Paul Bloch considered the challenge of hours of flying formation in difficult weather and the very real chance the target would be obscured, against the pressing need to hit this target. On the good side, it made it tougher for the krauts to find them.

"We've been alerted," Karl Ulrich said, sticking his head into Rudolf Steinfeld's office.

"Any details?"

"Same old crap, 'many enemy aircraft crossing the channel.'"

Steinfeld got up, arching his back to relieve the ache. He had confidence in the Wurzburg radar

71

system, but he had also been on many unsuccessful intercepts brought on by faulty interpretation of the data by the controllers.

Picking up his flying helmet, he joined his friend as they walked to the flight line.

"You know, they're not going to stop coming," Karl said.

"The yanks?"

"Every day, more bombers, more raids. Hell we've been shooting down more than they should be able to replace, but they keep coming."

Steinfeld knew his friend was right. While he had seen the intelligence estimates, it was clear to the men flying against the Eighth Air Force that the enemy was getting stronger and smarter every day. Rumors about the arrival of long range fighters had been rampant recently. The monopoly of the air by German fighters would end someday and Rudolf knew that would signal the beginning of the end for the air war. Even today he wasn't getting the replacements he needed and when they did arrive they had fewer hours and less gunnery training than anyone could consider satisfactory.

"We have to trust Galland, I know he's working to get us the fuel and new aircraft we need."

"Dolfo's a fighter pilot, not an ass-kissing, boot licking politician. He stands no chance in Berlin," Karl said, his voice angry.

As they split up to head for their own aircraft, Rudolf called after him, "Worry about keeping yourself alive, my friend. Let Galland take care of himself."

Sean noted 14,400 feet on the altimeter and knew that Paul Bloch was scanning around them, having thrown Don Parr out of the upper turret. It was just hard to call. It looked like the weather in front of the formation was breaking up a bit, but any lower and they would be torn apart by the 88mm flak guns that surrounded Kassel.

"Your airplane," Sean said to John Forster, taking his hands off the yoke.

"Right-o," came the rather non-regulation reply, but both men knew what it meant.

He turned as Parr and Bloch swapped places, the wing commander squeezing back into the jump seat.

"Whaddaya think?"

"I don't like the weather, but I think we can make it. What about you?"

"We're only forty or so miles from the IP. Fighters are nowhere to be found. I say we press on, hit the target then get the hell out of there."

"I'm going to leave altitude control to individual wings, if the weather is changing fast enough maybe they can step it up near the target."

Sean nodded. At least they would be a lot more accurate from a lower altitude, provided they didn't lose aircraft before they dropped.

"Bandits, right, three o'clock high," came the call from the top turret, the electric drive now alive moving the twin machine guns around to starboard.

"A dozen FW's," Kucinich called from the waist.

"Here they come," Parr continued, "Three o'clock going to two."

The staccato roar from the top turret was immediately repeated from the starboard waist and ball turret, tracers reaching out toward the small shapes now hurtling toward *Jezebel*.

Twenty minutes in and out the clouds, trying to follow the fighter director's calls with two divisions of fighters had pushed Steinfeld to the limit. His anger was reaching a boiling point when they flashed through a layer of clouds to see at least a dozen B-17's flying two miles parallel to them off their left wing, 2000 feet lower.

Blind luck, he told himself as he pulled hard left and commenced a turn to set up for his attack. Fighting the 'g' forces, he confirmed guns selected, checked quickly for his wingman and rolled wings level, his gunsight framing the lead B-17. As he began to fire from 1000 meters, he saw the orange tail and knew he'd found the American 23rd Group again.

Sean felt the airframe shudder as the top turret rotated behind him trying to bring the twin .50's to bear on the attackers.

"Starboard wing," John yelled as the FW flashed over the cockpit so low they heard his engine.

Turning, Sean knew the aircraft had been hit hard.

"Fire in number four," John yelled.

"Roger four," Sean called back, pulling the throttle closed and flipping the fuel boost pump off. "Feathering four," he continued slamming the feather button hard to drive the propeller blades to a neutral position.

"Smoke only, no flames on four!"

"Rog, opening cowl flaps and locking them out."

"Christ, flames on number three...three's on fire," John called.

"Shutting down three," Sean answered, desperation creeping into his voice.

Jezebel was now losing altitude and Sean knew he couldn't hold her.

"Gingerbread Two, you've got the lead," he transmitted using Mike Sullivan's call sign for the day. Already pre-briefed, the experienced aviator would take over the lead for the 23rd's formation while the 504th's wing commander would assume control of the entire strike.

"Anvil, Anvil, this is Jupiter. You now have the strike lead, acknowledge."

Paul Bloch understood without asking McGowan. They would no longer would they be doing anything but trying to survive.

Pushing the throttles up on the two remaining engines, Sean began a left turn to the north.

"Nav, heading for base, right now."

"Roger," O'Loughlin said as he drew a pencil line on the chart.

"Bombardier, stand by to dump our bombs. We're over empty country right now."

Hass checked the armament fuzing was safe and then opened the bomb bay doors.

A moment later the aircraft's gentle descent was arrested as almost 4,000 pounds of ordnance were jettisoned.

"Steady on mag heading 355."

"Number three cowl flapped open and locked. All fuel switches off on both engines, how's it looking out there?"

John Forster nodded after one more look.

"No smoke."

"Roger heading 355," Sean said, beginning an easy turn to the left.

"Criminy," Forster said, "We're losing fuel."

Sweating despite the cold temperature, McGowan pulled off his mask to wipe his face. "How far to the nearest base, nav."

Steve O'Loughlin had already been measuring the new pencil line across his chart.

"280 miles, skipper, we could land at Manston or Ramsgate."

Only a number, Sean thought, only a number, remembering the frigid English Channel that lay between them and safety.

"Roger."

He turned to Bloch who'd been listening on the intercom.

The older man shrugged. They both knew it would be close.

"Let's get a fuel check, John. Better to know in any case."

"Right," came the terse response.

"Okay, we're on our own. Keep your eyes open for krauts."

Looking left and right, Rudolf was irritated but not angry with his new wingman, Albert. Only two months in combat, he was still learning. However that would not prevent him from chewing the young pilots' ass when they landed. The lieutenant's job was to stay on Rudolf's wing, no matter what the lead did. Now he was nowhere to be seen.

It was time to go home in any case. He was almost out of ammunition and had less than thirty minutes of fuel left. And, he admitted to himself, he was tired. A quick navigation check and he turned north for Dortmund. Scanning around he noted that there was some amount of clearing to the east, always better to avoid the heavy weather in any case. Then he caught a shape down and to his right.

They might just make it, he thought after John reported their burnable fuel. Of course they could still lose more, there was no telling where all the damage was after that final attack. *Jezebel* was going to be in the hangar for some time if his guess was right. He'd seen aircraft with less damage written off if there was damage to any of the main structure. Better treat her gently on this trip he thought, remembering the wing coming off Todd's fort on landing.

"John, I don't want to pass up any suitable landing field. Check them out and let me know what you think."

"Can do."

The B-17 was flying on two engines, but there was no smoke or other visible damage and the vertical stabilizer was orange. Rudolf realized the aircraft might very well have been the leader he had attacked on the first run. He knew he'd scored multiple hits on the starboard wing and now both of those engines were feathered. Could it possibly be the same one? Whoever it was, they were a long way from England and likely wouldn't make it home anyway. He found himself pulling power and starting a slow descent parallel to the crippled bomber. He knew he should make one run, targeting the cockpit and try to finish the bomber off. At the very least he should be calling the controllers to lead a flight after the orange tail and destroy it.

He continued his descent, leveling at the fortress's altitude perhaps two miles abeam. Ahead a line of clouds lowered well below where he flew now and would engulf the American shortly. Why was he holding off?

"SHIT, single kraut fighter three o'clock level. It looks like he hasn't seen us." Don Parr slewed his turret out on the bearing, but knew the distance made shooting futile.

"He sees us alright," Sean said. "Probably calling the entire Luftwaffe to come join him would be my guess." England suddenly seemed very far away.

John Forster said nothing, he knew how this would play out and he didn't want to dwell on the end.

"Should be in the goo in two or three minutes," he said.

Sean had already thought about it, but the German knew that too. Why wasn't he attacking? Jammed guns? No ammo left?

The distance had now closed to a mile and Rudolf was drawn to the detail that he never really saw during attacks. On the nose was what looked like a big-breasted woman, with some name painted underneath. The Americans are obsessed with boobs he thought. Well why not, he laughed to himself, but German breasts were better, much firmer too.

"For now, hold your fire," Sean commanded to all stations. "I don't know why he isn't attacking, but I'd just as soon not provoke him."

"Jesus, would you look at that," Kucinich said. "It's one of those orange-tailed bastards."

"You're right," Harry said, leaning over his friend's back at the left waist station.

"Well I don't see anyone else back here," Huggie added.

The crew wasn't sure what to do, but they all continued to watch as the FW-190 slowly moved closer, the pilot now clearly visible in the cockpit.

"Maybe he just wants to take a look," Tommy Moore said, peering out the small window over his radio station.

"This makes no bloody sense," Forster said. "But what the hell, none of this ever makes sense."

Paul Bloch had traded places with Don Parr and said nothing but kept watching the fighter close to just outside 1000 yards.

"Train your turrets aft," Sean said. "Let's make sure he knows we're not looking for a kill."

Steinfeld knew he should break off, his fuel was getting short, but then he saw both the top and bottom turrets train their guns aft simultaneously.

Damn.

I will do it, he told himself and moved the stick slightly to the right, closing slowly just forward of the B-17's wing line. He could see right into the cockpit, the pilot's face turned directly at him. This must be a veteran crew, he thought. Rookies would have panicked by now. What am I doing, he asked himself, closing the distance to 100 feet. He reached up and unhooked the right side of his mask, letting it dangle open and turned to look at the pilot.

Sean McGowan watched the clouds approaching as the fighter closed with him. Okay he thought, his guns are pointing forward, he apparently is just coming in for a look. Then he saw the pilot drop his mask. Damn it. McGowan undid his mask and looked at the other pilot. He was a big man who filled the FW's cockpit. Probably has blond hair too, Sean thought. Then the pilot made a casual salute. Without thinking, Sean returned the salute, watching the fighter move down just as the bomber entered the clouds.

"Shit, I've seen everything now."

Chapter Eight

Two days later, Sean was in his office when the Assistant Chief of Staff for Intelligence of the Eighth Air Force arrived unannounced.

"Wanted to show you something," Colonel Steve Bernier said, with little ceremony. They knew each other from Sean's time as Eaker's aide and had developed a friendly relationship.

Sean stood up as Bernier spread three large black and white photos on his desk.

"First of all, you need to give your radio operator a three-day pass for taking these photos. We were able to gather information from our folks, the RAF and I think we know what we have here. This is an FW-190 model A6. It's from the 95th Fighter Wing of the 7th Aeroflotte, currently based near Dortmund. But here's the icing on the cake. See that black and white lighting symbol?"

Sean could see it painted below the orange tail cap.

"Okay, what does that mean?"

"We think this may be Steinfeld, Colonel Rudolf Steinfeld, one of the original core of Luftwaffe fighter pilots. These guys fought together in Spain and kicked everyone's ass when the war started. Some of them have over a hundred kills."

"So why did he do what he did?"

"Don't know," Bernier said, as he pulled out a pack of cigarettes and lit one. "Probably doesn't mean a fucking thing, but it drives intelligence officers crazy. Anything you've thought of since you got back?"

Sean remembered the long and painful flight back after the fighter left. They didn't see another aircraft and were able to land at Manston. *Jezebel* was still there having the number three and four engines changed along with a complete inspection. Other than the punctured fuel tanks, there appeared to be no structural damage.

"Nothing. It didn't make sense then, but I'm glad it worked out the way it did."

"We'd just as soon keep this as quiet. What we don't now could be important, so get that word out if you would."

"Hell, no one would believe it anyway."

Steinfeld. Colonel Rudolf Steinfeld. A Luftwaffe ace who, for one strange moment in time, wanted to see a B-17 up close. Next time we meet, he'll try to kill me.

"Colonel, he hates my guts, but he deserves it. And he'll be able to do more as a captain than as a master sergeant, even if he doesn't believe it."

Paul Bloch said, "It will be a temporary rank, but I have to think that in the long term he can convert to regular."

"Will he go along with it? He's a pretty hard headed son of a bitch, as you well know."

"I think I know how to pull it off."

On the next stand down day, it was time for an awards ceremony to recognize those men whose awards for combat had come in for presentation. The normal routine was to have the group at morning quarters and then the men being honored would be called up front and center, awards read and Colonel Bloch would pin on the medal. While the majority of awards were Air Medals and Purple Hearts, there would be Bronze Stars, a few Distinguished Flying Crosses and the rare Silver Star.

Today seventeen men had been called forward, the tinny public address system echoing inside the main hangar at Paddington.

Each awardee saluted the colonel, then their citation was read, the medal pinned on, a hearty handshake, one more salute and on to the next man.

Next to the last, Colonel Block returned the salute of Staff Sergeant Anthony Fortino, who in recognition of conspicuous gallantry above and beyond the call of duty in combat against the enemy was being awarded the Silver Star for gallantry.

Fortino's eyes remained fixed ahead, almost as if he was in a trance. The wise guy from West Orange, New Jersey was scared to death.

Paul Bloch pinned on the medal and turned so the photographer could take a shot.

"Smile, sergeant, this is for your mother," Bloch said, trying to relax what was obviously a very uncomfortable hero.

After the flash bulb went off, Block offered his hand.

"I'm proud of you son, and you should be too."

Fortino saluted, a small smile on his face.

"Yes, sir."

Next to the diminutive gunner, Master Sergeant William Joseph Hass stood like a mountain. He had been surprised at being called up in front of the wing. In any case, he knew the drill.

Snapping off a sharp salute, he said. "Good morning, colonel."

Bloch returned the salute.

"This is important for the good of the Air Force and the good of the group. Do we understand each other?"

The tone of Bloch's voice surprised Hass, but a career in uniform resulted in the answer that the wing commander expected.

"Yes, sir."

The group adjutant began to read over the public address system: "From the Secretary of the Army to Master Sergeant William J. Hass. Effective immediately you are promoted to the rank of captain in the United States Army Air Force, to serve with a date of rank effective 1 November, 1943. Signed E.G. Rutherford, Chief of Army Personnel."

"Congratulations, Captain Hass."

Paul Bloch raised his hand in salute to which the newly promoted Captain Hass responded automatically.

"Gotcha," Bloch said grinning as he walked away.

Standing in front of the squadron, Sean McGowan felt good about what had just happened. He hates me, but he's a hell of a soldier, he thought.

"I'm not exactly sure how to tell you this, but Jamie doesn't want to see you." John Forster looked uncomfortable sitting in a chair across from McGowan in his office.

"Why?"

"Aubrey wasn't specific, but Jamie lost her fiancé when he went down in a Lancaster. I guess she isn't ready to go through that again."

"Shit, I'm not her fiancé. I just want to see her."

"Hey, mate, don't piss on me, I know that. But she's a woman and as you and I both know, women don't make any sense.

How could I be such an idiot, Sean asked himself? He had felt what they had was something special. Apparently not.

"So you're headed for London and yours truly isn't invited."

"I'll tell you what. We go into town and have a good time, then I'll zip off to Mayfair to collect Miss Rose and you can head off wherever your American heart desires."

"What a shitty way to fight a war."

"I had the PX folks put this stuff together for you," Paul Bloch said handing a large brown package to Billy Hass. "Insignia, cap, all the crap you need. And you now have a bunk in officer's quarters."

"I haven't said yes."

"Are you going to hide behind some bullshit antiquated idea that all officers are assholes who don't work for a living and every sergeant is the brick upon which the army is built?"

Billy sat with his tie loosened, a glass of scotch in his hand.

"Sergeants make the army work."

"I know that, but damn it the army needs officers who know what they're doing to make the sergeants effective. You and I both know one dumb shit officer can cancel out ten sergeants."

Paul Bloch was a West Point graduate and Billy knew the commander's only goal was for his group to be the best. He wasn't bad for a regular army type.

"All right, colonel. I'll do it. But don't expect me to play any games. I'll still call 'em as I see 'em."

"Captain, I never expected anything else. Now are you ready to leave the flying to the younger ones so you can run things?"

Billy drained the glass.

"You lead from the front. If you want me to wear these bars, I'll do the same thing. I still fly."

He had tried, Bloch told himself, but he knew Hass would never take the easy way out.

"Come on Tony, let's get shit-faced and celebrate your medal. That's a slick deal." Corporal Anthony Auferio was lying in his rack, in a sleeveless undershirt and fatigue pants.

Staff Sergeant Fortino looked at his friend and said, "Anthony, I can't. I told Hass that I'd keep my nose clean."

"That's bullshit. Who's he, some kiss ass who ends up with bars? What a crock."

Tony looked at his friend and shook his head.

"Auferio, you're full of shit," he said and without another word walked out the barrack's door.

"Yeah, he gets fucking stripes and now he thinks he's God," Auferio said, rolling back on his bunk. He pulled a cigarette from behind his left ear and lit it. "Shit."

The small pub began to fill with customers getting off work from the surrounding government offices. John Forster had spent enough time in the area that he knew the bartender by name and two beers materialized as soon as the flyers sat down.

"When were you last home?"

Forster looked up from his glass, "Australia?"

Sean nodded.

"Over three years ago. Got here in February of '40."

"So you've seen the worst of it."

"Maybe the newspaper writers would say that, but hell, every day we go up is just as bad. Blokes keep getting killed and I guess it doesn't matter what the 'big picture' is if you're the one getting killed."

"How about this town?"

"That's different. You can see the damage now, even some of the rebuilding. But there was a time there when I thought the krauts would burn London to the ground."

"Now we're trying to do the same thing to their cities," Sean said.

"Too right. They started this stinking war."

After ordering another round, they both loosened their ties and sat back against the high-backed wooden booth.

"How about switching from night to daylight raids?"

"Bloody terrifying to see those bastards coming in on you, I'll tell you. But no doubt the bomb hits are better."

"Is it worth it?"

John laughed. "Ask me when the war's over."

From outside a siren began to wail.

"Damn. I was supposed to meet Aubrey in thirty minutes, now this will bollix up the whole night." John put his drink down. "Come on, let's go."

"Hey, Fortino."

Tony turned and saw Don Parr and Larry Kucinich down the street. He'd taken the bus to Paddington just to get away from the barracks. For the last hour he had been walking the quiet streets with no real purpose.

"Hey, guys."

"What ya doing out here by yourself?"

Fortino smiled. "Just gettin' some fresh air."

"Come on, I'll buy you a beer."

The three men began to walk north toward the town's most popular pub.

Jogging down the street, Sean could hear the anti-aircraft batteries firing from near the river. Glancing up he saw what first looked like a cloud then realized it was one of the many barrage balloons that swayed about the city in a now darkened sky.

"Hey," came a cry from behind them.

"Keep going, it's just some bleedin' air raid warden," John called as he turned down an alley that cut through a long row of houses and into the next street.

The dull roar of engines could be heard above the broken clouds. As they ran full tilt north, the air was split with the shriek of a stick of bombs slamming into the next street, the concussion hitting the men like a hammer followed by a roar that seemed to burst Sean's eardrums.

Both men found themselves thrown to the pavement, dust and debris completely obscuring everything around them.

"Christ," John yelled and he rolled on his back in agony, his arms held close to his chest.

Sean got to his knees and staggered to his friend's side.

"Are you hurt?" McGowan yelled, his ears still ringing from the blast.

John shook his head, "No...... just give me a minute," he gasped.

Looking toward the next street, Sean could see flames starting to show through the dust and smoke that continued to roil above the destruction.

Rolling onto his stomach, Forster pulled himself to his knees, still gasping for his breath. "It's their street," he cried, stumbling to his feet and staggering toward the smoke.

Sirens could be heard in the distance as the two men ran into the street, which was littered with rubble from several houses that had been leveled by direct hits.

"Over there, thank God," John yelled and ran forward to a two-story house that looked undamaged save for smoke rising from the rear of the structure. The fashionable townhouse next door had been torn apart by a bomb and flames were spreading through what remained of the inside. He stumbled up the steps to the door and tried to open it. "Damn it," he said looking around desperately.

"Around back," Sean said.

Running to the gap left by the bomb damage next door, the two men scrambled over broken masonry and shattered furniture.

Coughing from the thickening smoke, Sean felt his eyes watering from the acrid fumes as he tried figure out what he was seeing.

"Down here," John called, climbing over what remained of a low wall.

"Aubrey, where are you?" he yelled. "Aubrey, it's John, are you in here?"

Sean jumped down next to his friend, realizing that the lack of damage to the front of the house didn't tell the real story. A maze of broken wood and bricks covered what looked like a kitchen. From inside the wreckage he could see flames beginning to spread.

"Damn it, the shelter is down the stairs under there," John said, pointing to a wooden door partially blocked by floor beams.

"Quiet," Sean told John, grabbing his friend's arm.

They knelt down, their heads turned, listening.

The plaintive cry was barely audible.

"Damn!" Forster yelled in frustration. "We need help."

Watching the small flames spreading, Sean knew there wasn't time. He threw his feet over the remains of the outer wall and slid down toward the blocked door. Dust and smoke made him cough violently as he slammed into a beam that blocked the doorway.

John slid down next to him, throwing more dust into the air.

"Down there, right?" Sean asked.

"Leads to the cellar, but there's no other way out."

"Jamie, Aubrey, are you all right?" Sean yelled, his voice cracking from the effort.

A muffled reply was inaudible but they at least knew someone was alive.

"Come on!"

Sean threw himself forward, grabbing the wooden beam and pushing with all his strength to dislodge it.

Forster joined him and they both strained trying to move the largest barrier to the doorway.

"It's no use," Sean said dropping to his knees, his breath coming in gasps.

They could both hear the crackling of flames as the fire continued to spread through the broken wooden structure.

"We need an axe......"

Forster turned his head as the sound of a fire siren rose over the clamor.

Sean grabbed his arm, "Get help down here."

"I'll be back," he said and scrambled up the broken wall.

"We're gonna get you out," Sean yelled. He slid down to the door and wedged himself against the beam then kicked with all his strength. The door was solid and barely moved from the impact of Sean's kick. Looking around for anything to attack the door, he saw a piece of metal leaning against some broken bricks. Reaching down he saw it was a fire poker which must have come from an upstairs fireplace. Using it like a pike, he smashed the sharp point into one of the decorative panels on the door. Again and again he swung the poker, even though he could tell it was doing little good, at least they would know someone was trying to get to them.

"Watch out," John yelled, sliding down next to Sean and holding a fire axe.

Pulling himself out of the way, Sean watched as John brought the axe over his head and slammed it into the door with every ounce of his strength. Jerking the handle, he broke the axe free and quickly swung again striking a rhythm.

Sean watched as the axe blade dug deeper into the door. Small pieces of wood began to fly off, as the panel started to buckle.

"Here," Sean said, taking the axe from John who was breathing hard, sweat running off his face, glistening in the light of the flames that were building around them.

Two more swings and the upper part of the door crumpled into the cellar sending a plume of smoke upward toward the men.

"Aubrey, we're here,'" John yelled, pushing forward into the smoke, which was now clearing, showing a hole in the door wide enough for a person to crawl through. "Jamie.....Aubrey?"

"I'm going down there," Sean said, his voice grim. Grabbing the door frame he kicked viciously at the ragged edge of the hole, breaking out the remaining panel. In one motion he pushed his feet through the hole and lowered himself down into the cellar.

Taking one last breath he reached down and began to feel for the cellar steps. Coughing violently, Sean called, "Jamie, Aubrey!"

From the blackness he heard Aubrey's weak voice. "Here."

Working down two steps in pitch blackness he reached out finding her collapsed across the stairs.

"I've got you," he said. "JOHN!"

"I'm here, mate."

Quickly they had Aubrey through the door and into John's arms.

Without a word McGowan went back down into the darkness.

"Jamie, Jamie, where are you?"

He began to feel his way down the stairs like a blind man. Stumbling, he caught himself on the handrail, his other hand touching an outstretched arm.

"Jamie," he said quickly but there was no response. He found her waist and slid down so he could support her weight on his shoulder. Looking up he saw enough light to orient himself and began to climb.

"Here!"

John stood in the opening, his hands reaching down. They struggled with the limp body, but managed to get her through the jagged hole in the door. Emerging right behind Jamie, Sean began coughing violently. The fire had grown and now the front of the house was totally involved, flames shooting up behind the broken walls.

Several firemen had appeared on the top of the rubble and scrambled down to assist.

"Here you go," a big man with a Cornish accent said as he picked up Jamie in a fireman's carry and struggled up the rubble with another fireman pushing him from behind.

"Best we be getting out of here," another blue uniformed man said. "Here, lend me a hand."

With moves that had obviously been practiced too many times, the stocky firefighter helped Aubrey to her feet and put one arm over his shoulder.

"We'll have you out of here in no time, young lady."

Sean and John helped the man carry Aubrey up the rubble and away from the flames.

Fires were burning brightly in several buildings as they made their way into the street. One old fire truck was parked at the end of the block where three firemen directed a thin stream of water toward a burning building. Next to the fire truck was an olive-drab ambulance, the white and red cross stark in the light of the fires.

"Christ," Sean exclaimed at seeing the destruction, smoke and flames around them. So this was what it was like, he thought. Aubrey coughed, her body convulsing as they laid her down on the sidewalk. He looked around to see two firemen lifting Jamie into the ambulance. He suddenly realized he was afraid.

Tony Fortino was used to drinking until he could forget about everything around him. But tonight was different. He'd enjoyed the quiet conversation and camaraderie of the other sergeants. There hadn't been any bravado or bullshit, just four airmen trying to take a break from what they all faced on missions. They had talked of the current baseball season, their favorite foods and what they wanted to do when the war was over.

"How 'bout you," Don asked.

Tony had been wondering quietly to himself, what the hell will I do?

"Guess I'll go back home and get a job."

"Doin' what?"

"Never thought about it much. All I did before the war was hang out on the corner with my buddies and play stickball."

Larry Kucinich laughed, "That sounds like me, waiting for the weekend or something to happen. Guess we won't do that anymore."

The four men nodded, realizing that time was something that had become more precious.

Huggie Loggins finished his beer, "That's it for me. I have a rack with a soft pillow that's crying my name."

They all laughed and stood up.

Chapter Nine

It took Sean almost an hour to locate the Welbeck Hospital in Marlybone. The three-story brick front was clearly marked with large red crosses, the windows crisscrossed with tape to protect against flying glass. Racing up the steps, he hoped the ambulance driver had been correct. Was this the right hospital?

The confusion seemed insurmountable as he entered a lobby that was crowded with people, many wearing hastily applied bandages.

"Excuse me," Sean said to a nurse standing behind the main counter.

"You'll have to wait," she said and turned away with a clipboard, walking to a recessed back office.

With no option, he leaned on the counter and waited for the woman to turn back.

"I'm looking for someone," Sean blurted out as she returned, clipboard still in hand.

"As is everyone," she said, her voice tired but surprisingly pleasant. "Now can you tell me the name?"

"Miss Taylor-Paige, Jamie Taylor-Paige."

"Age?"

"I guess twenty five or so……"

"And when did she arrive?"

"In the last hour. She came by ambulance from Mayfair."

The woman flipped through several pages of notes.

"You're in luck, she's in the treatment room now. You may see her when they're finished."

Almost an hour later the nurse from the desk called to him. "Miss Taylor-Paige is in room 204."

"How is she?"

"Resting," she said, her voice friendly. "Smoke inhalation, but she should be fine. We'll keep her overnight just to be safe."

Sean McGowan hated hospitals. As he walked up the stairs to the second floor, the smell of disinfectant brought back memories from his childhood, but now it didn't seem to matter.

He found the small placard for room 204 outside a closed door. Slowly he turned the door knob and cracked the door open. He could see two obviously occupied beds. Quietly entering the room, he saw Jamie in the closest bed and was relieved that there was a portable screen blocking the other bed.

Jamie's eyes were closed and she seemed to be sleeping. Sean sat down carefully in a chair next to the foot of the bed. She looked peaceful he thought, a godsend after the terror of being trapped in that basement. He found that he was happy to sit in the quiet room with this young woman. Strange, he thought, I barely know her, but I want to be here with her. His thoughts drifted back to their first meeting and when she had kissed him good night.

"Sean?"

He stood up and went to her side.

"Hello Miss Taylor-Paige. How are you feeling?"

She thought for a moment.

"Tired.......where am I?"

"Welbeck Hospital. A little too much smoke, they said."

He could see she was trying to remember.

"The door was blocked.....Aubrey...is she alright?"

"She'll be fine, just a bit knocked about. John stayed with her."

"The house?"

He shook his head, "Not much left, I'm afraid. But you should be out of here in the morning, good as new."

She smiled at him.

"Thank you."

He took her hand but said nothing.

Jamie gently squeezed his hand and closed her eyes.

On the first day of December, Jagdgeschwader 95 had intercepted the American bombers fifteen miles south of Essen. On his second scramble of the day, Oberstleutnant Rudolf Steinfeld instinctively picked out his target, the lead B-17 at his two o'clock. Quickly crossing his wingman to the left wing, he rolled the fighter hard right and pulled around toward the bomber. One last check of the sky for other fighters and he turned his attention to the attack. From the radio calls he knew there were Messerschmitts attacking from the north as the might of the Luftwaffe converged on the attackers who appeared heading for Cologne. Either a new tactic or the American's poor formation flying, the high and low squadrons of this group seemed to be too close to the lead. They would pay for that mistake when their own defensive guns were blocked by friendly aircraft.

Adjusting his gunsight reticles slightly above the Fortress' cockpit he fired, knowing that he would score deadly hits on this run. Catching tracers in his peripheral vision, Steinfeld rolled hard left and began his dive away from the Americans. Enough of this, he thought, something didn't feel right.

In a blinding instant the forward section of his aircraft was torn apart by a concentrated burst of machine gun fire. Smoke began to billow over the cockpit and his experience told him the damage was fatal. A terrible vibration shook the airframe as the engine began tearing itself apart and igniting at the same time. No question now, he must get out before the entire aircraft burst into flames or exploded.

Desperately, he jettisoned the canopy and released his seat restraints. Engulfed in thick oily smoke he coughed hard, his eyes watering despite wearing goggles. He grabbed the canopy edge and pulled with all his might as he pushed his feet against the seat bottom. Searing pain worse than anything he had ever felt engulfed his body as he fell away from the stricken fighter.

Fighting for his breath, the waves of pain seemed to slow the world around him as he tumbled in a whirling nightmare of sky and ground. He knew he had to find his ripcord, find it and pull it. Ignore the pain, fight it with all your will until you can find the square metal handle. Tumbling he searched with his right hand as a feeling of panic began to overcome him. It had to be there.

The opening shock came moments after Rudolf had found the ripcord and between waves of pain, pulled with all his strength. As the canopy inflated, the last thing he felt was a violent jerk and his world slipped into blackness.

"Remind me we don't want to go back there again," McGowan said, adjusting the rudder trim on *Jezebel*.

Forster nodded without looking at the pilot.

"No arguments, mate."

"We got a problem," Billy Hass said as he moved up between the two pilots.

Sean turned to the bombardier, seeing the look in his eye.

Hass continued, "We still have one five hundred pound bomb aboard."

"Can you tell what happened?" McGowan asked.

The big man shook his head.

"Not for sure. It looks like the front latches opened and the aft stayed shut. It's hanging nose down."

Sean knew what that meant, a "hung bomb" could drop at any time or might stay secure until the armorers down-loaded it.

"Nobody down there but Germans, let's try to drop it again," Forster offered.

"The fuse is still attached?"

Hass nodded.

"Okay, see if it will drop. When the bomb bay doors are open, let me know and I'll yaw the aircraft gently."

"Gotcha."

"Shit, the ball turret's jammed." Fortino's voice was harsh on the intercom.

"Engineer, get back there and give 'em a hand."

"Roger."

McGowan took off his mask and rubbed his cheeks.

"What next?"

John Forster laughed, "Sure you want to know?"

Putting the mask back on, he activated his throat microphone.

"Okay, stay alert, we're still over krautland and as I recall they still don't like us much."

Hass reappeared in the cockpit.

"No luck on the doors. They closed fine, but there must have been some damage from that flak after the target."

"Got any more good news?" McGowan asked.

Hass nodded his head again.

"The bomb fell far enough that it snapped the arming wire. I don't know if there was enough wind in the bay to arm it."

Normally a bomb that isn't armed was considered safe, although "safe" bombs had been known to explode. But if the bomb had armed, the jolt at touchdown might jar it loose and it could go off. The only safe thing to do was to bail the crew out and let *Jezebel* head out to sea.

"I can try to unscrew the fuse," Hass said.

"Are you out of your bleedin' mind?" Forster asked.

"He's right," Sean said. "We just don't know. Trying to take it out might very well set it off."

"Over here, over here."

Steinfeld lay on his side in a shallow muddy ditch, parachute risers entangled around his body and hanging from a small tree. He rolled over despite terrible pain to see a very young private standing on the edge of the ditch with a model '98 Mauser pointed directly at him. The helmet seemed much too big for the boy and for a moment the colonel almost laughed.

"Point that damned rifle somewhere else before you hurt someone," Steinfeld said in his most Prussian voice.

"Ah...sir, I thought you were an American....sir."

"Would you like to check my identity disc or perhaps I should show you my Iron Cross?"

"Uh, no sir, of course not."

"Then help me get the hell out of here!"

Several infantrymen and a sergeant appeared from the woods. In several minutes Colonel Rudolf Steinfeld had been rescued from his ditch.

"I don't think we have any options. We need to find an area we can bail out and point her somewhere that won't kill anyone."

"Never crazy about parachutes, but it makes too much sense," John Forster said.

"Controlled bail out, daytime, no one's hurt, maybe 5000 feet, nice and slow?"

"Right."

"Skipper, we got a problem back here," Don Parr said on the intercom.

"Standby. John, go back and see what's going on."

Forster made his way back, crossing the walkway into the radio compartment where he saw Don Parr kneeling down next to the turret assembly. Behind him, the two waist gunners maintained a watch for enemy fighters.

"What's up?"

"Fucking thing won't move. There must be metal jammed in there and we can't get it around to let Fortino out."

Forster eased back in the co-pilot's seat. He and Billy Hass had worked for fifteen minutes with Parr to no avail. *Jezebel's* ball turret was badly jammed. The only way Staff Sergeant Fortino was going to get out of it was on deck with the assistance of a team of mechs.

"God damn it!" Fortino yelled as he moved the control grips left and right, trying to get the turret to move. He heard the hydraulic pumps screaming, but nothing was happening. His worst nightmare was happening and there was nothing he could do.

"You have fractured your pelvis, herr oberst. Not the most romantic of injuries, but surely one of the most painful."

In a drug-induced fog, Rudolf listened to the doctor, trying to concentrate on his words. Steinfeld had survived the ride to the hospital only to collapse on arrival. Since then he had been in and out of consciousness as the hospital tried to immobilize him as much as possible.

"We won't know if there is nerve damage until the medication wears off. You must have hit the tail when you bailed out and the bruising is very bad. All you can do now is rest. It will take a great deal of time for this to heal. I have to warn you, this type of injury may result in your inability to control your bladder, or possibly your sexual functions. I'm sorry."

Rudolf didn't care at this point, he just wanted the pain to stop. And he wanted to get the hell out of this hospital.

"I need to get back to my squadron," he said slowly, each word causing pain in his gut.

"The army is contacting the Luftwaffe. But nothing will happen today. So sleep, it's the best thing for you.

"That's the plan," Sean told the crew over the intercom.

There was no response from the rest of the flyers to Sean's intention to have them bail out over Paddington. He would then try to land *Jezebel* as carefully as possible.

"Go over you procedures, check your chutes and be ready. We'll be at the field in thirty minutes."

"I'll stick with you," Forster said across the cockpit.

"John, these guys need to see you go first. That's leadership by example."

"That's a load of crap and you know it!"

"I need you to do it for me."

McGowan thought about what he was about to say. Would he regret it?

"If something happens, I want you to talk to Jamie."

Forster turned but said nothing.

"Tell her she's someone very special and not to forget that."

"Sean, if something happens to you that would only make it harder on her."

"You and Hass make sure everyone is squared away and ready to jump on my signal."

Fifteen minutes later Forster returned with Hass right behind.

"I'm sticking with the ship," Hass said without any ceremony.

"You're following my orders, captain."

"You owe me this one."

McGowan began to protest, but held himself.

"Fortino is back in that turret by himself. I'll be damned if I'll leave him there to die alone if that's what happens."

Forster turned to look at Billy Hass and nodded.

McGowan stared straight ahead, his eyes scanning the horizon for the familiar landmarks around Paddington.

"Okay," Sean said, his voice calm.

"How you doing down there, Tony?"

"Sweating like a pig, captain. Fortino was trying to sound in control, but knew he had never been so afraid.

"Yeah, me too."

"Okay everyone, get ready to bail out. Acknowledge individually when it's time. Two minutes."

"Well it's time, mate."

"See ya in a few minutes and you're buying the first round."

"It's a date, yank."

The two men shook hands, both grips firm.

It took two passes by *Jezebel* over the field for seven men to bail out. John Forster went last after he had made sure everyone was out.

"We're cleared to land, kid. You all set back there?"

Fortino thought he misunderstood.

"Captain Hass is still back here, skipper."

"Thought I'd keep you company," Hass said on the intercom.

Tony realized what was happening. He was still scared, but it didn't seem as important anymore.

Paul Bloch stood on the exposed deck watching the lone fortress roll on final for landing. He remembered back to Todd Smith. God don't let that happen again he prayed.

Nice steady headwind, ten knots, Sean said to himself. Gear down and locked. Everything was looking good, 250 feet per minute descent rate, steady, power back just a touch, don't float when you flare, he told himself. Easy braking, smooth, don't get carried away. Runway on the nose quarter of a mile, 105 indicated, keep the wings as level as you can McGowan. Hold the damn airplane steady.

The two main landing gear touched the runway simultaneously with the gentlest of bumps. Slowing *Jezebel*, McGowan gently stopped the big bomber on the runway centerline and began to shut down the engines. Now he could only hope that every man who jumped was alright.

"Christ," he said as he took off his headset and hung it on the hook. His shirt was soaked through with sweat.

It took almost twenty minutes to extricate Staff Sergeant Fortino from the belly turret after the ordnance disposal squad had taken care of safing the errant bomb. All seven of the "*Jezebel* Jumpers" as they called themselves later were present at one of the best parties Paddington had ever seen. And John Forster did indeed buy the first round.

The party was beginning to break up when Sean saw Billy Hass put on his cap and head for the door.

"Captain Hass."

The big man turned and shaded his eyes from the outside lights.

"Mind if I walk back with you?" Sean asked.

"We're both going the same way."

The two men walked on toward billeting.

"That was a pretty ballsy thing you did today," Sean finally said.

"Couldn't leave the kid," Hass answered.

"I'm glad you stuck around," Sean said.

Hass laughed." Hell, I'm just stubborn."

It had been a long time since Sean had heard Billy Hass laugh.

A week after bailing out, Rudolf Steinfeld arrived at the military hospital in Dortmund. The pain had been a constant companion and he couldn't remember what it was like to move normally.

"I wondered when you would find your way back here."

Steinfeld looked up to see Major Reinhardt Hanson standing in the door.

"Renni, did you bring any of your magic pills?"

Hanson was one of the Luftwaffe's most well-known doctors. The two men had been good friends for many years.

"Schnapps, that's all you need. But I did bring some pills, too."

The doctor sat down next to the bed.

"Damn this hurts."

"Good. It's about time you understood the power of modern medicine. A hundred years ago, you would die. But today, I will heal you. Actually, I don't have any choice." The doctor sat back in his chair. "I had a call from Galland. He told me, as only Dolfo can, 'get your ass down to Dortmund and fix Steinfeld.' I am to tell you that he needs you back in the air in two weeks."

"Two weeks?"

Hanson laughed.

"He's a general. He can order anything he wants to. But you'll be lucky to be ready to fly combat in less than two months."

Rudolf knew his friend was right. The pain told him that.

"So I will spend much of my time here patting you on the head and feeding you schnapps." He stood up. "So let's take a look at you and see what we've got. Hell, maybe I will do some magic – then Dolfo can make me a colonel. Until then, I'll drink and chase nurses."

Despite the crowds on the streets on a late afternoon in December, Sean found the address of the small flat just east of Hyde Park without too much trouble. But when he pushed the buzzer, there had been no answer. Not surprised, even relieved, he leaned against the brick wall to wait. Is this a good idea he kept asking himself? He kept remembering his thoughts that day approaching Paddington. He had faced danger and death many times, but suddenly it had become different. Jamie touched something in his soul that he knew he couldn't live without.

Their eyes met as she turned up the street past the red phone box. Her expression was quizzical but happily surprised.

"Hello?" she said.

"Hi."

They stood facing each other, both smiling.

"Why didn't you let me know you were coming into London?"

"You know, the weather was a bit dicey..."

"Of course, the ops types were talking about a possible scrub earlier today."

He nodded.

"So, here I am."

She smiled, her dimples accentuating her happiness at seeing him.

"Then please come in and pour me a glass of claret."

Hanging up her coat and letting her hair down, Jamie relayed that the flat was very plain compared to the house in Mayfair, but with the housing shortage, they had to put up with whatever they could find.

Sean found the bottle of claret above the fridge and managed to get the cork out, hoping that the crumbling stopper did not mean the wine had turned.

"Well done, sir," Jamie said as she came into the small kitchen.

Holding the remains of the cork, Sean smiled at her.

"Here's hoping."

Pouring the wine into a plain water tumbler, he sniffed, and then sipped.

"Not bad."

They took their glasses and moved to the rather tired sofa that covered the wall opposite the front door.

"Still no ill effects?"

Jamie shook her head.

"It was like a blur, actually. Not like the last time. I wasn't scared. It was almost as if I knew it was my time." She sipped her wine, holding the glass with both hands. "Then you were there."

"I'm glad I was."

"I guess I learned a lot about you and about myself that night."

Sean put down his wine and put his hand on hers.

"And what did you learn?"

Jamie put her hand on his cheek and said quietly, "That I could still care about someone."

Leaning over, Sean kissed her gently.

"I care about you."

She looked into his eyes and whispered, "I know."

Tears in her eyes confused Sean. "Is that a bad thing?"

Standing up, Jamie walked over to the window, glancing down into the street as she found her words.

"I lost someone very dear to me early in the war," she said in a measured tone. "Sean, I can't do that again, I just can't."

"But you told me you care."

"And I do," she said quickly, turning to face him. "That's why I can't let this go any further. I'm sorry."

Sean stood up, confused and not sure what had happened. Walking to the door he knew he couldn't look back and he closed the door behind him as he left.

Crossing to the sofa, she sat down, her hands in her lap and bowed her head.

"Gentlemen, the colonel."

Everyone in the briefing room stood as Paul Bloch walked to the front podium.

Turning, he looked over the room.

"Glad you could all join me this morning," he said, grinning broadly. "Thought a trip to France today would just suit, don't you think?"

The crowd laughed as expected and settled down for the first briefing.

John Forster sat next to Sean and took notes as the weather briefer, affectionately known as "Black Cloud," described the weak front that was now over central Germany and moving east. With the exception of high cirrus over England and the French coast, the route would, by and large, be clear.

McGowan, who normally took thorough notes sat with his arms crossed, watching Black Cloud point to the expected high altitude wind chart.

"Anything wrong?"

Forster saw a brief head shake and knew his pilot and friend was being less than truthful.

"Right, what would have ever given me that idea?"

"The target today is a railroad marshaling yard near the city of Le Mans. Each ship will be carrying eight 500 pound general purpose bombs with impact fuses. Bombardiers, good pre-flight on the weapons, the crews have been rushed this morning due to a last minute change. Never hurts to double check."

"Man your aircraft no later than 0715, expect engine starts at 0745, with the first aircraft taxiing at 0805. I will be in the lead ship and will be rolling by 0815. Expedite your takeoff. With the high overcast, we'll rendezvous overhead the field. You can see your assignments on the board. I want the high squadron at 14,000, setting the rendezvous circle, no more than five miles from the field."

The wing commander went through each item on a large briefing card, covering radio frequencies, codes of the day, fighter support, and emergency procedures.

"Alright. Bombardiers up front with Captain Hass. Navigators in the back with Captain Alford. If there aren't any questions, good luck."

Thirty minutes later John found his pilot examining one of *Jezebel's* main landing gear.

"If we're going to go battle the krauts, I need to know you're ready to go."

Sean stood up and walked over to the Australian.

"She told me she wasn't interested."

"What?"

He nodded.

"Last night, I told her how I felt and she said no go."

"Christ.........you okay to do this?"

Nodding, McGowan said, "Come on, let's get this show on the road."

It had been a hectic morning for everyone in the Air Ministry's Current Operations Section. A message from the Eighth Air Force had been misinterpreted and required a hasty round of calls and messages to Bomber, Fighter and Coastal Command.

Aubrey Rose knocked quickly and strode into the large office to see Jamie at her desk.

"Quite a flap."

Jamie looked up and just nodded.

"I saw the 23rd was on the operational sortie sheet," Aubrey said. "Just a quick trip to France, thank God."

"Men die over France every day."

Aubrey looked at her friend with a flash of anger.

"Yes, I know. But allow me a bit of hope if you don't mind."

Jamie continued to leaf through a stack of paper as she said, "I don't expect I'll be seeing Sean again."

"What does that mean?" Aubrey asked.

"I told him I couldn't deal with losing another flyer."

"So that's it?"

"I would assume so."

Aubrey stared down at her friend who continued to read the papers on her desk.

"End of story?"

Jamie looked up with tears in her eyes.

"It has to be."

Chapter Ten

As 1944 began, a new presence began to make itself felt in the skies over Europe. Finally, American long range fighters began to fly from bases in England, now carrying a powerful weapon all the way to the heart of the German Reich. No longer would the Luftwaffe own the sky over Berlin.

Jagdgeschwader 95 had not fared well against the P-47's and P-51's that were now constant companions of the American bombers. By the time Rudolf returned to Dortmund, four of his pilots had been shot down and two of those killed. It didn't surprise him that the casualties had been three of his youngest aviators. But "Frodo" Hartlein had been with Rudolf for almost two years and had nine kills to his credit. When your time was up, it didn't matter who you were, Manfred Von Richthofen or Hans Marseille, everyone died in the end.

Released from the main military hospital in Dortmund after six weeks, he was now fully supplied with a pain killer from Renni called Pethidine and enough aspirin to supply the entire squadron. He didn't like to take the drugs, but without them he couldn't function.

"What are their tactics?"

Several of his pilots were sitting around a table in their ready room. Cigarette smoke drifted up from an ashtray in the middle of the table. Steinfeld could sense their mood and it wasn't positive or aggressive. That wasn't good. Fighter pilots have to know they are better than everyone else, or they will fly like cowards and die.

"Divisions of four mostly, but if there are a hundred bombers, there will be at least fifty fighters around them."

Another pilot spoke up, "It seems that some are operating un-tethered, much like our fighter sweep, clearing a corridor for the bombers. Others are glued to the bomber formation, not straying too far away."

Logical, thought Rudolf, I'd do the same thing.

"Are they any good?"

None of the men said anything, their answer obvious by their silence.

"Then we shall adapt our tactics accordingly. We are the most experienced fighter pilots in the world. And we're flying over our own country. That was the only reason the Brits survived in '40. By God, now we'll use that advantage to win."

He could see some of the old fire returning to their eyes.

"Skipper, the tower's on the line."

Sean picked up the phone on his desk, wondering what the problem might be, as he had no aircraft in the air.

"Major, this is Sergeant Grant in the tower. We have a P-51 inbound asking to park on your line."

His surprise gave way to pleasure. McGowan knew who was in that aircraft.

"Absolutely, sergeant."

Standing on the tarmac, Sean watched the fighter taxi in, much faster than a B-17 would ever dare. But Major Randy Mahr had never played by the rules as

112

long as Sean had known him. Classmates and roommates at West Point, they had been closer than brothers and remained close as they both rose in the Army Air Force. Mahr was now the commanding officer of the 330th Fighter Squadron based at Bascome.

Chocks were shoved around the port main landing gear and the plane captain signaled the pilot to cut his engine. The big twelve cylinder engine wound down, the propeller slowing then stopping abruptly. Painted on the nose of the fighter in bright red letters, "*Joltin' Joan,*" obviously one of Mahr's many conquests.

"Hey, you got a bar on this cow pasture?"

Sean grinned up at his friend.

"We only serve milk to pursuit pilots."

The lanky pilot climbed down and the two men grabbed each other in a bear hug.

"Pursuit pilot, my ass. Good to see you, you old son of a bitch."

Sean laughed. "Wondered when you would figure out how to find England. I've been waiting."

Mahr's voice took on a serious tone for a moment.

"It took too damn long, pal. I should have been over here six months ago watching your back."

"Well you're here now, you asshole, and I'm glad you are.

The two men began to walk toward the ops building.

"So when do you start flying operations?"

"End of the week," Mahr said.

"Christ, when did you get here?"

"Three days ago."

"That's tough," Sean said. Learning the rules and lay of the land were critical to operational success. Most bomber crews had at least one month of indoctrination before going into combat.

"Hell, we'll learn on the way to Berlin. Now where's the bar?"

"First you gotta tell me who '*Joltin' Joan'* is?"

Mahr grinned.

"You'll need a drink to believe it."

Rudolf Steinfeld found himself grateful that it was the second hop of the day and the pain had been manageable, but the numbness in his feet was disturbing. Shutting the throttle, he switched off the magnetos and began to unstrap.

"Only fuel and ammunition, Fritz," he called down to his long time plane captain. Fritz Werner had been with him since 1940 and had become one of the few constants in Steinfeld's ever changing world.

"Yes, sir," the stocky sergeant said, walking off toward the nearest fuel truck.

Karl Ulrich came around the port wingtip as Steinfeld was conducting a quick post-flight of the aircraft.

"Three replacement pilots just arrived."

Checking the leading edge of the propeller, Steinfeld thought it was strange Karl would come out to the aircraft just to tell him that.

"Fine."

"One of them is your brother." Ulrich's voice was tentative.

"That's bullshit. He's only been flying for six months. He can't be a replacement here."

"Rudi, the other two are just the same. An average of 80 flight hours total. They have a few hops in the 109, mostly gunnery. We're supposed to get them operational in the 190 and into the battle."

Steinfeld stopped and stared at his friend.

"Karl, are they out of their minds?"

Ulrich shook his head.

"No, my friend. Out of pilots."

The three young officers were standing outside of Steinfeld's office when he arrived with Ulrich. Albert Steinfeld, while seven years younger, looked very much like his older brother. The honest face and bright blue eyes making him look like a teenager.

"Come in, gentlemen," Rudolf said as he walked into his office. Tossing his flying helmet on the desk, he sat down and inspected the new arrivals.

At attention in front of their new squadron commander, the three young officers were the picture of military correctness.

"Report," Rudolf said watching his brother who was staring at the wall behind Steinfeld.

"Leutnant Steinfeld reporting, sir."

"Leutnant Mossbach reporting, sir."

"Leutnant Bayern reporting, sir."

He felt the anger rising within him. Perhaps with another year of training these pilots would be ready to face the American P-47's and P-51's. But he knew the fuel for training was short and Germany's loss of experienced pilots critical. He would have to make do. Perhaps I can keep these youngsters alive long enough to make them combat pilots he told himself.

"You men have come to the best fighter wing in the Luftwaffe. Your job is to listen, watch and learn. I will pair each of you with an experienced leader. Do what he says and don't lose sight of him. You will spend ten days learning the 190. My goal is to have each of you log 25 hours before your first operational mission. You must learn everything you can in a very short time. Major Ulrich will conduct your training. He's one of the best. Pick his brain, do what he says and you'll do fine. Understood?"

In unison they all answered, "Yes, sir."

When they had left, Rudolf said quietly to Karl Ulrich who had remained standing near the door.

"You're off ops while you train our young eagles."

"But.."

"You're due for a rest, my friend. It should be a leave but I can't spare you."

"What about your brother?"

Rudolf considered Albert. He had always thought of him as a boy, the young man who would sit for hours listening to stories about flying. The two had become very close, the difference in their ages avoiding many of the conflicts that brothers often experience. Their mother had died in 1939, which brought them even closer together. When Albert was accepted for pilot training, Rudolf never imagined he would be in the fight this quick.

"Train him well, Karl. He's my only brother."

Steinfeld looked at his friend's tired eyes. They had seen so much together he considered Karl like a brother. Now he was asking him to keep his only real brother alive.

"It's good to see you, Bertie," Rudolf said sitting down at the foot of his brother's bed in the junior officer's quarters.

"Yes....sir."

"That's not necessary when we're alone."

Albert Steinfeld noticeably relaxed from what had almost been full attention.

"Where's your roommate?"

"Leutnant Mossbach went out to get his haircut."

Rudolf laughed. "That's not going to help him fly any better."

"We're ready, Rudi. We really are...."

The colonel stood up abruptly.

"No, Bertie, you're not ready. Those assholes in training have forgotten what combat is like. Don't confuse getting comfortable in an aircraft with being ready to fight it. This battle over our country has become as brutal as I've ever seen it. Hundreds of men die every day up there. A lot of those men on both sides are good pilots and experienced. Whether you stay alive depends on you listening to the old crew, keeping your wits about you and a lot of luck."

The younger Steinfeld looked at his brother with surprise. He had never talked to him like that.

"I understand. All I can tell you is that I will do my best."

Rudolf considered his newest pilot and hoped that Bertie's best would be good enough.

"I know you will."

Albert had finished putting away his gear and was reading when Dieter Mossbach returned.

"Hello, Bertie."

"Dieter, the locker over there is empty. I took this bed, but I don't really care."

"Fine, Bertie. What're you reading?"

Without looking up, Albert said, "Notes from Major Ulrich. He wants all of us to read and memorize them by tomorrow morning's brief."

"What's in it?"

"He called it 'Uncle Karl's lessons learned'. Mostly debriefs. My God, I never understood what was going on up there."

The tall Mossbach looked up from his now open suitcase.

"What does that mean?"

"There are many days when the squadron would be in two or three battles. They've lost a lot of pilots in the last six months."

Dieter walked over to his roommate.

"This is really it, isn't it?"

Bertie stopped reading and looked up.

"What?"

"We're in the war. This is finally it."

"Yes, Dieter, I guess we are."

"What's with the sober faces, you two?"

Konrad Bayern stood in the doorway, his grin infectious as ever. The three pilots had been together since the first day of training and had come to call themselves "the three musketeers."

"Just getting ready for tomorrow," Bertie said, realizing that Dieter was having a tough moment.

"I'm rooming with an ace. Really. Oberleutnant Rolf Siebert. He has seven kills, seven!"

"Did you talk to him?"

"He's on leave for three days."

Konrad had always been the most enthusiastic of the three. Son of an army colonel, he loved the military and the party.

"But when he comes back, I'll get all his secrets. You'll see.

Bertie wondered how things always seemed to work out for Konrad. The top flight student, now he gets an inside track to learning the ropes. He'll probably get the Iron Cross before the year's out.

Chapter Eleven

"Looks like our escorts have decided to join the party," John Forster said as he scanned right from *Jezebel's* cockpit.

"Viktor's squadron is listed in the air order for today. I wouldn't be surprised if we saw them."

Forster continued to scan forward as the squadron formation continued toward the Channel.

"Where did he get that nickname?"

"He liked to drink vodka on liberty, and after a few he would take on the persona of a Russian Cossack, so he became Viktor."

"Might be tough to pick him out from all the fighters."

"He never did anything in a small way, and I think you'll be able to recognize the 330th if you see them."

Forster looked at McGowan.

"Right."

For Major Randy Mahr, it had been a whirlwind getting his squadron ready to fly combat missions in such a short period of time. But after six missions to the continent, they were starting to feel like veterans. Luck had been with them so far, only one pilot lost, although everyone knew that more men would die before it was over.

Mahr smiled to himself. It had taken a little extra work by the mechs, but the 330th were now uniform in their battle markings. Each of the squadron P-51's vertical stabilizers was painted with bright orange. Mahr had seen McGowan's B-17's at Paddington and knew it would help unite the squadron going into combat. His wing commander fortunately liked the idea and now they were making themselves known over Europe. As of today, the squadron had four confirmed kills, three 109's and a 190. Mahr had one of those kills and had been surprised how natural he had felt, even knowing that he was fighting for his life. Six years of flying pursuit and fighters before the war had honed his skills as an aviator, but now he knew it made him an effective combat pilot. And that felt good.

Ahead and below him, Mahr could now make out the B-17's of the leading group, the 902nd and the 23rd. The bombers, their target the railroad marshaling yard at Koblenz, had been airborne for an hour forming up. Now on course for Germany, six fighter squadrons began to join on their big friends.

Mahr keyed his radio and transmitted, "Keystone leader, Phoenix leader tied on, three o'clock high."

"Roger, welcome aboard, Phoenix."

Slowly moving his squadron forward, Randy picked out the 407th with their bright orange tails flying in the low squadron position of the second group. Time to say hello, he thought and began closing on the lead fortress.

"Would you look at that? You weren't kidding."

Sean looked past John to see four P-51's with bright orange tails sliding abeam *Jezebel*.

"I feel better already," Sean said and realized he really did.

"Herr oberst, we have an alert from sector, expect to launch in fifteen minutes."

Steinfeld acknowledged the messenger from the operations room. He felt better today than most days. His night sweats and nausea had been minimal last night, actually allowing him to sleep for three hours. Fortunately he'd developed a tolerance for the pain killing drug Pethidine and flying was less painful each day. He started taking a few extra pills when needed and had seen no ill effects.

Standing slowly, he stretched his back and took a deep breath. The damned pain was still there, just not as bad. That was critical for Steinfeld. Today his three new pilots were being released to full combat duty. But he was going to keep a tight leash on his young tigers.

Happily his brother had turned out to be a competent aviator, as had Bayern. He didn't have as much confidence in young Mossbach. Eager and respectful, Dieter had worked diligently but never seemed to gain the feel of the FW or air to air maneuvering. All Rudolf could do now was put him with an experienced leader and hope he would learn quickly. If not, he would die. He had broken one of his long standing rules by assigning young Bayern as Rolf Siebert's wingman. Normally flying together and living together created problems, but in this case, he hoped Rolf's experience would help Bayern stay alive. Karl Ulrich flew with Mossbach on his wing. That would give the young man the best chance possible of surviving his first day of combat.

On Bertie's last five practice sorties, Steinfeld had exercised his discretion and put the young leutnant on his wing, as he would be today. His brother had done an acceptable job, but Rudolf had continued to hammer into him lookout doctrine, tight formation and shooting at minimum range. Today he would see if his younger brother had absorbed his lessons.

He walked into the briefing room to see all the squadron pilots sitting in the overstuffed couches they had salvaged from a bombed out hotel. The three young ones sat among their experienced comrades trying to look nonchalant.

"Last check of the weather?"

"On the board, herr oberst."

"Very well. Good prefights today, it promises to be a busy day, may be your last chance to go over your aircraft carefully. Let's go."

One by one the young men filed out the door toward the orange-tailed Focke Wulfs parked in staggered lines across the ramp.

"Scared?"

Albert Steinfeld began to make a denial, but then said, "Yes."

"Good. When you stop being scared you're dead. Use that fear to pump yourself up. You can fly this aircraft. I've seen you and flown against you. You are as good as any American. Be smart and keep your head moving. Understand?"

"I do."

Rudolf stopped when they got to Bertie's aircraft. Their eyes met briefly and he slapped the young pilot on the back.

"Fly well."

He hoped his brother really did understand.

A thin layer of clouds was the only weather to mar the view of southwestern Germany from the cockpit of *Jezebel.* To Sean this was the toughest part of a mission. Over enemy territory, fully loaded with bombs and waiting for the inevitable attack by enemy fighters. At least now they would have fighters to engage the Germans first. But nothing had been done to lessen the intensity of the German anti-aircraft batteries that ringed every major city and industrial target in the country. The damage from one 88mm shell could easily bring down a fort if it exploded close enough.

More men in the Eighth had been wounded by flak than fighter attack.

"Navigation checkpoint on the nose, skipper."

"Thanks, nav."

So far the mission had gone as briefed. On time and on course. As all aviators like to say, 'a piece of cake.' And the group's maintenance aborts were now the lowest in the Eighth Air Force. A good plan that had finally come together.

"Rumor is that we're standing down after this mission," John said as he noted the fuel levels in all tanks. "Fuel's good, actually a little ahead of pre-flight."

Sean scanned the engine instruments.

"Nothing definite. We're due for a break. Just as well, I can see it in the aircrews, people are tired."

John nodded.

"If we do stand down, why not come into London with me. You know, a few pints, a few laughs?"

McGowan checked the instruments, noting all in the green.

"Haven't been there for some time."

"I know and it'll do you good."

"I'll think about it."

The radio began to crackle as the fighter escort began to pick up enemy fighters closing the formation.

"Okay, heads up. Looks like our kraut friends decided to pay us a visit."

Randy Mahr saw two lines of aircraft descending at one o'clock, headed for the lead forts. He immediately jettisoned his drop tanks, knowing that his division of P-51's was following his lead. Jamming the throttle to the firewall, he felt the power of the Merlin kick in, pushing him back into the seat.

One last check of his gun switches and it was time to pick out a target. With the massive rate of closure, he knew that he had one chance to hit the enemy before they flashed by and attacked the bombers. Judging by the ragged formation, the lead P-51's had been able to get some hits.

With a 20 degree deflection angle, Mahr knew he would be able to get off a solid burst of his eight Browning .50 caliber machine guns. Picking out a single aircraft, he banked slightly left and began to track his target as it converged toward the reticles on his gunsight. Almost without thinking, he squeezed the trigger and felt the aircraft shudder as eight streams of bullets arced out to meet the enemy aircraft. Tracer rounds spaced in with armor-piercing incendiary rounds left bright red trails lacing toward the enemy. A lethal mix designed to rip aircraft apart and set fuel tanks on fire.

The sky was ablaze with red and green tracers as the two groups of aircraft merged, blurs of silver and gray hurtling past each other in the bright blue sky. Radios came alive as the Americans pulled hard to re-engage the Germans who continued pressing their attack on the bombers.

Grunting hard as he pulled over six g's, Mahr fought the crushing force to look back over his shoulder and reacquire the Germans. In the back of his mind, he realized that the enemy aircraft also had orange flashes on their vertical stabs.

Steinfeld watched the American fighters closing, but knew he had to focus on the bombers. Brief gun bursts as they passed might do damage, but it was all they could do.

In the distance, the lead group of enemy bombers had already come under attack by other squadrons, the tracers forming a lacy pattern across the bright blue sky.

Flashing past the Americans, he quickly checked on Bertie, who was in a good spread position behind his left wing. Ahead he saw the leading bomber in his gunsight, watching the range close quickly. With reflexes trained by hundreds of attacks, he began firing at the lead aircraft, scoring hits immediately.

Bertie's heart was pounding so hard he thought it might rupture in his chest. Gripping the stick hard, he kept scanning left and right, protecting Rudi's back. Suddenly tracers raced past the nose of the 190, so quick that he realized he had no idea who was shooting at him. An aircraft slashed past on the right and he knew it had been the American fighter firing on him. Follow Rudi, he told himself, follow Rudi.

Thinking ahead of the aircraft, Rudolf Steinfeld knew he would be able to reverse left and re-attack if Bertie could only hang on during the hard maneuvering. Pulling left he gave his brother a moment to understand what was coming and began to tighten his turn, climbing slightly to cut down the radius of the turn and stay away from the fortress gunners in the lower box.

Grunting against the g forces, Bertie realized what was happening and tried to work inside of Rudi's turn. Forcing his head left to clear the inside of the turn, he saw the deadly silver outline of a P-51 closing on them. The nose of the American was coming up, drawing a line on Rudi. Despite being new to combat, Bertie instantly knew the danger.

"Red Wolf One, check left."

Instantly Steinfeld snapped his head to see an enemy fighter behind his left wing line setting up for a deflection shot. There was one chance and he had to take it.

"Red Wolf breaking right, two, he's yours."

Hard forward stick, full right rudder and the Focke Wulf pivoted, its nose descending below the horizon. Steinfeld knew that the American would try to follow and that would give Bertie a chance to kill or distract his assailant.

1st Lieutenant Tim Callaghan saw the German reverse and he slammed his stick right in an effort to follow and get a firing solution. The Merlin engine screamed as he jammed the throttle forward to accelerate with the enemy fighter. Pulling hard he began to see a chance to fire as the fighter stabilized just above his gunsight. The young pilot had only flown eight missions and this was his first real chance to bring down an enemy. Let me do this, he thought briefly as the target slid under his gunsight.

The world seemed to be in slow motion to Bertie as he pulled lead on the American, just like in training. As the enemy fighter slid into a firing position on Rudi, Bertie pulled his gun trigger. The American was so intent on killing the lead German, he never saw Bertie close to lethal range.

For a brief instant as his aircraft began to come apart, Tim Callaghan was confused, then surprised and finally blinded as a terrible force crashed into his back, killing him almost instantly. The stricken Mustang slowly rolled over and began a smoking, ever tightening, death spiral toward the earth.

Randy Mahr watched as the melee broke into individual combat, some simply a vicious firing pass, others a fully developed dog fight. Fine, he thought, that's our job, keep the bastards busy while the heavies keep going. He was alone, his wingman missing since the first attack. But he had ammunition and fuel. He didn't need anything else.

To his right he could see two FW's in a tight turn, probably setting up for another attack on the forts. He had the advantage of height and also being up-sun. It was a perfect set up.

"What a difference a few P-51's make."

Sean laughed at Forster's remark, but there was a great deal of truth in what the Australian had said. While *Jezebel* had fired at the attacking Germans, the attacks had been blunted by the American fighters to the extent that not a single fortress had been lost and the IP was only minutes away.

"Never tell them that, it'll go to their heads. But I'll buy Viktor a large vodka the next time I see him."

Billy Hass checked the navigation chart one last time and knelt down with his binoculars to pick out the IP visually. A very distinctive lake south of Wunnenberg would allow them to comfortably turn to the attack heading, confident they were on course and ready to drop their ordnance. A full load of 500 pound general purpose bombs would be the perfect weapon against the trains and tracks in the marshaling yard. Hass thought about the last several weeks. When he and McGowan had talked about how hard it was to turn a group around, he never would have thought it could have moved so fast. And the most amazing thing to Hass was the catalyst. It had been a wise cracking Italian gunner who had been promoted, survived an almost certain death and then been decorated that had brought the aircrews and mechanics together. Hass shook his head, you just never knew. Now there was pride in the group, airborne and on the ground.

Despite the close call, Rudolf Steinfeld knew he had to push himself. Never let down, never lose your focus was built into him after almost five years of flying combat. Scanning the sky around him, the last five minutes were instantly forgotten as he picked up the lone P-51 high at their 4 o'clock. Instinct told him the fighter was ready to attack and most attackers will try to pick off the wingman before anyone in the flight knows what's happening. Steinfeld had done it himself more times than he could remember. Now this American was going to try to do the same thing.

Checking his instruments quickly, Mahr scanned behind both wing lines to make sure he wasn't about to become a victory for a Luftwaffe pilot. Rolling wings level briefly to gain some angles on the German, he smoothly put the Mustang into a forty degree dive, his nose pointing at the leader, but his target was the trailing wingman. Closing to 1000 yards, Mahr allowed the gunsight to stabilize, forced himself to wait briefly then fired.

"NOW!" Rudolf Steinfeld called on the radio and instantly Bertie pulled the FW up hard and left, bleeding off airspeed and changing his flight path severely to the left. Waiting two seconds, Rudolf then pulled up, reversing to the right and continuing the roll until he was inverted and looking down through his canopy at the American who had overshot Bertie. The advantage quickly changed.

"Oh shit," Mahr thought as the trailing German pulled into him, showing a plane view of the Focke Wulf. Pulling hard, he knew the enemy pilot had forced him to fly through any firing solution. His only hope now was to keep his airspeed up and get his nose pointed back at the German. Glancing up he saw the enemy leader had reversed and only then did Mahr realized the danger. He'd been set up.

Three minutes of hard flying told Rudolf Steinfeld that he was facing a very experienced pilot. The two aircraft rolled about each other, each one trying to gain the advantage, but each time superb flying kept either from getting a shot. Rudolf wondered where Bertie was, knowing a second aircraft could quickly turn the tables on the American.   Each turn became increasingly more difficult as the pain from his back shot through to his groin. Sweat dripped from his face and he felt a wave of nausea begin to envelop him.

In all of his years of flying, Randy Mahr had never been in a fight like this. It was taking every bit of experience and skill to simply stay neutral with the German. And he knew the moment of decision was on him. If he didn't disengage now, he would run out of gas trying to get back to England. But the aircraft that attempts to run is almost always at a fatal disadvantage. Up sun was his only choice. Perhaps in that brief space of time when the German was blinded by the sun, he could make his move. He had to try.

The wave of sickness changed to a cold sweat despite the effort expended by Rudolf to combat the American. His head pounded as he strained to follow the enemy pilot as he climbed toward the sun. A sharp pain lanced through his gut, bringing a muffled grunt as the g forces pushed him into the seat and the sun filled his windscreen. Projecting his opponent's flight path, he strained to re-acquire the Mustang. A moment of panic gripped him as he couldn't find the enemy aircraft. Where was he? Frantically Steinfeld searched the sky, expecting a hail of tracers at any instant. Perhaps it was his time and he would almost welcome an end to the pain. But as he continued to search, it became apparent that the American was no longer there. He lowered the nose and set a heading for Dortmund. Releasing his oxygen mask he allowed his breathing to slow as the cool cockpit air dried the sweat on his face.

Albert Steinfeld shut the throttle of the FW-190 and realized he might be sick. Sweat soaked through his flight suit, despite the cool temperature. Around him, he saw the aircraft from his squadron parking and shutting down, the ground crews running to start fueling and re-arming. Looking up the line of parked FW's he didn't see his brother's aircraft. A terrible fear grabbed the young pilot. He had failed to stay with his leader and now his own brother might have died because of it.

"Come on, check your aircraft and get into ops."

Steinfeld's thoughts were interrupted by Karl Ulrich standing underneath his cockpit.

"Sir, I lost sight. We were being attacked by a P-51 and he told me to break...... then I lost them.."

Ulrich heard the fear in the young man's voice.

"It happens. Don't let it happen next time. Now get in there and debrief the flight. We'll be back on alert in 30 minutes."

Again? In only half an hour? The idea of returning to that maelstrom stunned Bertie.

"Don't worry about your brother," Ulrich said quietly, "He's as good as they come, he'll be alright." But as Rudi would have said, when it's your time.....

Sean adjusted the throttles slightly. Never ready to drop his guard, the mission had been almost flawless. He hadn't seen any forts go down and the flak had been off altitude over the target. Would that every mission be like this.

Steinfeld knew that the violence of the last dogfight had done something to his insides. Pain flowed down his legs, arching into his back. With an effort, he checked the sky, still thankfully finding it empty. He would double up on his pain pills and hope

130

for some extra time before the next scramble. But now he had to get back to Dortmund. And what happened to Bertie?

Rudolf Steinfeld opened his eyes slowly, the light glaring. He looked left and right, his mind still foggy. Where was he? Bertie, the fight with the Mustang, returning to the field, but what then?

Trying to move, he immediately stopped, the pain gripping his insides. He grunted and lay back, realizing he lay in a hospital bed with some kind of restraint straps.

"Don't move, I'll be right back."

He turned his head to see a nurse exit the room.

Three minutes later the door opened and a young woman in a white coat entered.

"Rest easy, herr oberst."

"Where am I?"

"You're in the military hospital at Dortmund."

The thoughts began to form in his mind. How did he get here? What is happening with the squadron? Bertie?

"I am Doctor Spengler. Doctor Hanson asked me to keep an eye on you until he returns."

"Renni?"

"He was recalled to Berlin and left just as you were brought in."

"How long have I been here?"

Doctor Spengler looked up from a chart.

"Two days."

"I need to get back to my squadron."

She turned and looked at him over the chart.

"Doctor Hanson thought you might say that."

Reaching down, she took his wrist and began measuring his pulse.

Rudolf watched her count to herself, and then record the reading on the chart.

"Open."

A thermometer was inserted under his tongue with the warning, "No talking. If you want to return to flight status, you must follow my orders."

Despite his desire to ask her a question, Steinfeld decided to follow her instructions.

Three minutes later she withdrew the thermometer and read the data.

"Better than I would have suspected," she said in an officious tone.

"How soon can I leave," he asked.

"You were experiencing severe pain while you were flying, is that not correct?"

Steinfeld took a moment to consider the slender woman who was now standing over him. She was attractive in a clinical way, her dark hair framing a pretty face that was devoid of any makeup.

"It was manageable."

The doctor put down the chart and looked him in the eye.

"For your information, after you found your aerodrome and somehow landed your aircraft, you taxied into a ditch. It appears you hit your head hard and were found convulsing in the cockpit. By all rights, you should be dead. I do not call that a manageable situation. But then I'm only a doctor, not a famous pilot."

While her words were harsh, Rudolf could sense that she was there to help him. And if Renni trusted her, he must also.

"What must I do?"

"Be honest with me."

Rudolf considered the slender doctor with the dark brown hair.

"Very well, herr doctor. And what should I call you?"

"Doctor Spengler," she said and returned to the chart. "Also I was instructed by Doctor Hanson to call Major Ulrich as soon as you were awake. He is on his way."

"You look like hell," Karl said when he entered the room thirty minutes later.

Time had moved very slowly as Steinfeld waited to find out what had happened to the squadron. Now he would know.

"How are you?"

"I'm fine and the squadron is doing well."

"Bertie?"

Karl smiled.

"He feels he let you down."

"Let me down? He shot down his first aircraft and did exactly what I told him to do."

His friend smiled. "He is very demanding of himself, much like his brother. But he has done well since.."

"And the rest?"

Karl walked over to a simple wood chair and sat down.

"We lost two pilots, Rolf Siebert and the new one, Bayern."

Rudolf remembered Rolf, the enthusiastic, talented pilot who had done his job sortie after sortie.

"Any idea what happened?"

Shaking his head, Karl took a moment to light a cigarette. "Both aircraft crashed about 40 kilometers southwest of Dortmund, both pilots still in the wreckage. No witnesses, no idea."

Too often the case, he thought, death coming violently with no one to witness your end but the enemy bent on your destruction.

"We received one replacement aircraft, a re-worked piece of shit that had crash landed last year.

133

Also two new pilots with less experience than your brother."

Rudolf Steinfeld said nothing. But he knew that Germany could never win the war.

The bustle of London took Sean by surprise. He'd not remembered it this way was annoyed by the crush of people making their way up Regent Street.

But the truth was, he needed to get away from Paddington and John's invitation sounded too good. It would be his first trip to London in a very long time. He knew that Aubrey was waiting for John and it would be good to talk with her. He'd always liked her outgoing personality, so very different from Jamie.

It still bothered Sean to think about what had happened between he and Jamie. It had seemed so right. But he couldn't dwell on what was over. Maybe she would find a nice librarian or accountant who didn't have to fight in the war.

The pub was called "Scully's Crossroad," located in Kensington. John had told him to meet them at 6:00 pm for drinks and then they would go over to a restaurant that served what John said was the best chicken in London.

Entering the low doorway, Sean wondered how long this building had been here. He was only six feet tall and had to duck his head to pass the doorway. The noise level was lower than he would have expected for this time of night and he found the atmosphere welcoming.

"Sean!"

He turned to see John.

"We're in here," he said, leading Sean back into second smaller public room filled with tables. "I brought someone who wanted to say hello."

Jamie Taylor Paige sat opposite Aubrey at one of the back tables. She looked up at Sean, her expression tentative.

"Hello, Sean," Aubrey said lightly.

He said, "Hi," but his eyes stayed fixed on Jamie.

"It's good to see you," Jamie said, her voice steady.

"Sit down," John said.

"Thanks," Sean said, and sat down next to Jamie.

One round of drinks later, John and Aubrey excused themselves, leaving for "something that had just come up."

Once they had said good bye, Sean ordered two glasses of wine for them.

"I see a conspiracy here, indeed I do."

Jamie smiled.

"I cannot tell a lie."

"Then I'm confused. I'm not sure why you would want to see me again."

The waiter brought their wine.

She took a sip, considering her answer.

"Perhaps I need to ask a more important question," she said.

"Okay?"

"Do you still want to see me?"

Sean looked at her.

"Do I want to see you? Jamie, I told you once I cared for you and got cut off at the knees. That was something I would prefer not to go through again."

Jamie sat looking at her wine.

"Did something change?" Sean asked. "Did you change?"

"I was afraid of what might happen."

"Shit."

She looked up sharply. "I'm telling you the truth. I couldn't stand losing someone again."

135

"Then I'm still confused. Nothing has changed with me. I still get paid to fly airplanes over Germany. But you know that."

Jamie nodded.

"I see the flight orders every day."

"So what has changed?"

She turned slightly to face him and raised her hand to his cheek.

"I couldn't convince myself that I didn't care about you. Because, dear man, I do. And whatever happens, will happen. I can't hide from it."

A day of x-rays and multiple exams kept Rudolf from feeling bored, his normal feeling anytime in hospital. Late in the afternoon, Renni entered his room, with Doctor Spengler in tow. But the expression on the normally ebullient doctor said volumes.

"Rudi, how are you feeling?" Hanson said, his voice upbeat.

"Like warmed over puke if the truth be told. I need one of your little pills."

"That, herr oberst, is one of the reasons you're back in here."

His anger rising, Rudolf was immediately diverted by Renni.

"Rudi, the reason for your continued pain was a problem with your back that was masked by the broken pelvis. The force of the impact herniated a lumbar disc."

Renni continued in an even voice, "Your vertebrae are separated and cushioned by discs. If these discs are damaged, by trauma for example, their functionality is compromised. Your damaged disc is located between the fourth and fifth lumbar vertebrae. The damage put significant pressure on the spinal nerve which explains the pain and numbness you have experienced."

"You make me sound like an old man."

"Not so, herr oberst," Doctor Spengler interjected. "This is common among athletes."

"So what can you do?"

"Actually the repair is very straight forward," Renni continued. "The pain is caused by pressure on the nerves. The surgeon will remove a small amount of bone that will allow a return to normal activity without the pain. We could allow time to see whether you will get better without surgery, sometimes all it takes rest and time."

"How long?" Rudi asked.

"Six months, hard to say. Everyone is different."

"Renni, I don't have six months to sit on my ass in the hospital."

"We had already figured that out, herr oberst. Your surgery is scheduled for tomorrow morning. The sooner we operate, the quicker you're back in the air."

Chapter Twelve

"I checked his logbook, skipper. He's completed his missions. It's all he ever wanted to do."

Sean checked the memo from Lieutenant Allen which listed the twenty five completed combat sorties by Staff Sergeant Fortino, which qualified him for rotation back to the states.

"And he doesn't want to go home?"

The assistant adjutant shook his head.

They both turned as Captain Hass walked into the office and sat down in the chair next to Allen, facing the small desk.

"No, sir. He said he wants to stay with you as long as you're here."

"And rumor has it that the rest of your crew is going to do the same thing."

He thought about the odd mix of men who took *Jezebel* into battle. Good men all had already risked everything too many times. How could he let them continue to risk their lives with the odds mounting every mission? But that would be how this war was won, men willing to pay whatever price was needed to get the job done.

"Thanks, Pete. Better draw up the paperwork."

The young officer picked up his papers and walked quickly out of the office.

"You look surprised." Hass said.

"About Fortino?"

The big man nodded.

Sean leaned back in the chair. "I never expected it."

"Didn't surprise me one bit," Hass said.

"Why not?"

"Simple, for the first time in the service, hell probably his life, he's accepted as part of a winning team."

McGowan looked at the older man, who despite being his bombardier, was certainly not his friend.

"You might have something there."

"Paul Bloch called it right. He said these crews just needed some leadership. You gave them what they needed."

"I'd have to say the same thing about you, captain."

"Not necessary."

Sean shook his head.

"No, it is. We don't much care for each other, and that's fine. But I think we both respect the other's ability to get the job done right and you did just that. I'm not gonna gush over it, but it's the truth."

"Fair enough."

Hass stood up.

"You know I'm sticking this thing out too."

McGowan smiled.

"You still want to be there when I get it don't you."

Hass turned and walked out of the office.

McGowan found Tony Fortino sitting outside his barracks, his nose in a book.

"Skipper," the young man said, standing and stuffing the paperback book in his back pocket.

"Catching up on your reading?"

"Huggie loaned it to me, turns out he's a big reader, who knew?"

"Lieutenant Allen told me that you requested an extension on your tour."

Fortino paused then nodded. "Yes, sir."

"You sure?"

He nodded again.

"You told everyone all you wanted to do was fly your missions and go home."

"I guess I did."

"What changed?"

The young man looked uncomfortable, but said, "I like being in this crew."

Sean smiled.

"Funny thing about that, it seems everyone feels the same way. The rest of the crew has all extended for twenty more missions, so you'll all finish at the same time."

Staff Sergeant Fortino grinned.

"And you and the Cobber...I mean Mr. Forster, will be here, right."

McGowan laughed. The crew had nicknames for everyone.

"You bet. Now, we're standing down for two days, so put in for a pass, and get out of here."

Sean waved when he saw Jamie step out of the railway carriage at Paddington Station. The squadron stand down coincided with a string of beautiful spring days, hardly a cloud to be seen.

"Good trip?"

Jamie smiled.

"The train, no. Knowing I was coming to see you, yes."

He kissed her, smelling perfume.

"I'm glad you're here."

She took his arm as he picked up her case and headed down the platform. He hadn't seen her since they parted in London after meeting at Scully's

Crossroads. They had spent several hours talking over dinner and during the walk back to her flat. Tentative at first, they had become more comfortable as they talked. He had been pleased but also in a quandary. Over the months since parting, he had tried so hard to put her out of his mind. Now all of those emotions had come flooding back, almost overwhelming him.

When they had arrived at her flat, she had asked if he wanted to come in. He surprised himself when he told her that he had to return to Paddington. He needed time to absorb what had happened.

The cottage stood by itself next to a small lake ringed with Willow trees. At the water's edge a floating dock pushed into the quiet water, a single rowboat resting upside down next to the water.

"Aubrey told me it was pretty."

"Reminds me of summers back home, in Seattle," Sean said as they walked along the bank, watching the birds swoop playfully back and forth over the dark green water.

"Tell me about it."

He took her hand as they stepped up over a small hummock.

"Every day was warm and sunny, no school and it seemed like it would never end."

"We used to go the channel beaches every August."

"Your family?"

She nodded.

"Those were happy days." Jamie sounded wistful, "Sometimes I think it will never be like that again."

"You might be right. This war has changed so many things."

Sean thought of all the men who had died and the many that would die before it was over.

"God, what a waste," he said.

Jamie stopped and put her arms around him.

"Please just hold me," she said softly. "For two days, there is no war, only the two of us."

Holding her close, he felt her shiver, but it knew it wasn't the cold.

"Very good," Doctor Spengler noted. Her examination had produced very little pain from the patient and that was substantial progress.

"So I can leave?"

"I think it would be appropriate that you move to a convalescent ward. I don't want to put your recovery at risk."

Despite the official tone of her direction, Steinfeld knew her well by now, and he had learned to trust her.

A successful surgery had relieved his pain and a moderate exercise program was now returning his strength and flexibility.

"Will I still see you?"

She turned to see him smiling at her.

Normally ready with a quick retort, the doctor seemed at a loss.

"Yes.....of course, you are still my patient."

"Then I will, as always, follow your instructions."

"Thank you. Now, you have a visitor."

"One more thing, I don't know your given name."

The doctor looked at him with surprise, then her expression softened.

"Karin."

One month of combat had changed Albert Steinfeld. While he looked no different physically, Rudolf could sense the difference in his brother. Gone was the enthusiasm he had seen when Bertie reported to the squadron. Now he could tell his brother had begun the transition that would change him forever. Having survived a month against the ever increasing strength of the enemy, odds were now in his favor that Bertie might live to see his 22nd birthday. The young pilot had survived because he learned how to kill other pilots before they killed him. It was something that changed a man forever.

"The doctor said you are doing much better."

Rudolf nodded.

"I am. Almost feel human again."

Bertie pulled up a chair and sat down.

"Karl gave me a day off ops – first time since getting to the squadron."

"How's he holding up?"

Bertie pulled out a cigarette and quickly lit it.

"With you gone, he's holding everything together. But you knew that."

"We've been together for a very long time. Karl's a good man."

Bertie took a long drag on his cigarette.

"He's still alive after all these years, that tells me he's a lucky one too."

Rudolf lay back on the pillow.

"I told you when you reported, it's skill and luck. Now you're figuring it out for yourself."

"And I also know that you and Karl are the only two pilots left from the last two years." Bertie stubbed out his cigarette.

Pausing for a moment, Rudolf pushed himself back to a sitting position.

"That's true," he said quietly.

"We lost Siebert and Bayern. Panke bailed out and will be down for a month. Doesn't leave much doubt where it will end for any of us."

"You can't afford to think that way, Bertie. Put it out of your mind and do your best."

Albert stood up.

"Will you fly again?"

Rudolf laughed. "Of course I will. That's what I do......what we do."

That afternoon Renni Hanson arrived back from his last trip to Berlin in time to accompany Rudolf to his new ward.

The two men walked down the long corridor, Rudolf finally wearing uniform pants and a shirt after weeks of gowns and pajamas.

"I feel good, Renni.

"I still want you to take it slowly. Don't overdo it."

"How long?"

The doctor knew what his friend meant.

"Out of here in two, maybe three weeks. Two months of supervised convalescing. Followed by a quick check from yours truly and we'll see if we can put you back in the cockpit. Then we'll have to see how you hold up to hard flying."

"Christ, that's a long time. I'll go crazy."

"My friend, there's nothing you or I or even the Fuhrer can do to make your back heal any sooner. It could be much worse and you know it."

They walked on, Rudi remembering that last flight, the pain and almost giving up at the end.

"So what's the gossip from Berlin?", he asked the doctor to take his mind off the past. "Did you see Galland?"

Hanson motioned him into an open room. "Here we are." The doctor closed the door.

"Apparently Hitler is furious with Goering. The bombing is hitting us hard. It all has an effect, but the daylight raids are destroying too many key targets. Rumor has it that Galland is in trouble."

"Shit, that's all we need, to lose a real fighter to some political boot licker."

Hanson walked to the window.

"Nice view. Of course it didn't surprise me for Doctor Spengler's most special patient."

"And what the hell does that mean?" Steinfeld asked.

Hanson turned and flashed his famous smile at Rudolf.

"I do believe that Doctor Spengler has become infatuated with her patient. And if I read my Steinfeld correctly, the feeling is mutual."

The beautiful day had transitioned through a fiery sunset to a crisp spring night. A warm fire crackled in the cottage's stone fireplace. Sean and Jamie had spent the afternoon talking after their walk and opened a bottle of wine to watch the sun set.

"Thank you for a wonderful dinner," Jamie said as they cleared the dishes from the small dining room table.

Sean laughed.

"Master Sergeant Weller has several special contacts in the supply department, including the senior mess sergeant. We owe our bountiful feast to their imaginative packing of goodies."

"Rationing has gotten better, but we still can't procure steaks like that. And you can cook too, what other surprises are you hiding?"

He walked over to her.

"No surprises, sweet lady. I'm just happy to be with you."

She kissed him lightly on the lips and returned to the dishes.

Sean walked back to the front room and found the bottle of bourbon the master sergeant had slipped into the "picnic basket." He made a drink and called to the kitchen, "Can I fix you a drink?"

There was no answer and he walked over and peeked in the kitchen, which to his surprise was empty. He went back and sat down on the small couch. He thought that Jamie seemed a bit sad or maybe just quiet he told himself. They had made such a quick reversal of the direction they had taken six months ago. Perhaps she was having second thoughts?

He turned as she came around the corner of the couch and sat next to him. She was wearing a light robe and it opened to show her bare legs.

"Can I fix you a drink?"

She shook her head and slipped the robe off her shoulders, allowing it to slip to the floor.

"Later," she whispered and kissed him hard on the lips.

Chapter Thirteen

Over two hundred bombers crossed the Dutch coast north of Amsterdam as the late morning sun broke through the thin layer of cirrus clouds. While most recent missions had been pounding targets in France, today's target was an oil refinery near central Hanover. The 23rd had the strike lead and Paul Bloch was leading the group with Sean in command of the second squadron in the group.

"So what's your guess on the invasion?"

Sean checked the instruments then said, "Way past my pay grade, but it seems like something's up."

John said, "A mate of mine told me that they couldn't get another ship into Portsmouth harbor."

"Bet there're a lot of army guys with puckered assholes about now."

Forster laughed. "Never heard it put quite that way."

Keying the intercom, Sean passed to the crew, "Okay, gentlemen, we're in German fighter range, let's be ready."

Behind them, Larry Parr drove the upper turret in a full circle, scanning for enemy aircraft. On each side of the formation, he saw P-51's flying loose formation on the bombers. Things had certainly improved over the last few months. He was developing a real affection for the fighters, their "little friends."

In the waist compartment, Harry Baumstark and Larry Kucinich fought the cold while searching the sky for Germans. F-2 heated flight gear made the long flights bearable and were a significant improvement from only a year ago. With their oxygen masks on and goggles down, there was no bare skin exposed to the minus 20 degree air that swirled into the aircraft.

Each man staring into the hostile blue was alone with his thoughts. Guns had been test fired, checklists completed and now before the inevitable arrival of the enemy the bomber crews were allowed their last quiet contemplation before battle. For many it would be their last.

Below in the ball turret, Tony Fortino was humming a Dorsey tune as he slowly rotated around, checking for fighters. Other than getting a max load of crap from Auferio for extending, he liked how it made him feel. It was probably the first time in his life he had done something for any reason other than "an angle."

A large bell alarm sounded in the sector air defense headquarters outside Dortmund. The harsh sound alerted everyone that a raid had been detected by the long range search radars that protected Germany. From the duty commander, instructions would send aircraft airborne, alert anti-aircraft batteries, cause smoke generators to be started around major target areas and alert the civil authorities. By mid-1944 the German air defense network was sophisticated and efficient, having evolved through hundreds of day and night raids that had been launched against the Reich over the last five years.

In the main sector control room, men and women went about their duties quietly, relaying instructions to the telephone switchboard and radio room. Above the main floor, Oberst Kurt Meinheim watched the plot develop and began the daily guessing game. Was this a major raid or just a diversion? What targets might be in the general direction the raid was currently flying or would there be a directional change to throw off the intercepting fighters?

"Alert Hanover, Magdeburg, Leipzig and Berlin."

"Yes, sir," replied his assistant and he picked up the first of three telephones on the operations desk.

Meinheim had seen this too many times as the American's strength had grown over the last year. If he committed the Luftwaffe's major effort toward this raid, a larger attack might be thirty minutes behind it, headed for the real target of the day. But he had to go with what he saw.

"Scramble, large raid crossed over the Dutch coast, heading east."

Pilots grabbed flight helmets and pushed their way out the door, breaking into a run as they cleared the building. The entire ramp came alive as ground crews swarmed over the aircraft, readying them for starting. In less than two minutes from the scramble call, the first engine roared into life, the acrid exhaust fumes drifting across the squadron as one engine after another started and came up to speed.

"Attention, attention, enemy raid is approaching, man all gun batteries," came the tinny voice over the speaker,

Within five minutes, eight single barrel 88mm anti-aircraft guns were uncovered and prepared for firing.

The 244th anti-aircraft artillery battalion manned two sites on the west side of the river, protecting the south and west approaches to Hanover. Equipped with the improved Flak 36 8.8cm guns manufactured by the Krupp Works, the battery had been credited with six American bombers destroyed over the last nine months.

"Stand ready, but do not load," came the command from the battery commander.

Crews stood by their guns, the routine having become second nature. Ammunition was ready, control had been established with the battery controller and now they waited for the last critical step, setting the fuses that would determine at what altitude the projectiles would detonate. Until the range finders passed that information, the game was to wait.

Private Joachim Himmel knelt by gun number four and coughed as he inhaled the coarse cigarette smoke. He didn't really enjoy the ersatz tobacco, but it was all that was available and smoking passed the hours on alert. The seventeen year old had been with the battery for almost three of his five months in the Luftwaffe. From a small town outside Cologne, he felt lucky to be in the anti-aircraft regiments and not the army. Tales of the savage fighting in Russia scared him although he would never admit that to anyone. Life in the service had been all right, the food was tolerable and he enjoyed the camaraderie of the barracks.

"I don't like the look of that weather up ahead," Sean told John. On the horizon, a layer of dark clouds extended up above their altitude.

"No way we'll be able to bomb from twenty one."

Sean knew Forster was right and that Colonel Bloch had two choices, scrub the target or take the strike in lower. Descending would make the flak deadlier, but also might help keep the enemy fighters away.

"Bombardier, pilot."

Billy Hass answered. "Go."

"If the boss takes the strike in, plan on bombing from sixteen thousand."

"I saw that crap up ahead. What the hell, lower releases make for more accurate hits, right?"

"Always the optimist," Sean said, laughing to himself.

Hass took out his glasses and began to search for several navigation check points. Even though they had to follow the leader, he still wanted to be ready to identify the prime aim point. He also knew the flak over Hanover had been reported as heavy and accurate, it would make for a tough bomb run.

Steve O'Loughlin turned as they both heard a change in the engines.

"Pilot to crew, lead is taking it lower for weather. Heads up."

"Herr Colonel, we are getting updated information on the raid. They are coming in lower than normal, probably hitting the backside of the weather front."

Kurt Meinheim knew the radar units would be refining their aiming data to pass to the flak batteries. Perhaps today the Americans would pay a higher price.

"Where are the fighters?"

His assistant pointed to a young woman who had just placed a white marker on the large table map.

"Just coming on the plot, sir."

The colonel had flown fighters at the beginning of the war until a wound permanently grounded him. But he knew the tension and worry as the fighter leaders followed vectors trying to make contact with the enemy.

"Good, they'll have time to engage before the Hanover flak corridor."

"Bandits, right one o'clock," John Forster called when he saw the small swarm of dots that he knew were enemy fighters.

Above and behind the cockpit, Don Parr swung the twin fifties around facing forward and strained his eyes to pick up the Germans.

"Moving from one to two, now level," John continued.

"Got 'em," Parr called and he checked for any friendly fighters in the area. His pulse picked up as he realized the sky was clear of American escorts and the Germans were beginning their attack.

"Right waist, here they come," Parr said and began firing short bursts at the attacking fighters.

The guns of *Jezebel* began to hammer out at the enemy aircraft, lines of tracers flying toward the racing fighters, now flashing into the formation as each fortress gunner fought to put sights on target without hitting a friend.

The intercom came alive as another attack erupted from the left side of the squadron. Two lines of Me-109's, their propeller spinners painted bright yellow, sliced through the formation of lumbering bombers. Cannon and machine gun fire raked the B-17's and began to take a toll.

Both of *Jezebel's* waist gunners were firing now as attacks were pressed home by the 109's. Suddenly a burst of fire tore through the compartment, sparks arcing from severed electrical lines.

"Shit," Kucinich yelled, ducking involuntarily then resuming firing. "Harry, you okay?"

"Yeah," Baumstark called back, his attention focused on a section of Germans approaching from behind the left wing line.

"Four o'clock going low!"

Fortino heard the call, although he had already been traversing the turret from right to left.

Both guns of the ball turret began to hammer as the Plexiglas bubble swung hard to the right, tracers flying out to intercept the second enemy aircraft.

152

"Damn it," Fortino yelled at himself as the fighter flashed past, with no apparent damage.

"Approaching the IP," the navigator called, confirming the formation's location. "There will be a ten degree turn to heading of 072 magnetic."

"Roger, 072," Sean answered, filing the numbers in his mind so he wouldn't have to take the time to write it down.

"Four minutes from IP to target," John Forster noted, even though both pilots already knew the time. Sometimes talking helped to maintain composure and today's attacks carried a level of frenzy the crew hadn't seen in several missions.

In front of them, a B-17 began pouring smoke from both engines on the right wing, drawing the attention of McGowan and Forster. Neither man said anything, each aware that less than a mile in front of them, two men in a cockpit like theirs were fighting to save their aircraft and crew.

"Mark the IP," came the call from below in the nose compartment.

Sean smoothly brought *Jezebel* right ten degrees and steadied on course 072. Then he saw the flak.

An alarm bell rang at the flak battery.

"First aircraft are coming within range. Estimated altitude 5500 meters. Batteries released."

Next to each gun the ammunition handlers began to set fuses and pass projectiles to the loaders.

The crack of the first gun always made everyone jump, despite knowing it was coming. Within a minute each gun was firing, the azimuth and elevation guidance now released to local battery control.

Joachim Himmel began a practiced routine which he knew could last for up to an hour. Jog to the ready service locker, pick up the twenty pound shell, and carry it to the fuse setter, place the fuse in the mechanism, then hand the shell to the loader. The crack of the guns, the acrid smell of the cordite and the back breaking work would make each minute as the battery fired a small hell for the crews. But he knew they were fighting to protect their city from enemy bombers. He'd seen the terrible damage across the country in city after city as he travelled to Hanover from Cologne. It was up to everyone to fight the battle and he was proud that he was doing his duty.

Another blast from the 88 tore the silence apart as more shells screamed up toward the attackers.

The first black bursts were slightly above *Jezebel's* altitude, but that meant they had the top squadron in their lethal range and Sean knew when the 88's started with correct fusing initially, aircraft went down.

"Christ," McGowan said as he saw smoke trailing from the lead aircraft, *Irish Maid.* "Bloch's hit."

Half a mile in front of *Jezebel*, the wing commander's aircraft began to slowly drop back, losing power from the flak hit.

A short transmission from Paul Bloch transferred the wing lead to Tom Russell, the 409th's commanding officer, who had been designated as the alternate in the briefing and assigned number three in the lead division.

The stricken bomber now began to lose altitude fast, turning north in what appeared an effort to escape the deadly flak corridor.

Sean adjusted the throttles and rechecked the heading, which had deviated almost three degrees off briefed.

"I don't know where the fuck they're going, but we won't hit the target unless we come right."

The voice of Hass over the intercom confirmed that losing the wing commander had fouled up the bomb run and Russell's bombardier had his head up his ass.

Ahead of them, the lead squadron continued a slow left turn and McGowan knew the strike was going to hell.

"Billy, you got the target?"

"Affirmative," came the bombardier's reply.

Sean keyed the radio, "Thunder lead, this is Ripsaw lead. We have the target, I say again, we have the target."

He knew Tom Russell would understand his meaning – which was, 'where the fuck are you going?' and we can take it from here.

"This is Thunder, roger. All strike aircraft, Ripsaw has the lead."

"Okay Billy, it's your show," Sean quickly said as *Jezebel* was buffeted by a near miss.

They both knew it was going to be tight, for Hass to get the aircraft to the bomb drop line and take control using the auto pilot, but if anyone could pull it off, it was Hass.

Still alert during the respite from fighter attacks, the gunners checked their equipment and waited for the bomb bay doors to open and the shudder of the aircraft as the deadly load fell free. While it was a key point in the mission, they also knew the fighters would be waiting for them on the long trip home.

"Bomb bay doors coming open," Hass called as he selected the hydraulic lever that would expose the twelve 250 pound general purpose bombs.

"PDI centered. It's your aircraft," Sean said.

"Roger."

The bomb release 30 seconds later was almost anti-climactic.

Ready to shift control back to the cockpit, Hass was thrown violently into the forward Plexiglas bubble,

Jezebel yawing hard left. Stunned, Billy Hass collapsed on the aluminum deck.

McGowan instinctively corrected the sickening move by the aircraft while trying to absorb the violence of the explosion on the right side of the ship. Damage was evident through the cockpit from fragments of shrapnel that had sliced into the thin aluminum skin. Wind screamed through broken metal of the fuselage adding to the roar of the engines and cries on the intercom.

"All right," he managed to say on the phones, "Damage, I need to know, what we got?"

"Waist is good, skipper," Baumstark called.

Huggie chimed in, "Rear gunner good."

In a strained voice, Fortino said, "Ball turret, okay."

"Shit, Tommy's down," Kucinich yelled and moved toward the radio compartment.

Seeing the fire light illuminated on number three engine, McGowan closed the throttle and secured the fuel boost pump. He quickly looked over to see John, his head drooping to the right, the shoulder straps holding him upright.

"The Cobber's hit, get me some help up here."

Where the hell is Parr he thought. He's the damned flight engineer, he should be helping me.

Steve O'Loughlin's head emerged from below.

"Come left to 280. Hass is hurt too."

"Check on him," Sean yelled as he feathered three and opened the cowl flaps. "Where's Parr," he called.

The navigator turned back after examining Forster.

"I need some bandages. Parr's dead, his whole fucking head is gone."

Sean yelled over the wind streaming through the cockpit, "How bad is Hass?"

156

"Don't know. I'll be back."

The controls began to feel stiff and Sean knew his only focus now had to be get the aircraft home.....or as far from Germany as possible. There had been stories of angry civilians attacking airmen who parachuted into the cities they had just bombed.

"Skipper, Tommy took shrapnel in his side. We patched him up best we could."

Sean thought about the kid, him and his camera. Shit, he thought then keyed the radio.

"*Lucky Lady*, this is Ripsaw. You have the lead."

"Roger," came a tinny response over the strike frequency.

"We're on our own now," Sean passed on the intercom. "I'll stick with the group as long as we can. Keep watching for kraut fighters. The top turret's out."

The crew knew what that meant.

Jezebel was losing altitude as Sean fought her nose around north to escape the deadly flak corridor.

In the nose compartment, Steve O'Loughlin had Billy Hass sitting up, holding a compress bandage to his head. Blood covered the side of his face down into his flight suit.

"How bad?" Hass asked, his head throbbing with the worst headache he'd ever had.

"Parr's dead, the Cobber's in a bad way, took a shit-load of shrapnel. I bandaged what I could, but it's a bitch with him in that seat."

"Here, help me up to the cockpit," Hass said.

"What?"

"We'll bring him down here and you can work on him. I'll fly copilot."

"Co-pilot? What the hell good will that do?"

"Hell, I've got more B-17 stick time than most of the co-pilots in the Eighth Air Force."

Karl Ulrich saw the American bombers on his nose at no more than five miles. The vectors he had received turned out to be better than normal and their altitude advantage would help as the squadron broke into four plane attack formations. The veteran pilot looked back to see his number three, Bertie Steinfeld leading his section. Good man, he thought, must run in the family. Of all the new pilots, Bertie had adapted quicker and certainly better to the brutal life of combat over Europe.

Now clear of the flak, Ulrich knew they had a golden opportunity before enemy escort fighters rejoined the strike. Hit hard, kill bombers and get out.

He keyed his radio, "Red Wolf attacking," letting the ground controllers and his aircraft know they were committed. He added full power and selected the second aircraft in the lead box as his target. Already trailing smoke from the left wing, the wounded fortress was the natural choice. Wounded crewmen and damaged aircraft couldn't fight back as well as most and this was war.

Leutnant Albert Steinfeld forgot his fear as always happened when the attack began. The terror of his dreams at night or nerves waiting for the alert launch always left him when the guns were armed and he knew the rage of the attack would take over. He took a quick glance at his wingman, Leutnant Konrad Brecht, the "new guy." Bertie was now considered a veteran by Karl Ulrich, who was running out of pilots. That was the way of things now, grow up or die.

Cannon shells arced toward the bombers as the fighters closed on their targets. Ulrich saw hits on the port side of his target and watched as more shells tore into the thin aluminum. Twinkles of fire from the top turret told him the twin machine guns were aimed at him and tracers flying by his canopy confirmed the American still had some fight left. The FW slashed past the nose less than two hundred meters in front of the bomber as Karl masked himself from the enemy gunner.

"God damn it," Staff Sergeant Mike Allison yelled in frustration as the lead enemy fighter flew below his firing arc.

Vibration from the airframe began to worsen as the tall New Englander traversed the turret left to pick up any follow up attacks.

"Crew from pilot," First Lieutenant Stan Onan called on the intercom, his voice strained. "I don't think I'll be able to keep her straight and level for much longer, get ready to jump."

"Shit," Allison said to himself as two FW's turned toward the stricken ship. "Two fighters left nine o'clock level," he called hoping to hear the waist gunner or ball turret open up.

Tracking the lead fighter, he focused and his months of experience allowed him to track the attacking Germans, firing both fifties in a valiant effort to distract them. He was switching to the second aircraft as he realized the big bomber was dropping the left wing. Before he could make a call, the aircraft increased the roll, the left wing now straight down and the *Amanda Mae* continued to spin out of control, the intercom strangely quiet.

Mother of God, he said to himself as the nose of the B-17 pointed toward the German countryside three miles below.

Albert Steinfeld watched the fatally wounded American bomber fall toward earth. He felt the elation of victory, the target had been destroyed. He quickly looked for Brecht, happy to see he was flying a good spread one hundred meters to the right. A quick check

159

of instruments and he began to circle north for another attack on the retreating fortresses.

He thought of his brother, still recovering in the hospital. How he had never understood what Rudi had been going through for the last four years. The young pilot grinned to himself when he thought how proud his older brother would be of him, now leading his own section and flying on Karl's wing.

"Hey Cobber, you're gonna be fine, just need to get these bandages on you."

Forster lay on his back, directly behind the bombardier's station, his awareness finally returning after a blurred trip from the cockpit with Hass and O'Loughlin nursing him every step.

"Bloody hell it hurts," John said, his voice straining against the pain.

"That's good, they say you can't feel the bad ones."

The co-pilot moaned as the young navigator tightened the bandage on his arm. "Well I can sure as hell feel that, damn it."

"You've got shrapnel in your leg and arm. I've stopped the bleeding and I can't see anything else."

"Thanks, mate."

"I'm gonna go check on Hass. Lie still and I'll be right back."

"Where's Billy?" Forster asked.

"Flying co-pilot."

"Phoenix flight, bandits, left eleven," Major Mahr transmitted and pushed the throttles full forward. The two FW's were in a gentle left hand turn, flying a loose spread formation. "Three you take the wingman."

Two mic clicks told Mahr that Barney Jorgensen knew his assignment.

The P-51's opened fire at just under three hundred yards, almost point blank range for the .50 caliber machine guns with armor piercing and high explosive rounds.

The post flight debrief noted that both enemy aircraft, FW-190's, took multiple hits, coming apart with no parachutes sighted. Mahr was credited with his fifth kill, making him an ace while Jorgenson notched up kill number two. Both men celebrated at the Bascome Officer's Club that night and by the next day's launch, Mahr's aircraft had five small swastika's painted below the cockpit.

Leutnant Albert Steinfeld was officially listed as "killed in action," one of twenty three Lufwaffe fighter pilots killed that day over Germany. The notation on the group combat diary for Leutnant Konrad Brecht, also listed KIA, was "…second mission."

"Losing oil pressure on number four," Sean called at Hass. "Going to shut her down and feather."

Hass was using all his strength to hold the wings level, the aircraft responding slowly and erratically, almost as if she had a mind of her own. His head ached with a pounding he had never experienced before, but he had to ignore that now.

"Roger."

"Get ready, it may take both of us to hold her steady," Sean said as he shut down the failing engine.

"I'm not going anywhere," he said, " I wanna see how this ends."

McGowan looked over at his co-pilot and knew what he meant. "We'll keep her heading west as long as she'll fly. If we can make it to the water, maybe she'll make it home."

Hass listened to McGowan, knowing that *Jezebel* would never see England again.

"Okay, everyone, we're passing through twelve thousand, start throwing everything overboard, guns, ammo, air bottles, I don't care. And be ready to jump."

Sean knew he had to stop his rate of descent, which was now between two and three hundred feet a minute. If they couldn't lighten the ship, they were done.

"Nav, can you get up here?"

"On my way," O'Loughlin answered.

"And Steve, bring something to cover Parr."

After pulling the .50 caliber's retention pin, Larry Kucinich carried the gun to the waist opening and let it fall.

"Christ, I hope the krauts don't find us."

His .50 already jettisoned, Harry Baumstark moved to the opening, flinging belts of ammunition over the side.

"No shit," the other gunner replied, not breaking his stride as he heaved a walk-around oxygen bottle in the chilly blue sky.

Fortino opened the hatch to the ball turret and scrambled out, his radio cord tangling in the support assembly. The young gunner tore off his flying helmet and threw it on the deck just as Huggie Loggins crawled forward from his position. They all knew their procedures, the waist, tail and ball turret gunners were to bail out through the rear access hatch. All of them except Fortino had done just that over Paddington, but this was different.

"Keep throwing anything you can over the side," Baumstark yelled, but almost everything that could be jettisoned had been.

"Where are we?" Huggins yelled over the wind stream.

The tall gunner just shook his head, too hard to know.

"Maybe Holland," Fortino said.

Kucinich turned, "Big fucking deal. The krauts happen to own Holland if you hadn't noticed."

"Forget it," Baumstark said, "Everyone make sure you've got your chutes attached, then check each other. Keep your Mae West's on, but get rid of those flak vests. And check your weapons. Make sure all your straps are tight."

Billy Hass was a strong and powerful man, but now he struggled to hold *Jezebel's* wings level, the aircraft vibrating badly.

"Gonna need some help, here," the bombardier yelled across the cockpit, unable to key the throat microphone.

McGowan grabbed the control wheel with one hand, his already on the mic switch.

"Nav, get the bomb bay doors open, then jettison the lower hatch. Waist, jettison the rear hatch and get ready to go."

"Roger, and the Cobber's ready to go," O'Loughlin replied, then hit the bomb bay switch which would give the pilots their best chance of getting out of the ship.

"Waist, got it."

The four men moved aft to the hatch and Baumstark released the retaining pin, the oval door snapping free in the wind stream. Each of the gunners had their chest chutes attached to the harness they wore at all times.

"What about Tommy?"

The radioman still sat against the forward bulkhead in the radio compartment.

Steve O'Loughlin reached down and pulled the release handle, watching the hatch fall away below the stricken bomber. McGowan's orders had been clear, get Forster to the escape hatch and shove him out when time came. Suddenly the ship began to roll to the right and the navigator desperately grabbed the bulkhead rail to keep from being thrown out.

"Shit!" McGowan yelled as they both wrestled the control wheel, but the B-17 was rolling out of their control. He reached for the bailout alarm and slammed it desperately three times, the harsh sound easily heard over the two remaining engines. Next he hit the "Salvo" switch to make sure the bomb bay doors were open. If he and Hass were going to get out of *Jezebel,* that was the only way out.

"OUT, OUT," Baumstark yelled, pushing Huggins toward the hatch as *Jezebel* continued her sickening roll. Without a look back, Huggie exited the aircraft. Larry Kucinich, looked at Baumstark, his eyes wide with fear as the ship began her death plunge.

"GO.....GO....."

As if coming out of a trance, Kucinich shook his head and rolled out the hatch.

"TONY, GO!"

Fortino hesitated.

"MOORE...WHAT ABOUT MOORE?"

Debris filled the air as the big bomber slowly rolled left then pitched nose down.

"IT'S TOO FUCKING LATE......GET OUT!"

The hell with you, Baumstark thought and pulled himself into the brutally cold afternoon sky.

Thrown against the bulkhead, Fortino felt his body lift up as the battered B-17 tried to level herself. Looking forward he saw the young radioman holding on to the leg of the radio platform, hunched into a ball.

Pulling himself through the waist, Fortino reached Moore as the ship's wings returned to level. Christ, I gotta get this kid outa here, he thought and saw Moore already had his chute attached.

"Tommy, Tommy, gotta bail out, come on."

164

Moore turned his head, confusion on his face.

"Come on, I'll help you."

Tony tried to pick Moore's shoulders up, but stopped when the radioman screamed.

Sobbing, Moore's voice fighting through the pain, he said, "I can't, it hurts too much."

"YOU HAVE TO, DAMN IT."

Tommy Moore, the youngest man in the crew said nothing, but slowly pulled himself to his knees. Fortino helped him rise and stagger to the aft end of the bomb bay.

"PULL THE RIPCHORD WHEN YOU"RE CLEAR, UNDERSTAND?"

Moore turned back to Fortino and nodded, his eyes wet with tears. Then he rolled forward and out into the howling wind.

Neither man in the cockpit said a word as the bomber rolled back to wings level. *Jezebel* wasn't ready to die just yet.

"Skipper."

Hass and McGowan turned to see Staff Sergeant Fortino behind them in the aisle.

"What are you doing here?" Sean yelled.

"Had to help Moore bail out. Everyone's out back aft."

Those words took a burden off McGowan, at least four of the crew should survive this war. Now, what about the rest of us?

"Go down and help the navigator with Mr. Forster."

"Yes, sir," Fortino answered and disappeared down the crawl way.

"I don't know how much longer she'll hold out," McGowan said, gingerly moving the control wheel to the left.

"Eight thousand feet, looks like we're over Holland."

Nodding, Sean agreed, "Looks like Emmen on the nose."

"You gonna try to get across the water?"

McGowan thought for a minute.

"Sure as hell would like to try. But I just don't think she'll make it."

"Even if we end up in the water, there's a chance the Brits will fish us out," Hass said.

They could see the haze ahead that told them the northeastern end of the English Channel was on their nose.

"Skipper!"

Sean turned to Fortino.

"His chute is torn apart," the sergeant said, his eyes showing that he understood what that meant.

"What?"

We were getting him ready, but the flak that hit him tore the chute up. Mr. O'Loughlin doesn't think it will work."

John Forster had been sitting on his seat pack parachute, the standard arrangement for all pilots and co-pilots.

McGowan knew that they could bail Forster out with his injuries, but escape at sea from a ditched B-17? No chance.

"Okay, you and the gator get ready to bail out."

"But, sir."

"Get down there and get ready, damn it."

Hass watched the sergeant disappear down the crawl space.

"What do you want to do, skipper?"

In the heat of the moment, Sean realized that was the first time Billy Hass had called him skipper."

166

"I've studied the charts. I can belly her in. It's the Cobber's only chance.

Hass stared ahead at the hazy horizon.

"Nope. You?"

"Me neither. Saw one at Randolph, it turned out okay."

McGowan knew it was the only choice.

"Hell, gotta learn sometime. Help get Forster strapped in best you can. You three can go out together, stick close and maybe you can make your way to the coast."

"I'm not going anywhere. If you're gonna get this thing down, you'll need help. Four men can take better care of Forster than just one."

"How about Fortino?"

"You know damn good and well he won't leave either one of us."

Sean remembered after the emergency landing at Paddington. When the ground crew had freed Fortino from the jammed ball turret, the look in his eyes was something that Sean would never forget. A connection had been made between two comrades, different in rank, age and background, but together, they had survived.

"You know, I kinda like having him around."

Steve O'Loughlin appeared five minutes later, a chart in his hand.

"We're just past Emmen," he said, pointing to the folded chart. "Forty miles to those inland lakes, seventy miles to the channel and one fifty to England."

Sean knew *Jezebel* was almost done. If it weren't for Forster, he would have everyone bail out now.

"I want you and Fortino to get the Cobber back to the radio compartment and strap him in, good. Billy and I are gonna set her down on this side of the water. We'll take care of Forster. You and Fortino can jump or stick with us, your choice."

O'Loughlin looked at Sean and grinned.

"Jump out of the same airplane twice? I'm sticking with you."

Fortino stuck his head up from below.

"All set back aft, skipper. Mr. Forster is strapped in but good."

"I'll hit the alarm bell three times just before we touch down. Brace just like you saw in the training films. It may be a wild ride, but I think the old lady will take care of us one more time."

"Yes, sir." Tony hesitated, then said. "Thanks, skipper." Then he ducked aft.

McGowan surveyed the ground in front of them while checking the altitude. Descending through fifteen hundred feet, it was time to commit to putting the bomber down. He estimated two hours to sunset, making the shadows on the ground deceptive. The surface wind appeared to be light, out of the north, so that at least would be in their favor.

"Billy, with three and four out, keeping the wings level is critical. Whatever went on before with the controls will kill us down low. So watch that for me. If I need help on the controls, I'll yell for it. Otherwise, I want you to work the throttles. We'll set up for a shallow rate of descent and all you should have to do is pull the power to idle when I call for it."

"Got it."

"I may need your help with the rudders. When I think I see our touchdown point, I'll let you know. Once this thing stops, don't worry about anything except getting the hell out of here."

McGowan keyed the intercom, "Nav, have everyone meet back by the tail when we get on deck."

"Roger."

Ahead Sean saw what looked like a wide area with no obstructions. As good as any, he thought.

"Three miles ahead, see the light area just left of those trees?"

Hass paused then said, "Got it."

Sean pulled power slightly, then selected flaps down. He knew this was the most critical time. If the flaps had been damaged, the aircraft could do anything as they tried to extend. But he needed to be as slow as possible. His hand remained poised to reverse the switch if anything happened to his control.

Both men felt the big bomber slow, the lift of the flaps evident as the air speed dropped to 120 knots. *Jezebel's* nose slewed right and Sean corrected with left rudder. She still felt controllable and he kept telling himself to leave the landing gear up, fighting a habit that had been burned into him since flight training.

Passing over a small farm he saw there was smoke rising from the main house, confirming the wind was out of the north but remained light.

"Don't forget to lock your harness," Hass reminded him.

McGowan keyed the intercom, "Standby in the back!"

Holding the wings level, he called, "Idle!"

Ahead of the aircraft, he saw that the field was covered in high grass that looked like wheat.

A deafening roar engulfed them as she settled onto her two spinning props and then fully onto the fuselage. Sean had always heard 'fly the aircraft until it stops moving' and so he instinctively worked the rudders to hold the nose straight as *Jezebel* plowed across the field, dirt, grass and water flying over the windscreen. Terrible sounds of tearing metal and popping rivets filled the aircraft, the sound adding to a roar from below them.

With a crash, the front Plexiglas shattered, followed by a rush of debris back to the crawl space.

Suddenly they were stopped, a cloud of dust boiling up over the fuselage.

"Throttles off, switches off," Sean called.

The two men freed themselves from their straps and opened their side windows.

"GET OUT," McGowan yelled.

Emerging from the window, Hass looked aft and saw a man climbing out of the hatch. It was Fortino, who then turned and helped John Forster out, who was followed by O'Loughlin. They all made it, he thought, pulling his legs the rest of the way out of the cockpit and sliding down onto the ground, the impact making the splitting pain in his head worse, if that was possible.

The smell of burned metal and aviation gasoline hit Sean as he made his way around the two smoking engines and toward the tail. The threat of fire was very real and he wanted to get everyone away from what remained of *Jezebel.*

He found O'Loughlin helping Fortino with John Forster thirty feet behind the tail. They turned as Sean caught up to them.

"Everyone okay?"

"Yeah," came the reply from the navigator.

Hass joined them and they moved farther from the ship, finally kneeling down in the field.

"Now what?" Steve O'Loughlin said as he knelt down, helping John to the ground.

"Other than John, is anybody hurt?" Sean asked.

"Shit, we got company," Hass said.

They all turned to see two men approaching.

Karl Ulrich took a deep breath and opened the door to see Steinfeld sitting in chair, reading a book.

"Karl!" Steinfeld said smiling, but then he stopped. The look on his friend's face told the story.

"Rudi, I don't know what to say, I'm sorry."

"What happened?" Steinfeld said, not really wanting to hear.

"Yesterday, second mission of the day. We were northwest of Hanover attacking B-17's on the way back to England. Bertie was leading a new man as my section leader. We took out at least two bombers then got jumped by P-51's. It turned into a furball and the sections got split up. I really don't know what happened, but the police found the crash site."

Steinfeld listed to Ulrich's words, seeing it all in his mind. The story had played out so many times already, a violent meeting in the air over Germany and young men die. He got up, throwing the book on the floor. He walked over to the closet and pulled out his uniform tunic, slipping it on.

"What can I do?" Ulrich asked.

"Take me back to the field," he answered, taking his cap from the shelf in the closet and walking out the door.

Chapter Fourteen

Jamie Taylor-Paige looked up from her desk to see Aubrey standing in the doorway.

"Hello," Jamie said, then looked back up at her friend after realizing that there were tears in her eyes.

Aubrey walked to Jamie's desk, wiping her eyes.

"What's happened?"

"*Jezebel* didn't come back from the Hanover mission," Aubrey said, her voice strained.

The horror of what her friend was saying struck her like a blow. It had happened, what she had always dreaded.

Jamie saw the look in her friend's eyes.

"Are you sure?"

Aubrey nodded.

"I know a lad in operations who saw the post mission report and he called me. It's against the rules," she said, wiping her eyes. "But he knew about John."

A sliver of hope crossed Jamie's mind.

"But was Sean with him? Sometimes they make changes, I know that and you do too..."

"Jamie, listen to me. Austin told me that the squadron commander was listed as missing."

"But..."

The two women looked at each other, then put their arms around one another.

There was nothing else for either of them to say.

Staff Sergeant Tony Fortino watched as the sky slowly lightened in the eastern sky. Checking his watch, he decided he would give the navigator an extra thirty minutes of sleep before waking him to take over the next watch. Since they had arrived at the remote farm around midnight, it had been quiet. The main house sat fifty yards from the barn where they had spent the remainder of the night.

The two men had both spoken enough English to let them know they wanted to help the American flyers. He knew from training that there were people in France, Holland and Belgium that might help downed airmen. But they had also been told that the Germans had informants and an efficient system for capturing enemy aircrews that bailed out or ditched in occupied territory. The skipper had told them to stay alert and all they could do was hope these people were the good ones. No shit, Tony thought to himself, it sure ain't Jersey.

The wooden door opened and Steve O'Loughlin came out of the barn rubbing his face.

"Everything quiet?" the lieutenant asked.

"So far. A light came on in the house maybe thirty minutes ago, but haven't seen anyone come out."

Steve looked around to get his bearings, seeing the one story house, which appeared to be on a raised foundation. A small outbuilding butted up to the larger house and an enclosed yard ran toward a small wooded area. It looked a lot like the small farms where he had grown up in Blacksburg, Virginia.

"Go get some rest."

McGowan nodded as Fortino sat down on the floor next to him.

"See anything?"

"Someone's up in the house, that's all."

"Did you hear anything? Engines, aircraft?"

Fortino shook his head.

"Quiet. We must be way out in the country."

Sean smiled. "For right now, that's fine with me."

John Forster moaned slightly.

Billy got up and moved over to the makeshift bed they had fashioned from several blankets and straw. He stumbled slightly, his head still pounding.

The Australian was asleep, his face pale in the light of the two burning candles.

Hass returned and sat down heavily.

"He's still sleeping, but we gotta get him real medical help."

They had retrieved the medical packs from *Jezebel,* and used those to improve the hasty dressings which O'Loughlin had applied in the aircraft.

"You're not looking great yourself. Let me look at that head," Sean said.

"I'm fine, just a headache."

"Maybe so, but let me look anyway."

"I'm fine, damn it."

Sean snapped back, "I don't know how long it's gonna take to get back home and I'm not taking anything for granted. Now let me see your head."

Hass looked at him and nodded with resignation.

Dried blood matted Hass's hair and removing the bandage took hair with it. Underneath, Sean found a deep gash which revealed white scalp and exposed bone amidst fresh blood seeping from the wound. He wasn't a doctor, but knew what he was looking at wasn't good.

McGowan knew direct pressure would stop bleeding, but how do you apply pressure when there is a wound down to the skull? Maybe that would do more damage. If nothing else, he could sprinkle sulfa powder on the wound and reapply a dressing. That would have to do for now.

"Well? Hass asked as Sean reached for one of the medical kits.

"It's cut pretty deep. I'm gonna disinfect it and put on another bandage. You need to take it easy, it's still bleeding a little bit. My guess is we need to stitch it up when we know what's going on with our Dutch friends."

"Here they come," Steve called from the door. "There's three of them."

The two men, one carrying a wooden box had been joined by an older man, probably in his fifties. He looked rugged, like a fisherman or farmer and was in direct contrast to Pieter and Aart, their two companions from the previous night, who appeared to be shopkeepers.

"This is John. He will help us," Pieter said in passable English.

The older man, offered his hand to Sean, who introduced himself, then continued, "What can you tell us about the Germans?"

"North of here, in Groningen", he said in good English, "Twenty five kilometers."

"Around here?" Sean asked, sweeping his hand in a circle.

The man shook his head.

"How far from here to…our aircraft?"

John turned to Pieter who said, "Five kilometers."

"Where should we go?" Sean asked.

"West, near Pesse," John said. "Tonight, after sunset."

"Then what?"

The man shrugged, "We see what happens. Then decide."

Sean felt frustration, but he was in no position to bargain.

"You will eat, then wait," Aart said, pointing to the box, which had four milk bottles filled with water, several loaves of bread and a large dried sausage.

"John," Sean said quietly, kneeling down next to the makeshift bed.

Forster opened his eyes, blinked several times then focused on his friend.

"Top of the morning, sunshine." .

"You need to eat something."

John nodded slowly.

"Anything to drink?"

"We drank all the beer, but I've got some water."

The Australian grinned slightly.

After a piece of bread and some sausage, John seemed to perk up.

"What's your plan?"

Sean laughed.

"When I come up with one, I'll let you know."

Forster turned slightly, the pain evident on his face.

"I know I'll hold you up. Don't worry about leaving me here, I'll manage. I know they have beer in this country and I can just wait until they liberate this place."

"I'll keep that in mind, but if you think I'm going to go back, face Aubrey and tell her I left you here to drink beer and chase women, you're crazy."

John laughed as he knew he was supposed to, then turned serious.

"I mean it. If you need to leave me, do it."

Sean nodded.

"Get some rest."

Captain Billy Hass watched Sean step back from John Forster. He had watched McGowan feed the co-pilot and check his wounds. I used to hate that guy, he thought. Robin's death had unleashed a fury that he thought would never end. But since he'd joined the 23rd, he had come to understand why Robin and Sean had been friends and now knew that McGowan had been devastated by the young man's death. Time does heal all wounds, he thought. I just wish my damned head would stop aching.

A tired Renault truck driven by Pieter had picked them up just before eight o'clock. John was with him and they quickly loaded the Americans in the back of the covered bed, immediately heading south on the narrow road. Sean knew, as did everyone else, that they could have very well been betrayed and were on their way to be turned over to the Germans. But the two Dutchmen gave them no reason to suspect treachery. They could have easily contacted the Germans by now. The Americans simply had to trust them.

The next day found the remaining crew of *Jezebel* in a small house, which didn't appear to have been lived in recently. No explanation was offered and no one asked the question. They put Forster in one of the beds and took turns sleeping in the other one between watches. Fortino surprised them all by making a batch of decent soup on the wood burning stove.

"Someone's coming," Tony Fortino said from his watch post in the front window of the house.

A small sedan stopped in the front yard. John emerged from the tiny car, as did a young woman, carrying a satchel.

Doctor Tanna VanderRonhaar introduced herself in faultless English.

"She will help," the old man said, stating the obvious.

After an examination of Forster, she looked at Billy, then reported to Sean.

"The Australian has fragments in his arm and leg. He needs a surgeon to remove them, but it is not urgent. Nothing appears to be near major blood vessels. He does need to rest as much as possible. I think the threat of infection is low at this time, but you must watch for any high fevers. I'm more concerned about the man with the head injury."

"His name is Hass, Captain Hass."

"There is no way to tell what damage lies under the captain's skull. But the external wound certainly is serious. I will stitch and dress the wound, but it is very important to monitor him. Dizziness, blurred vision, nausea, unconsciousness, any of them would indicate this is a very serious injury, not just a bump on the head. The next several days should tell.

"Thank you, doctor," Sean said, taking in what she had told him. "I know you're risking your life by helping us."

She looked at him with no reaction other than to say, "Everyone does what they must."

"Who are these men?" Sean asked. "They help us, but haven't told us why."

The doctor shrugged.

"Sometimes it's better not to know too much. We've learned that the hard way." That seemed to be her answer, but then she added, "Since the Germans came, there has always been a resistance force in Holland. That is all you need to know."

"I'm sorry, I have no anesthetic," Doctor VanderRonhaar said as she bent over Billy's scalp with a needle and thread.

Bill couldn't care less. His attention was totally focused on the young doctor, who began to stitch his wound. He guessed she was maybe thirty, with long brown hair, pulled back in a ponytail. She was very pretty even though she was wearing no makeup. Just a wholesome country girl, he thought.

"You're Dutch?" he asked.

Without interrupting her work, she said, "I am."

"It's just that your English sounds so.....so English," Hass said, realizing how odd that sounded.

Tanna smiled. "I studied medicine in England for seven years."

Hass wanted to say something to continue the conversation, but found he couldn't think of anything intelligent to say.

"I don't want to put a bandage back on your head," she said, taking one last stitch. "But please be careful." She tied off the thread and sat back to look at her patient.

"All done," she said, smiling. And for the first time, Doctor VanderRonhaar noticed that her patient had striking blue eyes.

"I will return tomorrow to check on you. Until then, please remain as still as you can and rest as much as possible."

Billy Hass smiled.

"Thank you.....very much."

"You have made remarkable progress, for a broken down old fighter pilot."

Rudi had just demonstrated a range of motions to Doctors Hanson and Spengler in his office at the aerodrome. Two weeks after walking out of the hospital, Steinfeld wanted to get back in the air. Both of the physicians understood he was in a rage over the loss of his brother, blaming himself for not being there. Now he was putting every bit of his energy into receiving a medical flight clearance.

Renni Hanson, for all his bluster and bravado, knew his business. His job was simple, keep Luftwaffe pilots in the air. Sometimes that meant following a course that main stream medicine might find disturbing.

Karin Spengler was not in the military, nor did she specialize in aviation medicine. And her medical opinion on the best course for Rudi Steinfeld differed substantially from that of Renni Hanson's. She felt that the senior doctor had lost his mind or was at least guilty of gross malpractice.

"And you might be able to return to active flying in two to three months."

Rudi said nothing but his eyes turned to her with the message that he did not agree. His attention turned to Renni.

"What can we do?"

The doctor shook his head, knowing that arguments were futile.

"I've thought it over and I believe I can build a back brace you can wear in the cockpit. Using that to support the spinal structure during violent maneuvering in conjunction with pain killers could get you in the air very soon."

Karin Spengler's face showed surprise then anger.

"He can't......that's crazy," she said, her voice angry.

"It may well be, doctor, but these are crazy times. Would we be taking fifteen and sixteen year olds into the Wehrmacht if things were normal? I think not. Rudi in a brace is still a better fighter pilot than most of the children that we are sending against the Americans every day."

"Rudi, your brother is gone. What can you accomplish by getting yourself killed?" Her voice cracked and she turned away to the window.

"I will leave you two alone," Renni said, closing the door as he left the room.

"Karin, I know you don't like this, but I can't just sit here."

She turned to face him, tears in her eyes.

"This damned war. I hate it and I hate your twisted sense of duty. What about you, your future?"

"Us?" he asked and she lowered her head.

"And us," she said quietly.

Rudi looked at her, remembering that first day when he had been convinced she was the personification of Germanic efficiency. He had heard of patients falling for their doctors and he was guilty, but he hadn't known that it worked both ways. He marveled that it has been only a month since they had met. How can it happen that quick? But he knew he felt different about Doctor Karin Spengler than any other woman he had ever known. And now she was telling him not to get back in the cockpit.

Chapter Fifteen

Jamie Taylor-Paige looked up as Aubrey came in their front door.

Tossing her bag and gas mask on the couch, Aubrey walked to the kitchenette and pulled a bottle of gin from the cabinet.

"Ice?"

"In the box," Jamie answered.

The sounds of ice hitting the glass were followed by the ice box door closing.

In a moment the young woman sat down next to her roommate and took a long drink.

"Anything?"

Aubrey nodded.

"Having John in the crew gave our people a little more access to what's going on."

"And?"

"There are so many losses, it's hard to understand how they can sort them out, but they try," Aubrey said, taking another deep drink. "A division of fighters coming home after a low altitude strafing mission spotted a B-17 that had made a forced landing in Holland, about 30 miles south of Groningen. It turns out the fighter lead recognized the orange tail of the 23rd. They made several passes, but saw no sign of the crew."

"Damn."

"Maybe not. It turns out that the underground in that part of Holland is known to be pretty active. They might have gone into hiding. In any case, there have been no reports from the Red Cross of any of the crew being found or taken prisoner."

Jamie put her hands together as if she were praying.

"Please, please make it so."

Draining her glass, Aubrey got up.

"I think I shall have another one of these. Might I make one for you?"

"A large one."

Major Randy Mahr scanned the photographs that had just come in from the wing intelligence shop. A tasked photo-reconnaissance mission had sent a P-38 over the crash site to record what there was to see.

"Look at this, he said. Both side windows are open. Whoever was flying that aircraft was able to crawl out of it."

Mahr's intelligence officer, Captain Benny Driscoll bent over the table with a large mounted magnifying glass.

"I can only see one major hit. It looks like the starboard forward fuselage took a flak burst. The burn and scorch marks make it look like there might have been fires in number three and four and the props were certainly feathered when the ship bellied in. See the difference in the prop condition between one and two and three and four?"

"You're right."

"I think we have survivors of that landing and they are somewhere in Holland."

Randy thought about Sean and knew he had to try and help him get home.

"Benny, keep your antenna up on this one. One of those survivors on the ground is my West Point roommate.

Driscoll looked up at his boss and nodded.

"You got it, skipper."

Mahr remembered the last time he had seen Sean, who had stopped at Bascome on his way back to Paddington from London. He had told his friend about an English girl he had fallen for and that it was the real thing. Funny, Randy thought, in all the years I've known him, he had never gotten really serious about any woman. Now he finds one and this happens. Shit.

Steve O'Loughlin shook Sean awake as the sun began to show itself across the surrounding fields.

"Yeah, what's up?"

"Fortino just took the watch and told me he was worried about the Cobber. I checked him and Fortino's right. John's got a fever, sure as hell."

McGowan rolled over, and sat up on the edge of the bed. The last three days had been quiet for the crew, but also hard with nothing to do but talk among themselves. Food had been delivered two days ago, more bread and sausage, even some local beer. That had picked up their spirits, but now that the initial struggle to get set up was over, the real question of what would happen to them was weighing on everyone.

He knelt down and placed his wrist on John's forehead, remembering a trick his mother used when she had thought he had a temperature.

Forster opened his eyes as Sean lifted his hand.

Sean said, "A little warm. How do you feel?"

"Been better for sure, but I'm doing all right."

Small beads of sweat glistened on John's brow and Sean knew that his friend was not doing well. But how could they contact the Dutchman? His visits had been random and he might not even come by today.

"Let's get his boots and socks off," O'Loughlin said, kneeling down and untying Forster's right boot.

"What?"

"Best way to get his temp down." He pulled off the wool sock and began on the other boot.

"Where'd you learn that?" Sean asked.

The navigator pulled Forster's second sock off and said, "Eagle Scout. Lots of water, aspirin and keep him cool. Wet socks work great for that."

"Okay Florence Nightingale, do what you can."

That afternoon Tanna VanderRonhaar and John, who had never volunteered his last name, stopped by to check on the Americans. She took John Forster's temperature, which registered as 102.2 degrees Fahrenheit on her mercury thermometer. The doctor was pleased with what the crew had done to bring his temp down, but she also knew that the fever was an indication of a bigger problem.

"Wounds from shrapnel often become infected. The fever is the body's attempt to fight off the infection. Until the fragments are totally removed, there will still be problems."

"What can we do?"

She turned as Billy Hass joined them on the porch.

She continued, "Take him to the hospital in Groningen, but that would mean capture by the Germans."

"And there's no way to know if the krauts would take care of him anyway," Hass said.

McGowan knew Hass was right. There had to be another way.

"Can it be done here?"

Tanna VanderRonhaar thought for a moment, then said, "It would be difficult, but yes, it could."

"What do we need to do?" Sean asked.

"For now, keep his temperature down. I will need to get some equipment from Hoogeveen. Also we will need blood. Do you know his blood type?"

"Hang on," Hass said and went back in the house.

"You can really do it here?"

The doctor nodded slightly. "It's his best chance. I had hoped that he would avoid an infection, but now we must take action."

"Would he stand a better chance in a real hospital?"

"Of course, he would. But he would then be at the mercy of the Germans."

Hass came out the door, stumbling slightly on the rough wood planks.

"I think we're in luck. Forster is "O" positive. So are Fortino and O'Loughlin."

The doctor reached up and steadied his head, her hand on his cheek. She looked in his eyes.

"Have you been dizzy?"

Hass nodded, "Just a little."

"I want you to spend as much time as you can lying down, resting and keeping your movements to a minimum."

He looked at her, understanding she was serious.

"Okay, whatever you say."

"Ready?"

John Forster nodded slightly, "Right."

The doctor began probing John's right bicep, which was being held firmly by McGowan.

186

Two injections of Procaine had numbed the area, but gritted teeth told them that John was feeling the instrument working its way into the wound.

Tanna withdrew the probe and reached for long necked forceps.

"Good news. It appears there is only one large fragment and I should be able to remove it. Mr. Forster, there will be some pain. Please stay with me, it shouldn't take long."

The Australian nodded, his teeth clenched together.

In a moment she held a bent piece of metal the size of a quarter in the forceps. She put the instrument down and dabbed at the entry wound which seeped blood.

Five minutes of pressure and she closed up the arm wound with sulfa powder and a gauze bandage covered with wide adhesive tape.

Doctor VanderRonhaar found two pieces of metal in John's thigh. One appeared to be steel, probably from the German shell while the other was definitely aluminum, a piece of *Jezebel's* fuselage.

After closing and bandaging the leg, she gave John a pint of blood, donated by Sergeant Fortino. The Cobber was on the road to recovery.

Sean picked up one of the water buckets that they had found in the kitchen. The old fashioned water pump was a short walk from the house and he needed fresh air after the surgery. Scanning around for unwanted visitors, he stepped down and started across the wide yard. The small farm reminded him of the Midwest, but that world was a long way from northern Holland.

The sound of aircraft engines broke into his thoughts and Sean turned to see four P-51's in a line abreast coming toward him at no more than 200 feet above the ground. He dropped the bucket and began waving his arms. The roar as they flashed past echoed against the surrounding trees. As they turned south, he saw the orange tails. One of the fighters detached from the group and began to circle back while the remaining three climbed overhead.

Sean watched the lone P-51 level its wings and heard the engine slowing. The canopy slid back and he could see the pilot looking down at him from less than 100 feet. It was Mahr, son of a bitch!

Pumping his fist in the air, Sean yelled, "VIKTOR!" at the top of his lungs, knowing that Randy couldn't hear it but he didn't care. The crew of *Jezebel* had been found.

Sean forgot the bucket on the ground and ran back to the house. Not sure what the sighting meant, at least the world would know they were alive and on the ground in Holland.

He opened the door to find Steve O'Loughlin standing over Doctor VanderRonhaar, who was kneeling down next to Billy Hass.

"What happened?"

"He just fainted, went down like a ton of bricks."

Tanna turned to the men and said simply, "Help me get him into bed."

Sean saw the concern in her face.

Karl Ulrich stuck his head into Rudi's office.

"I heard you got a flight clearance."

"How are you," Karl asked.

Rudi lied, "A little sore, but I'll be fine. In fact schedule me for a warm up flight tomorrow morning. I'll go out solo, but make sure the aircraft is fully armed in case our friends show up."

The damned brace was uncomfortable, but it did what Renni said it would. Rudi rolled the FW ninety degrees to the left and began to smoothly apply back stick, noting with pleasure that he remained free from pain. Now he pushed the stick forward, unloading the aircraft and then slammed the stick hard right as he put in full right rudder. Rolling rapidly to the right, he then reapplied full back stick and reversed his turn. I owe the good doctor a large bottle of brandy, he thought and turned toward the aerodrome. It was time to get back into the fight. But he knew it was a futile battle they were fighting, a battle that with an inevitable end.

Lieutenant Colonel Thad Spencer was still shaking his head when he knocked and entered General Ira Eaker's office.

Randy Mahr's sighting of Major Sean McGowan on the ground in Holland was a first for the Eighth Air Force. As such there was no precedent or policy for what to do next. And as is often the case in the military, when in doubt, kick it upstairs.

Eaker looked up from his desk.

"General, it looks like one of our P-51's spotted McGowan on the ground in Holland." He handed the report to the general.

Scanning the paper, he said quietly, "I'll be damned."

"Apparently Major Mahr and McGowan were roommates at West Point and so the confirmation seems pretty solid."

"How can we get them back?"

Spencer said, "I have to find that out, sir. I know we'll have to get the Brits involved. They have the best connections to the underground in Europe and their Lysanders seem to be the a good way to get our men out."

Eaker knew the little English bi-plane had served the British well, ferrying agents in and out of occupied Europe, why not bring aircrew out?

"Thad, I want you to work on this full time – highest priority possible and I'll call in any favors we need to with my Brit contacts."

"Yes, sir, understood."

"How are you feeling?"

Billy Hass's face was pale and sweat covered.

"Not worth a damn."

The big man had been vomiting during the night and Sean knew he had to get water into him or Hass would get worse.

"Here, try drinking some water."

Billy nodded and began to sit up, but immediately lay back down.

"Shit, the whole world is swimming when I try to sit up."

"Someone's coming," Fortino called from the front room.

"Hold on, I'll be back."

Sean walked over to Fortino, who had pulled his .45 from its holster.

"It's John," Sean said, watching the wiry little man get out of the small sedan. Doctor VanderRonhaar was with him.

Meeting them at the front door, Sean saw that John had a small package.

"Tea and cheese." He handed it to Sean and stepped inside.

"Hello, doctor."

Tanna nodded and followed John.

"I wanted to check on our patients," she said, putting a worn brown leather case on the front room table.

"Our Australian seems to be much better. The fever's almost gone. He's been eating and drinking a little."

"Very good," she said. "And the big man?"

Sean hesitated.

She understood. "I'll check him first."

Chapter Sixteen

Thad Spencer sat in an outer office at 64 Baker Street, London. Two days of phone calls and memos had resulted in the American gaining access to a special operational section of MI-6, wondering what the future would bring for McGowan and the crew of *Jezebel*.

"Commander Stewart will see you now, colonel."

The yeoman opened the door for him.

A tall man in the uniform of a commander in the Royal Navy came around the desk to offer his hand.

"Jack Stewart, please sit down."

Thad Spencer was taken aback by the British commander's American accent. He noticed the wings and a row of decoration that contained the British Distinguished Flying Cross. At least he would be talking to another aviator. Most aviators speak the same language, regardless of the uniform they wear.

"Can I get you some coffee?"

"No thanks, but you might answer a question for me."

Stewart smiled. "I'll sure try."

"You sound more like an American than most Americans. Am I missing something?"

The tall man laughed.

"Not at all. I'm Annapolis, class of '35, grew up in Seattle."

"But how....?"

"That I can't talk about, but I assure you I do work for MI-6 and I think we can help with your B-17 crew."

"Then, commander, I'm all ears."

"Please call me Jack, we're pretty informal around here."

"Jack, I'm Thad."

"Now you're lucky because the crew is in a part of Holland that doesn't have a high concentration of ground troops. Many of the troops have moved south toward the invasion area. That being said, we're also fortunate that the resistance in that area is well organized and we have a good working relationship with them."

"Can I ask what that means?"

Stewart continued, "Sure. We supply them with weapons, money and equipment and they keep us informed of what the Germans are doing on the ground. By the way, everything we are talking about is top secret."

"I brought my clearance and your yeoman had me fill out several forms."

"Good. That will keep the security people happy."

"So you think there's a way to bring the crew out of there?"

Stewart nodded.

"Actually there are several ways, aircraft or motor torpedo boat. Both the RAF and the Navy's costal command have been ferrying people back and forth since the war started. The challenge is to decide what would work best for your people."

"What determines that? Spencer asked.

"We have to decide what is the best way to get your people out of Holland without compromising the locals who are left behind. The Germans have no problem with reprisals. Also one of the biggest threats is having a collaborator inform the Germans that something is scheduled and we end up with everyone dead or captured."

"Dropping bombs on Germany sure seems easier."

"Are you a bomber pilot?" Stewart had seen the wings on Spencer's left breast and the American Distinguished Flying Cross ribbon.

"B-17's."

"Did you know this crew?"

Spencer shook his head.

"The pilot worked at headquarters before I got there. I understand he's flown two full tours over here."

"Then he's a man that clearly needs to be saved. Let's go grab some lunch. My folks have been working on this and they should have something for us shortly."

It had been a cool spring, but now in the middle of June, Jamie began to see signs that spring was almost on London. It had always been her favorite time of the year. Watching the trees and plants shed their dreary winter colors and begin to bloom gave her a boost every year. But this year she knew that nothing was going to help the loneliness and pain she had felt since *Jezebel* was lost. The invasion must mean the war would be over soon. Why now, so close to the end?

"Colonel Spencer, this is Phil Hatcher, my operations officer.

Entering Stewart's office after lunch, the two men had seen a stocky man in his mid-thirties leaning over Jack's desk.

"Nice to meet you, colonel."

"What've you got, Phil."

"We see two options. Neither is perfect, but both look like they would work. Extraction by sea, preferable because we can accommodate a full B-17 crew, but hard because we need to get them to the coast. More chance of discovery and the German E-boats have been active lately, probably because of the invasion." He pointed to the chart. "It would be a forty to fifty mile journey depending where the underground felt the best pick up point would be."

Stewart nodded.

"The other option?"

"We schedule an aircraft to land near where they are and make it a grab and go. It would probably alert the Germans and who knows what the kraut bastards would do to the locals."

"What kind of aircraft?" Spencer asked.

"Probably a Hudson. Two could carry ten passengers easily, but not sure if they would all fit into one."

"Day or night?" Stewart asked.

"Night makes more sense. We could go in during the day with lots of air cover, but that would surely draw attention to the area. If they could get in near sunset and back out again, it might go unnoticed."

Stewart turned to Spencer.

"What do you think?"

Thad Spencer had learned a long time ago that you were stupid not to listen to the experts and this was certainly one of those times.

"The Eighth Air Force will support whatever MI-6 feels has the best chance of success with the least amount of casualties."

"Fair enough," Stewart said. "I'll talk to my brigadier and we'll get the wheels rolling."

"By the way, I'm West Point, '35. Were you at Franklin Field for that last Army Navy Game?"

Stewart laughed.

"Soaking wet, but happy as hell. I guess I owe you."

Breaking a thirteen year losing streak, the Naval Academy had defeated the Military Academy 3-0 in

Philadelphia during a driving rainstorm in 1934, much to the chagrin of the seniors of West Point's class of 1935.

Tanna VanderRonhaar closed the door and crossed the room to where Sean stood, looking out the window. The prior afternoon she had told Sean that she was even more worried about Billy Hass than she had been at the time of Forster's surgery. Now she was back again to check on her patients, but had spent most of her time in the darkened room with Hass.

McGowan looked at her expectantly, but saw the look in her eyes.

"Well?"

"Major, it's not good. I believe he has internal bleeding, the result of the trauma he suffered in the plane."

"But he seemed fine. Hell, he helped me land the aircraft."

"Sometime that is how these things progress. Perhaps there was clotting and the bleeding was arrested. But something, even the truck ride, might have disturbed the clot and then the bleeding could continue."

"So what can we do?"

Doctor VanderRonhaar shook her head.

"You have two options. Take him to the hospital or keep him totally still, quiet and rested, hoping the injury will resolve itself. In hospital, they would open the scull and try to relieve the pressure. That is a dangerous procedure and the staff at Groningen seldom does that type of surgery."

Sean felt frustrated.

"What gives him the best chance of living?"

"Hard to say. Surgery is more proactive, but there are times when doing nothing is just as effective and avoids the dangers of surgery. Major, I don't know in this case. He is a strong man, but the wound to his head was deep. The safest way in a normal world would be surgery. But when you bring in captivity by the Germans, I worry. The kind of care someone would need after that type of surgery, I doubt would be provided by the Wehrmacht."

"I think I have to leave it up to Hass."

"Give it a day. I may have a better feel for how the captain is progressing tomorrow. In any case, nothing can be done today."

The doctor sat carefully on the edge of Billy's bed.

"I'm leaving now," she said quietly.

He opened his eyes, smiling slightly.

"Thank you for everything you've done."

She looked down at him and gently put her hand on his cheek.

"I wish I could do more for my American."

His eyes turned toward her and he raised his hand. She understood and took it in hers.

Feeling his grip tighten, she returned the pressure, then gently kissed the top of his hand.

RAF Tangmere was the home to one of the Royal Air Forces most unique squadrons. 161 Squadron flew in support of the underground resistance in occupied Europe. As such, the squadron operated an odd assortment of aircraft, which were flown by an even odder group of aviators. Collected from all branches of the air force, the squadron pilots had proven they had the unique talent of flying where prudent aviators should not and doing it at times that made no logical sense if you wanted to die in your bed of old age. But the underground in Europe and MI-6 would be severely crippled if those men were not willing to go where they did.

Wing Commander Terrence Toms, DSC, DFC was the overall commander at Tangmere and also acknowledged as the most combat experienced pilot on the base. Because the mission to rescue the crew of *Jezebel* was so unusual, it had been his decision to go or not. Not surprising to his pilots, he not only decided to take on the mission, but he would fly the aircraft.

"Spencer, do come in. Damn nice of you to drive all the way down here."

Thad Spencer had asked around about "T" Toms before driving down to Tangmere. A career regular air force officer, the wing commander had started the war in Mosquitoes flying in France, Norway and during the Battle of Britain. For the last two years, he had been at Tangmere and his reputation had only grown.

A large grin and strong handshake did nothing to change Spencer's mind.

"Sit down and let's go over the situation. Presley, send in some coffee, please."

His assistant closed the door and Toms returned to his desk.

"I talked with Jack Stewart and he's working on establishing contact directly with the resistance in the area. Bit dicey, of course, trying to get the right hand talking to the left. But Stewart will figure something out, he always does."

"I think I understand what you mean. You need to get someone on the ground you can talk to and that person needs to get connected to our people."

Toms grinned. "Exactly so.

"How long would this take?"

"Rather quickly I would think," Toms continued. "The crates are ready to go, pilots briefed and the weather looks good for the rest of the week. Actually I expect we'll hear something very soon from Stewart's people. After that, we go."

What a character, Spencer thought, but he seems to know what he's doing.

Watching John and Tanna VanderRonhaar approach the house, Sean knew it had come time for a decision about Billy. He desperately hoped she would feel rest was all he needed. How do you turn a comrade over to your enemy, hoping they will take care of him?

The doctor entered, nodded to Sean and walked to Hass's door.

"We need to talk," John said.

"Sit down."

The two men sat opposite each other at the table.

"We've been contacted by a group we work with, and it was about your crew."

"How would anyone else know about us?"

"They were contacted by radio. The British."

Sean was now more confused.

"And what did they say?"

For the first time since he had met the wiry old man, he detected a small grin.

"They want to send an aircraft to fly your crew back to England."

McGowan wasn't sure what he had just heard.

"The Brits will land here and fly us out?"

John nodded. "We told them it could be done."

"Damn."

Sean had figured they would hide until the allied advance liberated Holland, which would likely take months.

"All they need from us is a landing location, time and how many men will be going out."

The door opened and the doctor emerged. She gently closed the door and came over to the table.

"He is better, thank God."

"That's great, doc," Sean said.

"Does she know about the flight?"

John shook his head.

"What flight?" she asked.

"The British will bring an aircraft to fly us back to England."

"When?"

"I would guess soon," Sean answered and turned to John who nodded.

"Captain Hass simply can't travel," she said, he voice flat. "Certainly not in an aircraft."

"Are you sure?" Sean asked.

She nodded.

"He is stable now. Any movement could worsen his condition or kill him."

McGowan looked out the window at the blue sky and made a decision.

Chapter Seventeen

Rudolf Steinfeld leveled his FW-190 at 10,000 feet and quickly checked on the other three aircraft in his flight. He was ignoring orders by splitting off from the main group, now on a vector to intercept an American raid heading toward Cologne, but he didn't give a damn. It had been obvious that to him that Jagdgeschwader 95 had lost the killer spirit. Constant attacks on the airfields coupled with more and more enemy fighters in the air each day had taken a toll. Now he'd decided to do something to bring his wing back into the fight with a vengeance.

Checking the operational logs of the sector air defense headquarters, it appeared to Rudolf that when there had been strikes to the east and south of Dortmund by the Americans, the field had been attacked. His theory being that they were flying targets of opportunity missions, much like his squadron had done in France in 1940. While aircraft in the landing pattern are vulnerable to enemy fighters, those same attackers are equally at risk if there are fighters armed and waiting for them. He was going to test his theory. If it worked out, he would tell Galland.

Flying on his wing were three veterans whom he knew were effective shots and could operate at the tree tops. Perhaps this would be a drill in futility, but he had to find out.

The radio crackled alerting the flight that low flying aircraft had been spotted approaching the field. Without signal, Rudi opened the throttle and pushed over. They would be at the field in less than one minute and approaching the maximum speed of the FW. Most attacks in the past had come from the south or east and for that reason he had made his approach from the southeast, moving the formation into a combat spread. Descending through four thousand feet, the German fighters were approaching 400 knots when they saw the enemy fighters down to their left.

Following the brief, Hugo Steinke, flying in the far left position, broke toward the fast moving targets, each FW following him in turn.

Hoping the anti-aircraft crews followed instructions and only fired at confirmed enemy aircraft, Rudi descended through 600 feet, flashing over the field boundary. Ahead he saw a P-47 crossing the flight line, its guns throwing tracers across the field, many bouncing crazily off the concrete. With a 50 knot speed advantage over his target, Rudi pulled into firing range and squeezed the trigger. From two hundred yards his machine guns and cannon tore into the American's fuselage. Smoke immediately trailed the American who began to pull up as Rudi hit the Thunderbolt with another brutal barrage. In an instant the fighter's right wing snapped off and it careened into an open field at the end of the runway erupting in a large fireball. So much for the theory, Rudi thought as he turned left looking for more Americans.

Looking at the ceiling, Billy thought that today the pain in his head was better, maybe. He'd come to hate the darkened quiet room as much as any criminal hated his cell. But that was the hand he'd been dealt and he would deal with it. I'll get better and back in this war, one way or the other, he thought. And if the

Germans find me, I'll stick this .45 in my mouth and pull the trigger. Even in his pain, he knew that Tanna's life would be worthless if he was caught and tortured. Her visits had made his injury bearable. Why couldn't they have met in a different world?

"You awake?"

"Come in," he answered Sean.

McGowan entered the room and closed the door.

"Doing okay?"

Hass tried to sound upbeat, "Pretty good. I think the doc's got the right idea, just need to rest for a while."

"Yeah, I think so. She's a sharp lady, pretty gutsy too."

Sean sat down on the chair next to Billy's bed.

"Fortino's making some of his famous soup. John brought us a couple of chickens this morning. Smells pretty good already."

Hass smiled in the darkness.

"Guess he can do more than just shoot down krauts."

Sean laughed dutifully.

"John told me that there's some scheme to have the Brits fly in here and pick us up."

"No kidding? Sounds too good to be true."

"Hell, I'll believe it when I see it," Sean said, now staring down at the floor. "The only problem is that the doctor said that you can't be moved."

Hass didn't respond, but he did turn his head slowly on the pillow to look at McGowan.

"I don't know what to tell you, I'm not a damned doctor. She said you could get worse or die."

"This just gets better......."

"John said you could stay here for now, but they'll probably move you when she says you can travel."

"Well," Hass said with resignation, "Maybe I can learn to speak Dutch."

203

Randy Mahr threw his flight jacket on the couch and walked over to his desk. Although he'd never actually been hit by a truck, he was pretty sure it couldn't feel much worse. He'd logged forty seven flight hours in the last nine days, flying in shitty weather to boot. Six engagements had resulted in two more victories, running his total kills to fourteen confirmed and three probables. But he was tired and he knew it.

Opening the lower desk drawer he took out a bottle of Tom Moore bourbon and poured two inches into a clear glass tumbler. He'd lost a young pilot today and he was going to have to write a letter to the man's wife. What a crock of shit, he thought and downed half the glass of booze. How the hell does a letter help a woman deal with having her husband blown apart over Germany.

"Skipper, the colonel's on the phone."

Mahr looked up at his clerk standing at the door.

"Tell him I'll call him right back."

"Yes, sir."

The major poured another measure of bourbon in the glass. But whatever he wants can damn well wait, he thought. I need a drink.

"Sir, he's very insistent."

"Shit."

He picked up the phone and paused before answering as professionally as possible, "Major Mahr speaking, sir."

"Major, I know you just got back from debrief, but something's come up. Can you come over here?"

Randy looked at the half empty glass. "Yes, sir, I'll leave shortly."

Arriving at headquarters, Mahr found six other fighter squadron commanders sitting at a large conference table with Colonel Ned Thomsen, his wing commander and Thomsen's counterpart from Boughton, Colonel Tony Hill.

"Gentlemen, thanks for getting over here so quickly. We've got a problem that the front office wants us to tackle and right now."

The men around the table said nothing, but it was clear their attention was fully on Thomsen.

"It seems that the Luftwaffe is not going to go quietly into the night as it were. We've had four incidents in the last two days of our fighter sweeps being ambushed over German airfields. I guess we should have expected this from them, but we honestly felt they couldn't afford to take anything away from their attacks on our bombers. Our job is to come up with a plan to deal with them."

Having flown on many low altitude attack runs in the last two months, Mahr began to think about how they would turn the tables. An interesting task and he felt some of his energy returning.

Thad Spencer had barely gotten back in his office when the call came in from Jack Stewart. Four hours later he was at Tangmere, where he met Stewart and Toms.

"Good luck all around," Stewart said when Spencer was shown into Wing Commander Toms' office.

"How so?"

"Our people were able to get a radio message through to the Dutch resistance. They confirmed there are five crewmen in hiding and we're ready to try for an extraction."

Only five, Spencer thought, what happened to the rest of them? He said, "How soon would you try?"

Toms laid a chart on the table.

"Here is the area we're talking about. You can see from the maps that the terrain is essentially flat.

With the exception of the few wooded areas, it's damn near a huge airfield. Which means we can probably land very close to your chaps. Furthermore, the weather is cooperating right now. I say we try for tomorrow at sunset."

"Can the Dutch be ready?" Spencer asked.

Jack Stewart nodded.

"They have asked us to select three landing areas and will let us know when they're ready. Although we know from experience that dragging these things out is never a good idea. Too many people end up knowing what's going on and that only cuts down your chances of getting in and out."

"With five, we would take one Hudson, land right at sunset, pick up your lads and dash back across the Channel. We'll lay on a small fighter escort just in case, but I suspect we would be in and out before the Germans even thought about reacting."

Stewart spoke up, "I'll send one of my experienced men who has been on the ground over there several times. He'll be able to provide a cool head and firepower in case things get dicey."

"How so?" Spencer asked.

"We never know what's waiting when we set down. Even with good recognition codes, you don't know if someone has informed the Germans and there's an ambush waiting. It's smart to have someone ready to deal with unexpected problems."

Toms lit his pipe.

"Most times it goes without a hitch."

"Sunset tomorrow," John said. "There is a large field about five kilometers from here. We'll take you there in the truck and be ready with a signal for the airplane."

"What kind of signal," Sean asked.

"Three lanterns, laid out in a triangle."

"Do we know what kind of aircraft?" John Forster asked.

The Dutchman shook his head, "No."

"There will be only three of us on that aircraft," Sean said quietly. "I'm staying here with Hass."

"I'll stay, skipper," Sergeant Fortino said.

"Thanks for offering, but I want the three of you out of here and back to England."

Forster said, "I bet the Brits will be bloody angry if they send an aircraft in here to get you and you say 'no'."

"Probably will," Sean agreed. "But I'm not leaving Hass, especially in his condition."

"But what good can you do? You're not a doctor, and he already has a good one. You don't speak Dutch and your German is bush league at best."

"I can come up with plenty of reasons why this is a dumb thing to do, I don't need any help."

"Colonel Spencer, this is Warrant Officer Terry Howe of my group."

Howe was an average looking man in his late twenties wearing army battle dress. But he carried himself like a man who is used to taking care of himself.

"Nice to meet you," Spencer said, shaking Howe's hand.

Jack Stewart continued, "You never know who or what's waiting on the ground. Terry's there to provide firepower if it's needed."

"How long will the aircraft be on the ground?"

Stewart said, "Long enough to load the passengers."

"I brought photos of the crew as you requested," Spencer said, handing a manila envelope to Stewart.

"Just to confirm who's actually aboard after the pick-up."

"Seems a little odd," Spencer said.

Stewart smiled. "You learn to be very cautious in this business. Things are often not what they seem."

They think this could be a trap, Spencer thought to himself.

"You're the experts, whatever you say."

"Let's get over to the briefing. It's two hours to takeoff."

Howe picked up his haversack and then a Thompson .45 sub-machine gun with a pouch of ammunition clips.

"After you."

"Here, skipper, I won't be needing these," Sergeant Fortino said as he handed two full .45 clips to Sean.

The two men were standing beside Pieter's' small truck as the sun began to set.

"Good luck," Sean said, shaking hands with Fortino. "Keep an eye on those two. We know they can't take care of themselves."

They both turned as John Forster came out the front door, supported by Steve O'Loughlin. Walking slowly, with Forster's arm around the navigator's neck, the men made it to the back of the truck where the Australian leaned against the bumper.

"Criminy, I feel like a damned old man."

"You are an old man," Sean said, helping him into the truck.

"That's good," Forster said, now sitting with his back against the side of the truck.

"In you go," Sean directed the other two as John came out of the house.

The old Dutchman had arrived with Doctor VanderRonhaar and Pieter, who now sat in the driver's seat ready to leave.

"We'll come back for the doctor after this is over," he said.

Sean nodded as John walked toward the cab.

"I know better than to try and change your mind," John said.

"There's no choice for me," Sean said. "Tell Jamie I'll be back, it's just gonna take a little longer."

Forster nodded and offered his hand. "Watch your ass, yank."

McGowan nodded and pulled the tarp closed over the back of the truck.

Pieter started the Renault, put it into gear with a crunch of metal and slowly drove off down the dirt road.

Sean watched the truck until it went around the bend then turned back to the house.

"That must have been a hard thing to do," Tanna said from the porch.

He walked up to her.

"Not really. Hass is my responsibility."

She followed him into the cottage.

"You take your friendships very seriously."

Sean smiled. "We aren't really friends."

The doctor looked at him, her expression asking the question.

"Captain Hass blames me for the death of his brother."

"What?"

He told her the story of the ill-fated flight when Lieutenant Robin Hass had died.

"And yet the two of you fly together and you are willing to risk your life staying behind with him."

"Yeah, I guess it doesn't make much sense. It's about doing what needs to be done. Simple as that."

She shook her head.

"I thought Dutchmen were hard headed, but you Americans are worse."

McGowan grinned at her.

209

"Yes, ma'am, I guess we are. How's our patient doing?"

Her expression changed, the worry obvious.

"Not as good as yesterday. Nothing obvious, but he seems very lethargic, which is not a good sign."

"When will he be able to travel?"

She shrugged.

"I don't know."

Sean opened the door to Hass' room, letting his eyes adjust to the dark.

"Getting ready to shove off?" Billy asked.

"Nah, thought I would stick around here for a while."

Turning his head, Hass said slowly.

"What does that mean?"

Sean walked over to the bed and looked down.

"They're gone. It's you and me now, so don't give me any problems or I'll put you up on charges."

"You stayed?"

"Yeah."

"You're a dumb shit then," Billy said.

"And you're the third person today who's told me that. But I wasn't leaving you all bunged up. We'll go home when it's time. Until then follow the doctor's orders."

"This is about Robin, isn't it?"

Was it, Sean asked himself?

Wing Commander Toms pulled back slightly on the control yoke as the coast came into view in the distance. Following takeoff from Tangmere, Toms had remained on the deck all the way, never getting above one hundred feet altitude.

"Bloody good navigation," Toms said to his co-pilot Dicky Thompson.

On the nose they could see the Lange Jaap lighthouse rising above the surrounding flat terrain.

"Standby to come right to one zero eight magnetic," Thompson said after checking his chart.

"One zero eight, roger."

Their route of flight had been designed to stay over water until the last minute. Now they turned inland, still over Lake Ijssel.

"Clock running," Thompson said after pushing the reset knob on the navigational clock.

"Roger, indicating one eighty on the nose."

"Twenty minutes on this course and we will hopefully find four lonesome yanks."

A half-moon was now visible through the scattered clouds as the sun continued to set. Pieter had parked the truck at the edge of the trees bordering on a large area of open fields. One hundred feet from the trees, three kerosene lanterns burned in a twenty foot triangle.

"How the fuck will they ever see those," Tony Fortino said quietly to Steve O'Loughlin.

Steve shook his head.

"Beats the shit out of me, as long as they do."

O'Loughlin walked back to where John Forster sat against a pine tree.

"You okay?"

"Right as rain," John answered, "Ready to get this bloody show on the road."

"Yeah," Steve said, the doubt obvious in his voice. "Wait a minute, I hear an aircraft."

"That's twenty minutes," Toms said, throttling back and beginning a climb. "Now let's find those lads."

Turning left he began to scan the terrain, looking for the pre-arranged signal.

In the rear of the Hudson, Terry Howe sat at one of the left cabin windows looking for the signal while the turret gunner, Sergeant Howland, searched the right side of the aircraft

"Tallyho, Toms called and immediately lowered the nose. "Triangle of lights at ten-thirty."

"Roger," Thompson replied.

"Landing checks," Toms called as he turned the aircraft toward the triangle and leveled one thousand feet above the ground.

Smoothly and methodically the two pilots worked their way through the landing checklist.

"Landing checks complete," the co-pilot reported.

Toms knew that the winds in the area were expected to be from the west and he leveled at five hundred feet heading east with the triangle about a mile off the left wing.

"I'll call for landing lights when I roll on final," Toms said as he rechecked the landing gear down.

"Prepare for landing," Thompson shouted back into the cabin.

Terry Howe strapped in next to Sergeant Howland, checking that his weapon was beside him on the seat.

Calm winds, Toms thought as he steadied up on a westerly heading. The only question, as always, were there any obstacles they couldn't see.

Pulling the throttle to idle, he held the nose up slightly and waited for the wheels to touch down. The aircraft bounced slightly then settled on the main landing gear as the airspeed bled off. Toms saw nothing in the glare of the landing light except short grass, perhaps the remains of the spring crop.

"Son of a bitch," Tony Fortino said in awe, watching the twin engine bomber slow to a stop and retrace its course back toward the point it had touched down.

John pointed a flashlight toward the aircraft and signaled their location.

"We must load quickly, hurry up."

Fortino and O'Loughlin supported John Forster as they headed toward the aircraft which was now stopped and had switched off its landing light.

Terry Howe swung the cabin door open against the propeller wash and locked it in place. He jumped down and immediately scanned the surrounding area. The last illumination from the setting sun was now totally gone and the woods off the right of the aircraft were hidden in darkness. A light was approaching across the field and he could make out four men. He walked to meet the group, his Thompson ready if needed.

"There were to be four of you," Howe asked when it was clear one of the men was an older civilian.

"The skipper is staying behind to take care of our wounded man."

Terry Howe had been on a number of these missions and he knew they never went as briefed. In any case there was nothing he was going to do about it now.

"Very well, let's get aboard and out of here."

As they began to help Forster into the Hudson, the night was ripped apart by the sound of automatic weapons fire.

"Damn," Howe said, turning to face the woods and kneeling down. "Get in the aircraft!"

Howe scanned the dark woods and saw muzzle flashes as bullets whined by in the darkness. Shit. He grabbed the civilian and pushed him into the Hudson as Sergeant Howland opened up with the twin Browning machine guns in the turret. One more check around the aircraft and the commando jumped into the Hudson and pulled the hatch closed.

"GO, GO, GO," he yelled toward the cockpit, pushing the civilian forward.

Toms jammed throttles forward and released the brakes. The Hudson began its takeoff roll with a continuous fire from the turret, sweeping the edge of the woods.

"Airspeed's off the peg," Thompson called, they both knowing the bomber needed at least ninety five knots to get airborne at their current fuel load.

"Sixty......seventy......"

Wing Commander Toms could feel the aircraft trying to break free, there was nothing to do now but press on.

"Eighty.........ninety.....NINETY FIVE."

With the slightest back pressure, Terry Toms nursed the Hudson off the ground. Falling back on his thousands of hours, he knew they needed to get the landing gear up. If they settled back for any reason, they were dead. He slammed the gear handle up, checked the throttles full forward and watched the vertical speed indicator. "Climb you beauty," he said aloud, but his thoughts were focused on the airspeed and altimeter, both which were increasing ever so slowly.

"Christ," Dickey Thompson said as they passed two hundred feet and Toms retracted the big Fowler flaps.

"Better check in back for any casualties," Toms said evenly.

Chapter Eighteen

"General, this is Spencer. I'm at Tangmere. The Hudson landed thirty minutes ago with McGowan's crew. There were only three of them."

General Eaker asked, "McGowan?"

"Sir, he stayed behind with his wounded bombardier who apparently couldn't be moved."

"How are the rest of them?'

"Two are fine, the ball turret gunner, a Sergeant Fortino and the navigator, Lieutenant O'Loughlin. His co-pilot, an Australian exchange officer named Forster was wounded in the arm and leg but is moving on his own."

"Thad, I'd like to see that sergeant and the navigator as soon as the intelligence folks are done with them."

"Yes, sir. Also, they were taken under fire in the landing area. A Dutch civilian, apparently a member of the resistance ended up on the Hudson."

"Quite a night it seems."

"Yes, sir."

"Thad, please pass on my personal thanks to the Hudson crew. Let's look at some kind of appropriate decoration for the crew. So what happens now with McGowan."

"General, I'll call Commander Stewart at MI-6 and find out."

Doctor Tanna VanderRonhaar looked out the cottage window wondering where John could be. She checked her watch. They had been gone over four hours. Every minute that went by raised the chances that something was very wrong.

"They should have been back by now."

"Yes," she said.

"What do you want to do?" Sean asked.

She shrugged her shoulders. "Wait. There's nothing else to do."

"If they don't come back by morning, I think we have to figure that the Germans are involved."

Tanna knew what that meant. Pieter and John, she thought, could it have finally caught up with them? She had known the younger man her entire life and he was one of her closest friends. Had he been caught by the Germans? The Gestapo? She had heard the terrible stories. And John, it was too hard to think about.

Pieter Vandenbergh moved through the woods, alert for any sounds of pursuit. He knew this area and hoped the Germans didn't have enough troops to surround the forested area he was now making his way through. The events at the landing field still seemed like a nightmare to the young man, machine gun fire, sharp orders in the darkness and the trees around him being shredded by bullets. Somehow he had avoided being hit or spotted by the Germans and now he knew he had to make it back to Meppel and let Aart know what had happened. But one question kept coming to back him. Had John gone on the aircraft? Perhaps he was lying dead in the field or had been captured by the Germans. The second possibility is what drove Vandenbergh on through the thick underbrush. If the

Germans had John, everyone was at risk, particularly the Americans.

The street was eerily quiet as Pieter made his way to the small house on the corner of Lueten Street. Aart Boonstra served the small town of Meppel as its only pharmacist. But the middle aged man was much more. He had been the leader of the local resistance since the fall of 1940. The lack of a heavy German presence in the area had kept their direct attacks on their occupiers infrequent. Their real value had been maintaining the flow of material and people from England through Holland and into Europe.

The front door opened slightly then swung wide.

"Come in, but be quiet, Lois is asleep."

Once inside, Pieter waited while Aart lit a small candle on the front room table.

"What's happened?

"Germans. They were in the woods west of us. I don't know how many, but there were machine guns."

"John?"

"I don't know," Pieter said. "The airplane got off, but I don't know what happened to John."

Boonstra knew what that meant as well as Pieter.

"And the American is still in the house?"

"Two Americans, one stayed behind with the other."

"Damn them. Don't they understand the danger?"

Pieter went on, "Tanna is still out at the cottage with them. I need a car to go get her."

"The roads will be full of Germans. You have to wait until things settle down."

"I can't do that, she's expecting me to come back for her. If I'm not there, who knows what she'll do."

"Then take my bicycle and stay off the main roads. At least you can tell her to stay out of sight.

We'll use my car to get her, but it might take several days."

Sean McGowan knew that something had happened to the Dutchman and by association to his three crewmen. It was also logical that if any of his men or the Dutchmen had been captured, then he and Hass were in danger. He had to do something.

"Doctor, we need to get out of here."

"And go where?"

"That's what I'm asking you. If the Germans saw the aircraft, they might search the area."

Where could they go, she asked herself? And in any case, her patient was still very much a question.

"I don't know," she answered. "And your friend really shouldn't be moved."

"I understand that, but he'll be in worse shape if the Germans get a hold of him. Isn't there somewhere close we could take him?"

She crossed her arms and walked to the window. Head injuries were so unpredictable. She considered their options.

"We could take him to Vanderhoek's. It's a small farm south of here. No one has lived there for the last year and it's well off the main road. But we have no way to get there."

"Doctor, I'll find a way."

"We've had a good debrief with the Dutchman," Jack Stewart said.

Colonel Spencer had driven into London after talking to Stewart the day prior. Although it had only been two days since the Hudson rescue flight, Stewart told Spencer that MI-6 thought they had a plan that would get McGowan and Hass back to England.

Stewart continued, "There was another man with him at the pickup point. If that fellow was captured, all bets are off. He likely would have been tortured and give up the location of your men. But if he was killed or escaped, they may still be hiding out in the cottage."

"No way to confirm?"

"Actually there is, but we aren't scheduled to make radio contact with the local resistance until tonight. Once we can confirm that this man Vandenbergh wasn't captured, we'll put our plan in action."

Spencer asked, "Can you fill me in? I know General Eaker is very interested."

"It's a variation of the last go, but with a twist. Because the krauts were waiting, we have to assume something or someone might have been compromised. A bad card in the deck, so to speak. So we'll stage a fake landing as a diversion while another aircraft picks up your two pilots."

"But I thought Captain Hass couldn't be moved."

Stewart nodded. "That's what we understand. But it turns out that this man's daughter is the doctor who's taking care of Hass."

"So how will you work it?"

"We're going to take Mr. VanderRonhaar back to Holland and let him work the diversion and have him contact us when Hass can travel."

"This is quite an effort by the British to rescue two American flyers," Spencer said.

"I'd like to think the Americans would do the same thing for us," Stewart said.

Colonel Paul Bloch motioned for the two survivors to enter the general's office.

The two men walked to Eaker's desk and saluted.

"Reporting as ordered, sir."

"Stand at ease, please," the general said. He rose and came around the desk and extended his hand.

"Glad to have you back," he said as he shook hands with Staff Sergeant Fortino and Lieutenant O'Loughlin.

"Please have a seat."

"Yes, sir."

"Colonel, would you ask my aide to have them send in some coffee?" He turned to O'Loughlin and Fortino.

"The docs told me you both checked out okay, any problems?"

"No, sir," O'Loughlin answered.

Fortino shook his head.

"Sergeant, I understand you have four German fighters to your credit."

"Yes, sir."

"And I read the debrief of your actions during the forced landing and on the ground."

Fortino looked uncomfortable.

"You're a credit to the Air Force, sergeant. For your performance in the air and during this mission, you are being meritoriously promoted to tech sergeant. You are also being recommended for the Bronze Star. Well done, son. Lieutenant, you will also be recommended for the Bronze Star. And on the advice of Colonel Bloch, we are recommending your immediate promotion to captain."

"Thank you, sir," Steve said, grinning.

"Now, I'd like you to go over what happened on your last flight. It's not often that we get an opportunity like this. I know the intelligence officers have given you the works, but I want to ask you some questions that might help crews in the future. Now why don't you start from the top."

Over the next hour, the two crewmembers debriefed the general and answered his questions.

"I understand both of you have over twenty five missions?"

They both answered, "Yes, sir."

"Well this will be sending you both back to the states," the general finally said.

"Sir, what's gonna happen to the skipper?" Fortino asked.

"We're doing everything we can to make sure that Major McGowan and Captain Hass get back to England."

"General, the krauts almost got us in that field," Steve said. " It seems to me that it doesn't look too good for them."

Paul Bloch looked uncomfortable, seeing the look on Eaker's face.

"I'd be lying to you if I told you it was going to be easy to get them out. But we have some pretty smart people working on it."

"Yes, sir," Steve answered.

Fortino hesitated then said, "General, I'd just as soon stay here in England if that's okay."

Eaker looked hard at him.

"Got a girl, right?"

"No, sir, nothing like that. What I mean is maybe I can help out the new guys, the new ball turret gunners. Kinda get them ready."

"What do you think about that, lieutenant? Would Technical Sergeant Fortino make a good instructor in the OTU?"

"Yes, sir, no question about it."

Eaker said, "I'll have orders cut."

O'Loughlin hesitated then asked, "Sir, can I ask a question about the skipper?"

"Go ahead, lieutenant."

221

"General, the intelligence officers told us we can't say anything about the skipper or what's happening."

Eaker nodded.

"I understand it's standard procedure to protect the underground and in this case give Major McGowan the best chance of making it home."

"Yes, sir. I understand that. But he has a girl in London. She's the roommate of the girl who's seeing our co-pilot. We think she should know."

The general understood the dilemma.

The invasion had provided an even larger challenge to the Air Ministry as the details for inter-service operations only became more complicated. Routine days became sixteen hours as the staff, particularly in Current Operations dealt with difficult logistic and operational problems on a constant basis. Solace for the overworked staff was the apparent success of Operation Overlord and the hastened end to the war.

Jamie Taylor-Paige found the mind-numbing workload a godsend. The crazy schedule resulted in little contact with Aubrey. Sleeping and working kept both of them completely occupied. They had stopped talking about Sean and John. It was if they both had come to the conclusion that dwelling on it would only made things worse and right now neither could afford it.

"There is someone to see you in Conference Room B."

Jamie turned to see Mr. Hawthorne, her supervisor.

"To see me?"

"Right. Down you go and try to make it short, we have several deadlines coming due."

Walking down the dim corridor, Jamie wondered who would be coming to see her and why in the conference room?

She knocked on the door, opened it and stepped inside.

"There she is," Aubrey said to an army captain who sat in front of an opened folder on the large table.

"Aubrey. What's this?"

"Miss Taylor-Paige, my name is Baker. Please have a seat."

Jamie sat down opposite the two of them.

"I work in one of the intelligence organizations," Baker said. "We are involved in an operation, while extremely sensitive, we feel you should be made aware of it. Before I brief you, I am required to have you sign an acknowledgement that discussing anything of what I am about to tell you would be a violation of the Official Secrets Acts. Do you understand?"

"Yes."

"Please sign this affidavit, right here."

Searching Aubrey's eyes, Jamie saw something that made her hopeful.

"This about Sean, I mean Major McGowan?"

"Quite right."

"Is he all right?" she asked quickly.

Baker's face softened.

"As far as we know, yes," he said. "Several members of his crew were rescued and returned to allied control."

She looked at Aubrey, who smiled and nodded.

"The rescue operation is ongoing. We should know more in the next few days. Major McGowan is in Holland with another member of his crew, Captain Hass. Lieutenant O'Loughlin, Staff Sergeant Fortino and Squadron Leader Forster are here in England."

"Thank God," Jamie said quietly.

"He stayed behind to take care of Captain Hass." Aubrey interjected.

Jamie felt her eyes welling with tears.

"But he's alive," she said softly, "He's alive."

Chapter Nineteen

The ache would probably always be there, he thought, the pain of getting out of bed always reminding him of his injury. Rudolf Steinfeld sat on the edge of the bed in his darkened room and took a deep breath, wincing slightly. He reached over and turned on the small lamp, allowing his eyes to adjust to the light.

"Rudi, what time is it?"

He looked over at Karin Spengler. She lay on her side, the sheet just covering her breasts. And I once thought she was a witch, he thought and smiled.

"Just after five. Get some more sleep, my dear."

"I wish I could," she said sleepily. "But I have early rounds at the hospital."

She got out of bed in one smooth motion, the sheet dropping away from her bare body as she walked around the foot of the bed and put her arms around Steinfeld.

Karin looked up at her lover. "Today?"

"We go on alert at 0700."

Her arms closed tighter around him.

Randy Mahr knew that the success of the "Bushwhacker" missions would depend on timing and discipline by everyone involved. But if they did their jobs right, the Germans would pay a heavy price.

Today's target would be the Dortmund Luftwaffe base. Conserving fuel, the squadron would arrive with full tanks and ammo when another squadron from the wing was attacking Dortmund on their way back from the mission to Wilhelmshaven. If the Germans had an ambush waiting, they would find a fully armed P-51 squadron jumping them. If there was no ambush, then Mahr's squadron would attack the anti-aircraft batteries that surrounded the field. In any case the Germans would pay a price.

Rudi found Karl Ulrich in the small room off the operations office. Any other officer in the wing would have jumped to attention for the wing commander, but Karl Ulrich knew better.

"Good morning," Rudi said, walking to the small window. "What's the word from maintenance?"

"Twenty two available, three more possibles."

"They busted their asses last night."

Ulrich grunted his agreement.

Steinfeld looked at a status sheet on the desk. "Anything come down from sector yet?'

"All quiet for now."

The major lit a cigarette and threw the match into an ashtray.

"Weather?" Rudi asked.

"Nothing worth noting, some lower layers over the coast that should burn off. Some mid-level clouds in our area. All in all, a beautiful day to go flying. Wouldn't you agree, my colonel?"

Looking at his friend of many years and many dogfights, Steinfeld smiled. "Remember what we said when we first started this fucking war?"

Ulrich nodded.

"As good a day to die as any."

The phone rang on the desk.

"Ulrich."

Karl replaced the phone receiver.

"Sector just called. Launch and check in, no scramble."

Steinfeld considered what his friend had said. Were they beginning to marshal squadrons in the air because the size of the raid was so large, or just being cautious?

"Come on, my Bavarian friend, time to defend the Fatherland."

"Shit."

As the Mustangs crossed the English coast, Randy Mahr looked down at the Channel. God I hate flying over water, he thought. The windswept water had claimed too many victims from both sides. Once in the water your chances of living began to dwindle fast. How do those naval types do it? Flying hundreds of miles over the open ocean, then having to come back and find a single ship to land on. Enough of that, he told himself, focus on today's mission or you might just find yourself floating down there.

Three four plane divisions followed Mahr as he adjusted the squadron's course toward the navigation check point at Zeebrugge, where they would cross the Dutch coast. From there, Dortmund was due east. They had been at low altitude since takeoff, never climbing over five hundred feet. Now they skimmed the waves only one hundred feet below. Perhaps the German radar would not see them coming.

He checked his watch, knowing that timing was going to be critical. Too early would destroy the element of surprise, while too late would let the Germans off without a beating. Almost without thinking, he adjusted the power to slow the Mustang just slightly. The only wrench that might be thrown into the operation was if they were intercepted by German fighters. If that happened, Mahr would press toward

Dortmund with his four fighters while the rest of the squadron occupied the krauts.

Climbing past ten thousand feet, Steinfeld scanned the sky in front of him. In a move that was now subconscious, he slowly rolled the fighter ten degrees left then back to the right as he surveyed under the formation. While every pilot was responsible for lookout doctrine, he had found that flying formation always took priority until they were at altitude and in combat spread.

Looking forward, he checked the rate of climb, shit – there was something down there. The wing, now broken into three flights climbed another thousand feet as Steinfeld stabilized his flight and keyed his microphone.

"Red Wolf, lead squadron stick with me. Karl, take the rest for sector control."

Eight fighters began to turn right and descend, following their commander, while the rest joined on Ulrich and resumed their climb.

This could be a fool's errand, Steinfeld told himself. Lowering the wing's strength by eight fighters on what might turn out to be a complete waste of time. He pushed the nose over and allowed the sleek fighter to accelerate. Whatever he saw down there would not outrun a 190 coming down from altitude unless it was a British Mosquito.

Scanning the terrain on his nose, Steinfeld methodically moved his eyes across the low country that made up the Dutch/German border. Descending through five thousand feet he began a very slow turn to the right. Nothing. Damn it. The rest of the Focke Wulf's had spread into their combat formation, ready for the attack.

Still descending, he began a slow turn back to the left. There! A formation of fighters, low, heading east about three miles, on the nose. He pushed the throttle to full military and quickly charged his guns. In the other seven fighters, each pilot repeated the procedure. Now it was simply a matter of chasing the enemy aircraft until they were able to attack. The sun angle was working against the FW's, making it more likely the enemy would spot them before they could open fire. But every fight was different. Pilots flying close to the ground were going to be more attentive to maintaining altitude and might not see the attackers.

Mustangs, Rudi told himself, P-51's, down low, heading toward Dortmund and these Mustangs had orange tails.

"Phoenix! Bandit! Break, break brea...."

Randy Mahr looked right to see one Mustang plow into the ground, cartwheeling in flames. Tracers flew past him as he began a hard turn to the right and keyed his microphone, "Phoenix, sections, sections, sections!"

Desperately climbing and trying to locate their attackers, the P-51's were now broken into two plane formations using a tactic that Mahr had drilled into them. In short order frantic calls were coming over the tactical frequency, each group of Americans fighting to neutralize the German's initial advantage.

Knowing that Bobby Mitchell could hang with him, Mahr jettisoned his drop tanks and rechecked his guns armed and ready. He saw an FW-190 behind his right wing and knew the attacker was closing to a firing range. At full military power, the American knew their only chance was to force an overshoot long enough to give them some breathing room.

"Mitch, go high," he broadcast, then he pulled hard on the stick, feeling the force slam him into the seat and his vision begin to grey. Hold it, hold it. Now. He stuffed the stick forward, fighting hard to keep the big fighter's altitude constant, then he slammed the stick hard right while pushing full right rudder, whipping the fighter through one hundred and eighty degrees of roll before he again pulled back as hard as he could. Fighting the "g" forces, Mahr looked over his left shoulder and picked up the German who had switched his attack to Mitchell. Pulling hard, he brought the Mustang's nose around toward the German, who had begun firing at Mitchell. *Now it's your turn, asshole.*

He let the gunsight stabilize for two seconds then fired his eight machine guns, immediately scoring hits on the enemy fighter's fuselage. Smoke began to trail from the FW, who now began a hard turn to the left which forced Mahr to pull power to avoid an overshoot just as tracers whipped by his cockpit, then slammed into his engine. Dense black smoke began to pour from the engine compartment as the engine began to tear itself apart.

Steinfeld had seen enough damaged aircraft to know the Mustang was finished. Scores didn't matter anymore, what mattered was surviving to continue the fight. He pulled off the wounded American, confident the aircraft would be a flaming wreck in short order. Quickly scanning the sky, he saw one P-51 in what looked like a stalemated turn with one of his aircraft. One versus one, the outcome was always in doubt. Two versus one, seldom.

Too low, too damned low, Mahr knew jumping wasn't an option. *It's easy to make a decision when you have no other options,* he thought and knew he was going to have to set *Joltin' Joan* down. He'd done it once before in a trainer in Texas when the engine failed on takeoff. He'd walked away from that one and he intended to do so again.

Drop tanks are gone, shut off fuel master and magnetos. Safe the guns, get the canopy open. Methodically he worked through his mental checklist to prepare for the inevitable as he searched for a field to set down. At five hundred feet, the decision was made, flaps down, one hundred knots indicated, but slowing. Okay, lock your harness, get ready, God looks after drunks and fighter pilots, he thought as the wide field opened on the nose and he let the big fighter settle. Keep the nose up, keep the nose up, hold the attitude, nose straight, use the rudder, fly it, fly it.

The impact was loud as the Mustang slid across the plowed field and lurched to a stop, throwing him hard into his straps. Get out, he told himself, stay calm but get out. He hit the quick disconnect and ripped the radio cords out the instrument panel. Stepping on the seat, he put one foot on the cockpit rail and jumped.

Chapter Twenty

The Vanderhoek farm had not impressed McGowan when he had first seen it the previous morning. One small cottage and a barn that appeared ready to collapse. But it was far from the main road and had no close neighbors. Pieter had returned to the old house with a car after telling them to sit tight for several days. The small number of German troops still in the area had not been on the roads after the first day and the drive south had been uneventful.

Now it was just a matter of waiting until they could establish contact with the British and make a plan. Sean hated inactivity, but knew there was nothing he could do about it. Billy had shown no ill effects from the car journey and the cottage was comfortable enough.

"All quiet?"

Sean turned to see Billy. He nodded.

"Haven't seen or heard anything. How're you doing?"

Hass sat down on the small couch.

"Better, I think. The headaches aren't as bad. Or maybe I'm just getting used to them."

Sean laughed.

The two men looked at each other.

"Quite a story to tell our grandkids," Hass said.

Major Randy Mahr kept thinking about the uneaten donut he had left on his desk just prior to the mission. His stomach had stopped growling, but the hunger was stronger than the day before. He'd stumbled upon a stream at mid-day, drinking his fill, but found nothing to eat. Last night had dragged on as he remembered, then dwelled on that damned glazed donut.

He'd considered his options and the only one that made sense was to take a chance and contact a local. What a crap shoot he thought, hoping most Dutchmen were anti-German. He would find out.

"They found Karl, sir. I'm sorry."

The adjutant stood at attention in the doorway to Steinfeld's office.

"Where?"

"Just north of Reimgen."

Karl Ulrich had been missing for two days. Leading the rest of the wing while Rudi had attacked the low-flying Americans, Karl simply disappeared after engaging a large number of American fighters. No one saw him hit or go down, but that was the way of aerial combat.

"He had been severely wounded, but was able to jump. They found him in a wooded area."

Karl Ulrich, his friend, a good man and one of the best pilots Steinfeld had ever known. Damn this war. He thought back to the old days, the names he could remember, but the faces were harder each day. Not many of us left.

John VanderRonhaar knew he wasn't a coward. But as he listened to the engines accelerate his stomach felt more than a little queasy. The parachute straps cutting into his crotch didn't help either. He looked across at the commando, Howe, who would be jumping with him. The Englishman appeared relaxed and very comfortable with all of the jump gear attached to his body. VanderRonhaar had been surprised when Commander Stewart told him they would be returning him to Holland by parachute. When the Dutchman had asked about training, Stewart had told him that experience had shown them that practice jumps did little more than injure people. They could teach him everything he would need to know to successfully make his first jump.

He did feel ready, if a little sore from the landing practice. Extensive lectures had prepared him for what to expect and how to handle any problems. Although, as Howe had told them, they were jumping low enough that there was no need to worry about using a reserve chute.

Ten minutes after takeoff, John heard the engines slow and he assumed they had reached their cruise altitude.

"Are you all right?"

Howe's question broke VanderRonhaar's thoughts of what waited on the ground in Holland.

"Yes......Yes, I am. How long?" he asked over the interior noise.

"Forty five minutes would be my guess. Watch for the red light."

John knew the red light above the main door of the Hudson would light up five minutes prior to the jump signal. When the green light illuminated they were to exit the aircraft. A cargo container would precede Howe, then he would follow. The very large RAF flight engineer would be there to make sure the interval wasn't too long. Howe had explained it to him, "Jump right after me, close as you can. If you freeze, Sergeant Waltham will assist you out the door."

It would be all right, he told himself, if not totally believing himself. Once on the ground, everything would be fine.

His thoughts returned to Holland. While there had been no information to the contrary, he worried about Tanna. She was a stubborn woman and sometimes let her feelings cloud her judgment, particularly when it came to taking care of her patients. Now it seemed to John that this American had become more than just an injured allied airman to her.

Terry Howe saw the red light come on and reached over to shake the Dutchman's arm.

"Gear check," he said.

John stood up for Howe to inspect his chute one last time.

"Looks fine. Ready?"

VanderRonhaar nodded.

Sergeant released the door hatch pins, pulling it into the cabin.

The cargo container lay just aft on the door. Web straps connected the cylinder to the smaller parachute and a long lanyard was attached to the ripcord assembly. The sergeant pushed the package to the edge of the door.

Howe moved to the door, standing right behind the cargo pack.

John followed the commando to the door concentrating on the procedures that had been drilled into him, knees together, arms crossed hard on chest and roll forward. He could feel his heart pounding in his chest. My God, roll forward into the darkness, he thought, what am I doing?

"Green light," Waltham shouted, shoving the package out the door.

Before the sergeant could yell "Go," Howe had rolled out the door, his static line pulled hard against the door edge.

"GO!!"

John rolled into the black night.

Terry Howe quickly released his harness and began rolling up the dark green parachute. Gone were the days of white parachutes and Howe was damned glad. Less likely to be spotted and easier to conceal, he thought, but harder to see someone following you in the jump.

He stood up and looked for the Dutchman's chute. It was nowhere to be seen. Picking up his parachute bundle, he put it under one arm and began to make his way across the field.

Lying on his back, John felt like he had fallen out of a truck, but nothing seemed to be damaged. He took a deep breath and then remembered to release the main quick-disconnect. Sitting up, he pulled his left arm out of the harness, then his right, rolling onto his knees. My God, he thought, I really did it. He grinned to himself.

"Are you all right?"

VanderRonhaar turned to see Terry Howe coming out of the night.

Standing up, he said, "Yes....yes, I think I am."

"Come on, we have to find the cargo pack."

It had taken John only minutes to determine they had been dropped within one kilometer of their intended landing site. The cargo container had proved more elusive. The small package and chute was eventually found in a drainage ditch but took up forty minutes they couldn't afford. Howe retrieved extra ammunition for his Thompson .45 caliber sub-machine gun and a rucksack that included fragmentation grenades and flares. He passed six loaded clips to John for the Sten gun he'd been issued.

With the sun coming up in less than six hours, John knew he and Howe would be pressed to make it to Zylstra's farm where they would be able to get help from one of the members of his group, Raymond.

After covering their chute and the container in a copse of trees, the two men set out across the countryside under a quarter moon.

The young British officer was at least twenty five years younger than the Dutchman, but the pace set by the older man impressed the commando. Howe had seen action in the western desert and on numerous raids into occupied France. His specialty was weapons and ordnance originally, but his experience now made him one of the best behind the lines operators in MI-6.

In a small concession to the rules of war, Howe wore his standard battle dress, knowing that the men he was going to rescue were uniformed members of the service and if captured he would be able to at least maintain the appearance of a regular soldier. While that was a slim protection at best, VanderRonhaar had no cover for what he was doing other than his ability to blend into the populace. If caught actively assisting the British and Americans he would certainly suffer torture and death at the hands of the Gestapo.

"How much farther?" Howe asked as he saw the sky starting to lighten. It had been a long night, but thankfully they had only seen the lights of a lone car far across one field. Other than that, they could have been on the moon.

Without looking back, John said, "It's over the next little hill, we'll be there in ten minutes. Then he suddenly stopped and put his hand back to stop Howe.

"Listen!"

The sounds of a vehicle came from the distance.

"Hurry," John said and began to run.

Emerging from the low line of trees, the Dutchman dropped down to a knee and looked over the small valley. In the first light of the day, Howe could see several men next to a large Mercedes sedan which was parked in front of a two story farmhouse. A smaller Renault coupe had pulled around to the side of the house.

"Germans," John said. "Mother of God, no."

Howe knew the farm belonged to a member of the underground named Raymond Zylstra. John had counted on the man to get them to McGowan's hideout.

They watched two men get out of the Renault and move around behind the house while the men in front waited.

"You're sure they're Germans?"

"The local police don't have cars like that, only the Gestapo."

"Who's in the house?"

"Just Raymond, he's a widower."

The two men in front moved to the door and pounded on it.

"Let's get closer," VanderRonhaar said.

As they moved through the underbrush, they heard yells.

Moving to within a hundred feet, they knelt down and watched two men manhandling another out to the sedan. The man, his hands bound behind him, looked disheveled and disoriented.

Howe watched John lower his head as if he had just seen a death sentence carried out.

"Raymond knows everyone in our group. They will make him talk. I have to warn my people to go into hiding."

The men returned to the house, leaving Raymond sitting in the back seat of the sedan.

"Are there other farms near here?" Howe asked.

"What?" VanderRonhaar seemed stunned watching his friend locked in the police car.

"Other farms, houses, what else is around here?" Howe asked, his voice urgent.

"There's one small farm about four kilometers south."

Howe surveyed the area, seeing the single road leading into the farm.

"Is there another way into the farm besides the road?"

"No"

"Stay low and follow me," Howe said and headed for the larger vehicle.

They moved to within ten paces of the car, taking cover in a ditch behind high grass.

The commando knew what he had to do.

"When the two in the house come back outside, we'll take them out. That should bring the other two around the front of the house, then we kill them. Got it?"

John VanderRonhaar had never shot a man. The two times his group had exchanged fire with Germans had been at night and totally confused, but he knew he hadn't hit anyone. Now the rising sun would leave no doubt. He hoped he could do it.

A yell of pain came from within the house and the two policemen emerged dragging another man between them.

"Christ," Howe said, pausing for an instant. "Stay here, watch for the other men."

Howe leaped forward and ran toward the three men with his pistol already aimed at the man on the left. The .45 barked and the policeman spun away, his face still showing surprise. Without slowing, Howe fired one round into the second man who had let go of the prisoner and was trying to pull a gun from under his jacket. The man staggered back, blood erupting from his right shoulder. Now three feet away, the commando fired two rounds point blank into the man's chest throwing the German backward in a spray of blood. .

John, watching with disbelief as the British officer attacked the two Germans, saw one of the other Germans run around the right side of the house, a pistol drawn. Without thinking, he aimed the Sten and sprayed bullets until the magazine ran out.

Howe saw the third German collapse as the Dutchman's fusillade took its toll. He flattened himself against the front wall and slowly moved behind a small tree at the corner of the house.

John fumbled with the release lever, trying desperately to free the empty magazine from the Sten. He looked up and saw a fourth man running toward him, a pistol in his hand. His mind told him to run, but he was frozen in place, watching with horror as the man leveled the gun at him.

Howe fired once at the German then took three steps toward him, aiming down and firing one more time. Without stopping he turned to face the man who had been dragged from the house, leveling the .45.

"Who are you?" he asked in English. "John, get up here."

"I'm an American pilot! Christ, don't shoot."

The American accent told Terry Howe that this man was genuine.

"My name's Howe, warrant officer."

""Mahr, major."

The lanky man got off the ground and offered his hand.

"Thanks."

"My pleasure, yank."

"Please help me," John called as he tried to help his friend out of the back seat.

Raymond's face was already swollen from where the Germans had hit him and he looked dazed.

"John?"

"Let's get him inside."

"Bad idea," Howe said. "We need to get away from here, now." Four dead Germans would not be missed for long and certainly someone knew where they were going. "Move your friend to the other car. Major, help me load these bodies into the Mercedes."

Major Randy Mahr was comfortable in the cockpit of a high performance fighter. He was decidedly uncomfortable in the back seat of the small Renault sedan winding its way down the two lane road in German occupied Holland. The events of the last hour were hard to take in. He understood the violent battle in the skies, but this was different. He had seen men shot to death only feet away, then loaded their still warm bodies into the back seat of a large German touring car. Now he found himself heading for who knows where in the company of two men he didn't know and a Dutchman who had taken him in the day prior. And the damned Brit wasn't talking. All he knew is that they were going to a safe location. Fifteen minutes before, the commando had driven the Mercedes into a stand of trees and covered it with underbrush.

Chapter Twenty One

Sean McGowan rubbed his eyes and decided some fresh air might help him wake up. Taking a majority of the "watches", he and Billy Hass had kept one of them awake at all times. But he was tired and frustrated. How long before they would know something? Pieter told them he would return as soon as they heard anything. That was two days ago. He stood up and stretched his arms above his head.

The door opened from the bedroom and Billy Hass emerged.

"Good morning," Sean said.

"Yo."

"How're you feeling?"

Billy gave him a thumbs up.

"Best I've felt in a long time."

He did look better Sean thought to himself.

"There's some tea on the stove."

The sound of a car motor froze both of them.

Sean moved to the window, pulling the .45 from his holster.

"Small car, haven't seen it before," he said.

Hass went into the bedroom and emerged with his pistol.

The two men had talked about their options in the event the Germans found the house. The woods behind the building provided some cover and it had been decided that unless the odds were overwhelming, one man would hold them off while the other tried to escape. Reluctantly, Sean had agreed that Billy was the least capable of making an escape on foot, so McGowan would go out the window. Using the fence as cover, he would make his way to the woods and try to find Aart or Pieter.

Hass moved to the window.

"Get ready to go," he said raising the gun and chambering a round.

"Still only one car?" Sean asked.

Hass nodded.

"Wait. Hell, that's John. Damn, he made it back."

McGowan peered out and saw a second man in British battle dress. Suddenly, the idea of their rescue wasn't so farfetched. Then he saw something he never could have imagined.

Opening the door he yelled, "Viktor!"

Randy Mahr looked across the car and stared.

"I'll be damned."

The two men met each other in a huge bear hug.

"I take it you two know each other," Terry Howe said, the sarcasm evident.

"Americans are very strange people," John said as they watched Sean and Randy shake hands and slap each other's arms.

"That has certainly been my experience," Howe said. "Let's get your friend inside."

"How in the hell did you end up here?" Sean asked Randy as they went into the house.

"It's a long story. You got any booze?"

One hour later, with Raymond Zylstra resting in the bedroom, the five men completed a discussion of the plan for their rescue.

"So what kind of diversion would you try?" Sean asked John. Perhaps blowing something up he assumed.

"We have someone who the Germans think is working for them who can provide them with false information. That would put their forces in the wrong place when the pickup takes place."

"Wouldn't a bomb planted somewhere do the same thing, and you'd be more certain of the results?"

John shook his head.

"Bombs result in reprisals. Innocent people die and I won't do that to save the three of you. It will be bad enough if they discover the Mercedes."

"I didn't think about that."

"The Gestapo are animals. They have no honor. When Holland is liberated, we will hunt them down and kill them."

Sean heard the anger in the man's voice. He didn't doubt his words.

Rudolf Steinfeld examined the pictures his intelligence officer had laid on his desk.

"And they confirmed the tail marking was orange?"

"Yes, sir. It was in the crash site screening. It seems that you likely did shoot down the commander of the American's 330th Fighter Squadron. Our intelligence lists a Major Randolph Mahr."

Steinfeld remembered several engagements with the orange tailed P-51's. Funny he thought, we both have the same colors.

"And we don't know if he was killed or captured?"

"No, sir. No information on the pilot was passed along."

"Judging by the photo, whoever was flying that aircraft was well enough to pull off a dead stick landing. Of course he could have been wounded."

"Yes, sir."

"Very well, it's not important. But if you get any more information, let me know."

"I will, herr oberst."

The sound of high performance engines came from outside and he knew the morning alert launch was returning. What would be the butcher's bill today?

"So far we have three pilots confirmed losses, sir. Steinlacht, Posen and Brecht. All seen going down, no parachutes observed."

Steinfeld looked at the head de-briefer. A pile of after action reports lay scattered on his desk. The last two pilots were completing their post mission reports at the next table.

"What happened," Steinfeld asked. "Keep your seat, just tell me what you saw."

Hauptmann Gerhard Krueger put down his pencil and said, "May I smoke, sir."

Rudolf nodded, and the man lit a cigarette.

"Sir, we scrambled on a call from sector. I had four in my flight. The target was an enemy formation approaching Hannover at an estimated altitude of twenty three thousand feet. Before we ever saw the bombers, we were jumped by a squadron of P-47's. The two new men, Munsch and Jurgen didn't have a chance."

Steinfeld heard the bitterness in his voice, but Krueger was one of his most experienced pilots and he'd earned the right to speak his mind.

Steinfeld looked hard at his subordinate.

"Krueger, walk with me."

The two men left the debrief room and walked in silence to the administrative building and into Steinfeld's office.

The wing commander pulled a glass from his desk and poured a full measure of brandy, handing it to

Krueger. He poured another shot into a mug and added tea for himself.

"You're angry."

Krueger drank half of the brandy.

"It's pointless. Will anything we do now change the ultimate result of the war?"

Considering his young officer, Rudolf knew he had been flying in combat for almost two straight years. Krueger was probably twenty five years old but looked ten years older. He deserved an honest answer.

"No, it won't."

"Then why do we keep taking these young men out to die?"

"Because we are German officers."

Krueger shook his head.

"That's not enough."

Rudolf Steinfeld felt very tired, but he understood the anger and frustration of Gerhard Krueger.

"It is, Gerhard. It's always been enough and it always will."

"Orange-tailed 190's?"

Major Randy Mahr nodded.

"We've run into them before, a tough bunch."

Sean thought back to that afternoon over Germany. "The commander of that outfit should have shot me down."

"What?"

McGowan told the story of his encounter with Lieutenant Colonel Rudolf Steinfeld.

"Steinfeld?"

"Their fighter wing commander out of Dortmund. Apparently this guy was one of the original Luftwaffe fighter pilots, even fought in Spain. We've heard some of them have over a hundred kills."

The thought of one hundred kills was hard for Mahr to imagine. How many missions, how many years? What are the odds of surviving?

"I wonder if he was the guy who shot me down?"

"What makes you think that?" Sean asked.

Mahr continued, "On one of our earlier missions I ran into an orange tail. It was the toughest fight I was ever in. It was everything I could do to just stay even, then this guy disengages. The pilot who shot me down flew the same way, like the damned plane was controlled by the hand of God."

"Well, we'll never know."

Mahr smiled, "I'd like to run into that guy one more time."

"Relax, let's work on getting home first."

Aart Boonstra could not feel his hands. He knew, through a fog of pain that they were behind his back, tied together with wire. Sitting on a worn metal chair, the Dutchman was supported by a large rope around his chest holding him upright, his legs secured to the chair with straps of leather. Dried blood crusted around his nose and mouth, the result of a vicious beating earlier in the day. He was losing his grip on time. What had gone wrong he kept asking himself? Who talked? Was there a traitor in their group? Trying to focus on questions helped him to avoid thinking about what would ultimately happen to him.

The door opened and a tall man in the grey uniform of the SS entered the darkened room. He moved in front of the prisoner and looked down over a prominent nose. Obersturmbannführer Otto Krebs was the Inspector of State Security for Department D1, northern Holland.

"You look terrible," the man observed.

Boonstra looked up into the man's eyes.

"You know you're already condemned?"

247

Through the pain, he slowly realized it was easier now that there was no doubt. Death a welcome alternative to the horror he'd been suffering. The hell with these people, he thought, it doesn't matter anymore.

"You can ignore me, Aart Boonstra, but I think not for long. Bring her in," Krebs said casually.

The woman gasped when she saw him.

"Oh no."

Aart raised his head in response to the female voice and immediately jerked against his restraints.

"Anna!"

She moved to the chair, expecting the guards to restrain her, but they watched as she knelt down next to her husband. She carefully put her hand on his cheek.

"What have they done?"

Their eyes met, both knowing their lives would never be the same.

A uniformed guard reached down and pulled the woman to her feet.

The tall man stood in front of the Dutchman and said, "I am not an unreasonable man, Herr Boonstra. If you work with us, your wife will be released. If not, she will take your place in that chair. It is your choice."

Aart felt totally helpless, there was nothing to do but submit. He couldn't let anything happen to Anna, nothing else mattered.

"I...what do you want?"

"Where are the Americans?"

"You will let Anna go?"

"Of course," the man said.

His mind desperately trying to think through what was happening, Aart asked, "How do I know you are telling the truth?"

The man smiled slightly.

"Quite frankly, you don't. But you have my word that if you don't give us what we want, she will never leave this place alive. So, I repeat, it's your choice."

The German saw Boonstra lower his head and knew the man had broken. Now to catch the Americans.

Terry Howe heard the sound of an engine approaching. He looked out the window to see the approaching vehicle was the small Renault truck belonging to John. The resistance leader had departed the Vanderhoek farm early the day prior, leaving the four allied airmen to await his return.

The expression on the man's face told Howe that all was not well.

"Hello."

"We need to talk," John said as he stepped inside the small house.

"What's happened?" McGowan asked

"Aart Boonstra has been arrested."

By now, all of the Americans had come into the living room.

"The Germans have had him since yesterday. He knows you're here and they will make him talk. We must move."

"Now?" Howe asked.

"As quickly as possible. Any delay could put the Germans on us."

"There are what, four, five hours before the sun goes down?" Major Mahr asked. "How do we move on the roads in daylight?"

"There are no Germans if we move south on the forest road. I know a place we can hide out."

The sound of engines made them all turn.

"Shit."

Moving quickly to the window, Sean saw two German light military trucks and a larger civilian sedan, stopping on the road. Grey uniformed soldiers jumped from the small kampfwagens, running for cover in the wide ditch next to the road.

Terry Howe watched the large car pull to a stop, its occupants quickly exiting. He knew from talking with John and making a quick reconnaissance, that there was no viable escape route out the back. That had bothered him then and now he wished he had pressed the issue. In one way it made his decision easy.

"Stay low and keep their attention," Terry said, grabbing his rucksack and sub-machine gun. "I'll work around behind them from the left."

"Gotcha," Mahr said, kneeling down next to McGowan.

Hass moved to McGowan's left and unholstered his .45.

"You all right?" Sean asked.

"I'm fine," the big man said, carefully peering out the window.

"John, go to the right. Get behind them." Howe ordered, motioning with his hand.

The Dutchman nodded and picked up the Sten gun.

A heavily accented demand in English came from behind the large sedan.

"Come out. Come out. No weapons."

"Watch your ammunition, but keep them looking this way," Sean said as he raised his .45 and broke the window with a quick blow from the gun butt. Briefly sighting the pistol, he fired a single round at the sedan.

Immediately the German soldiers began firing at the house, the crack of their Mausers echoing off the trees.

The airmen instinctively took cover behind whatever might protect them as bullets began to pierce the thin walls of the cottage.

Kneeling down behind a small bookcase, Mahr fired a round from the left edge of the largest window, ducking for cover.

Crawling across the floor, Sean reached the single kitchen window that faced their attackers. He carefully raised his head to peer outside as the window shattered from a single rifle shot.

"Shit!" he said, dropping on the floor among the broken pieces of glass.

Howe climbed out the single side window and sprinted toward a low hedge twenty feet from the house. Sliding hard, he rolled under the leafy bushes and pushed through to the other side. Crawling toward the road, he watched the men in the ditch firing at the house. Green troops he thought, they're simply firing at random. He couldn't see the other men who had been in the sedan. Reaching the end of the hedge, he caught his breath, wiping the sweat from his face. With knowledge and a practiced hand, he pulled two Mark II fragmentation grenades from his rucksack and slowly rose to his knees. The Germans who were thirty feet away remained unaware of him as he pulled the first pin. Allowing the safety spoon to detach, he waited one second then threw. Reaching for the second grenade, he pulled the pin, released the safety and threw it, dropping flat as the first one exploded.

Howe grabbed the Thompson and ran around the edge of the bushes, firing one burst dead ahead then rolled right into the ditch. Up again, he ran forward, firing two quick bursts into the bodies lying against both sides of the ditch. The commando threw himself to the ground, taking what cover he could.

A Sten gun was firing from his right and Howe forced himself to move up, looking desperately left and right for any threat. He saw two men in grey uniforms firing over the hood. They never saw him as he closed to fifteen yards and emptied his magazine into them.

The sound of silence echoed around the small room. Cordite fumes filled the air and dust floated in the early morning sunlight.

Randy Mahr raised his head slowly and looked out the broken window.

"I think he did it."

Billy Hass rose up, also looking cautiously out his window.

A burst of fire made them all drop back to the floor, but nothing hit the house.

"Howe, you okay?" Mahr yelled.

"Right."

The men rose and moved to the bullet riddled door.

Hass looked back behind the couch and saw McGowan on the floor, a pool of red under his body.

John VanderRonhaar sat in the right seat of the large sedan as it sped down the forest road. How had things gone so wrong? The American McGowan lay in the back seat, his face deathly pale, bleeding from a gunshot wound. Raymond Zylstra sat next to the wounded man, his face a mask of shock. The big man, Hass, held McGowan in his arms, blood soaking his shirt and pants.

Driving the sedan with Major Mahr next to him, Terry Howe went over their options. No radio available to contact England. The local network probably compromised. A number of Germans had gone missing and the Gestapo would likely start a local search. What the hell, he thought to himself, I never expected this, but Stewart did and that's why Stewart is the boss.

"Can we get word to your daughter?" Howe asked, knowing they needed a doctor to look at the American.

John nodded.

VanderRonhaar had done a hell of a job when he had to, but now he seemed stunned.

"Do you know the place I described?"

"Yes."

"That's our best chance," Howe said. Hell, it's our only option he thought to himself.

Chapter Twenty Two

Tanna VanderRonhaar had done all she could for Sean McGowan. The single bullet had entered his lower left chest and exited several inches above his waist. His breathing told her that the left lung was slowly filling with blood. He likely needed a thoracic surgeon, but that would have to wait.

She looked across the small clearing at her father. A courageous man who had risen to the challenge like few men would have. The exhaustion evident on his face concerned her, but did nothing to diminish her pride.

Billy Hass knelt over McGowan, using a wet cloth to mop the pilot's face. In the fading sunlight, the lack of color told everyone that the wound was taking its toll. He looked up to see Raymond standing next to him.

"Can I help you?" the Dutchman asked. He appeared to have regained his strength and looked eager to help.

"Nothing really to do, but thank you," Hass replied. The man's face still showed the result of the blows from the Germans, two ugly bruises and a swollen lip telling the tale. Raymond sat down next to McGowan, almost as if he was standing guard.

Howe and Mahr stood at the end of the clearing, surveying the open field beyond.

"What do you think?" Howe asked.

"There's nothing I can see that would be a problem. But I'd really like to get out there and walk it to be sure."

Terry Howe wanted to do the same thing. If a Hudson was going to set down out there, he wanted to make sure there weren't unseen obstacles. He did know that Commander Stewart wouldn't have made the field the alternate pick up point unless someone had checked it out. But that was most likely done by photography and pictures never told the whole story.

Always planning for the unexpected, Jack Stewart had selected a location for pick up in the event radio contact could not be established. Each evening an aircraft from 161 Squadron would check the field, ready to land if a green flare was observed on the ground. Now seven fugitives from the Germans waited for that aircraft as the summer sun began to set.

Tanna knelt down next to Billy Hass.

He turned to look at her and smiled.

"Hello," she said quietly. Reaching down, she began to take McGowan's pulse. He had lost a great deal of blood and she was concerned for his life.

Sean opened his eyes and turned his head slightly. His breathing was labored and his eyes seemed dull. He looked at Hass, who continued to dab at the sweat on his face.

"Thanks." His voice was strained.

"Major. I know it is hard for you to breathe. There is fluid in your lung. I'll do my best to keep it drained and that should make it easier for you."

McGowan nodded.

Hass looked down at the crude patch over the wound. Gauze coated with petroleum jelly covered the bullet hole to prevent air from flowing back into the lung. Once the doctor had put the bandage in place, Sean's breathing had been easier. Watching his friend struggle to breathe, the brutal truth hit him. The only reason McGowan is lying here in a Dutch forest fighting for his life, is because he stayed behind to take care of me.

Hauptman Reinhard Luetje always enjoyed flying at sunset. The demarcation between night and day was especially keen at altitude where the sun might be shining, while below you the world had already turned to darkness. That vision was clear today and made up for the fool's errand he had been scrambled on to search for a phantom radar signal. His irritation had been evident to the ground controller who, after several heading recommendations, had stopped making any transmissions.

I will just enjoy flying, Luetje told himself. What flying had once been, when each flight hadn't been a desperate fight against the overwhelming strength of the enemy. The smooth sound of the Daimler Benz engine seemed to transcend everything as he began a slow roll to the right, pulling the nose up above the horizon then expertly coordinating the stick and rudder to smoothly roll the Messerschmitt through three hundred and sixty degrees. As he passed through inverted, he glanced down as he always did. It was then that he saw the aircraft.

"By God, there's a green flare. See it?"

"Tally ho," answered Flight Lieutenant David Bennett.

Dicky Thompson banked the Hudson and began to set up for a landing.

"We're going to set her down, keep on your toes," he passed over the intercom.

"Bandit!! Nine o'clock high, it's a jerry fighter," called the turret gunner, Sergeant Bradley.

The Hudson was a good aircraft, but Thompson knew they stood no chance against a fast mover. Now his job had to be survival.

"How far out?" Thompson asked, hoping the answer was the right one.

"A mile, no more, but he's tracking away from us, just starting his turn."

There was a chance, only one.

Luetje was angry with himself. Trying to get into a firing position, he pulled hard into a split S but buried the fighter's nose. As he reduced power and rolled the aircraft level, he was completely out of phase with the enemy aircraft, which he recognized as a British Hudson. He jammed the throttle forward and turned toward the target. An easy kill he thought, just get into gun range.

The weather system which had moved through the lowlands was mostly gone, but lower layers of clouds still spread toward the horizon westward.

Thirty seconds, Dicky's mind screamed at him. Just give me thirty bloody seconds and I'll have her in those wonderful clouds.

"He's closing," Bradley said evenly, trying to keep his heart from beating out of his chest. No deflection, the bastard was coming up from dead astern. Knowing he was outgunned by the 109, he still knew that tracers attract attention. With full ammunition canisters, he had nothing to lose.

Dicky felt and heard the turret open up, hoping the reduced visibility was making it hard on the German.

Ignoring the tracers floating toward him, Luetje opened up on the Hudson, knowing his fire would strike home. Then it was gone, lost in a layer of swirling grey clouds. Damn it, damn it, damn it. He unleashed one more three second burst at the clouds then pulled up hard, climbing above the darkening mass that stretched for twenty miles.

"Nice job, Dicky. The maintenance chief told me the port engine was destroyed along with the flap mechanism.

Wing Commander Toms had just returned from checking the damaged aircraft, now parked outside 161 Squadron's hangar. He reached in his lower drawer and pulled out a bottle of scotch. Without asking, the senior officer poured three drinks, handing one to Thompson then Bennett.

"To another day, gentlemen."

"Yes, sir," David Bennett echoed.

"Skipper, they're down there. The green flare was clear. I just hope the kraut fighter didn't see it."

"I have a call into Jack Stewart. I think we have to assume that the longer those people stay there, the less chance we have of getting them back. I'll take a Hudson in at first light. Get with Fighter Command. I want some cover, just in case."

"I'll let Jack Stewart know what's going on also," Thompson said.

Terry Howe knelt down next to the prone figure of Sean McGowan and looked at Billy Hass.

"How's it going?" he said quietly.

Hass nodded slightly.

"Okay, for now. What happened out there?"

Howe continued, his voice low so he wouldn't wake McGowan.

"We heard the Hudson and popped the flare. They were turning toward us when a single fighter attacked them."

The exhaustion in Hass's voice was evident as he asked quickly, "What happened?"

Shaking his head, Howe replied softly, "I don't know. They both disappeared heading west."

"Now what?"

"We try again tomorrow night."

Neither man voiced the obvious problem – had their position been compromised? He walked over to John VanderRonhaar.

"Tell me what else is around here," he asked the Dutchman. "We may have to move."

Rudolf Steinfeld read the typed message from the sector air defense commander.

"Fools," he said, crumpling the paper and throwing it across the operations office. "We don't have enough aircraft to play these silly games, chasing phantoms."

"What do you want to do, sir?" Leutnant Fritsch asked.

"If they want a patrol over that area, we will give them what they ask for."

"Sir?"

"One aircraft, launch at first light. That will allow it back on deck in time for the normal launch times. And I'll fly the hop."

He turned to leave and saw Hauptman Hans Dieter.

"Herr oberst, I have some interesting information."

Thirty minutes later Rudolf Steinfeld sat back in his desk chair, his mind going over the reports and information from his senior intelligence officer. Several folders lay on his desk with two photographs showing aircraft crash sites. One photo showed the nose of an American B-17 that had made a forced landing in

Holland. On the nose he saw the same image he had seen on the lone bomber near Frankfurt. The buxom lady was a bit worse for wear, but now he could still read the lettering, "*Jezebel.*"

"What is your analysis of this information," he asked Dieter.

"The area where the two aircraft were found, both the B-17 and the P-51 has seen active resistance for most of the war and increased activity more recently. The airmen have not been captured, which makes it logical they have contacted the Dutch resistance and are hiding out.

"And you said there had been several times when allied aircraft have landed in the same area."

"Three that the Gestapo confirmed, one occurred within the last month."

Steinfeld looked at the photo of the P-51. Beneath the cockpit, in addition to a row of small swastikas, it read, "Major Randy Mahr."

Terry Toms sipped the hot tea, the steam providing a sense of comfort in the raw early morning hours. He felt the normal apprehension prior to a tough mission, but he also knew that he wasn't going to ask anyone else to go on this one. He had learned since 1939 that the Luftwaffe was a force to be respected. If the fighter that shot up Dicky Thompson had any idea what the Hudson was doing, they could be flying into a trap. The weather might help them, a system having moved through during the night, leaving some cloudiness over Holland.

"Sir, Commander Stewart is here."

Toms turned to see Dicky Thompson's head in the open door.

"Please have him come in."

Jack Stewart walked into the office, carrying a kit bag over the shoulder of his battle dress. At his waist he wore a U.S. Colt Model .45 ACP.

"You appear to be ready to do battle, Jack."

"Good morning, wing commander," Stewart said, grinning at his friend. "Thought you might need someone to keep you company."

Toms had expected that MI-6 might send someone to handle any landing zone problems.

"Delighted to have you along," Toms said, his tone humorous. He then asked soberly, "Any idea if the Germans suspect anything?"

Stewart sat down on the couch and took the tea from Toms.

"Nothing obvious in message traffic. We don't know what might be happening over land lines. So far, we've had two radio messages from the local resistance group, no indications of any increased activity on the ground."

"That's encouraging."

Stewart nodded. "But we both know you can't underestimate the bastards."

"Right," Toms said. "Finish your tea. I want to check the weather one more time. Dicky's in my right seat. He'll run you out to the kite."

Fighting back a yawn, Rudolf Steinfeld rubbed his face, wondering if taking this flight had been such a good idea. Still, an early morning launch for a solo flight was a luxury he had missed. No scramble order or worrying about a dozen other aircraft trying to rendezvous and climb toward the enemy. The weather was the only negative for the mission, the cloud layers making navigation harder, but the system was clearing out. His plan was straight forward, climb to 4,000 feet and patrol north from Arnhem to Groningen then reverse back south and home. Mission accomplished and the fat-assed paper pushers at headquarters would be satisfied. But in the back of his mind, there remained a question he knew might never be answered. Looking right, he cleared the area and pulled onto the runway.

"Tanna," Billy said urgently, shaking her arm.

Opening her eyes, the confusion immediately left her and she sat up.

"He's having trouble breathing."

She rolled on her knees and stepped across the small clearing, kneeling down next to McGowan.

"How long has he been like this?" she asked.

"Not long, maybe ten minutes."

Even in the reduced light, Tanna could see the bluish pallor and sheen of sweat covering McGowan's face. His breathing was rapid and she immediately knew what was happening.

"Help me."

She motioned to Billy, who had been joined by Mahr.

"Help me get him on his left side."

The two men gently rolled Sean on his side as the doctor reached down, and removed the bandage from the wound. Blood oozed over the doctor's hand and pooled on the ground.

Sean struggled for breath, taking short hard gasps. He looked at Hass who was supporting his head and tried to form a word, but nothing came.

"All right, roll him on his back," Tanna ordered.

"Try to relax," she told Sean as she began to take his pulse. Turning her head she told Billy, "We have to keep him warm."

Mahr pulled off his leather flight jacket and lay it over McGowan.

Feeling the coat on his chest, Sean opened his eyes and saw Mahr.

"Hang in there, buddy."

A stab of pain lanced into McGowan's chest, contorting his face into a grimace. He fought the pain and let his body relax as the pain subsided. Then he winked at his old roommate.

Mahr knelt down and tucked the flight jacket.

"I'm always taking care of you," he said with faked exasperation.

McGowan's raspy voice could just be heard above the wind moving through the trees.

"Damned...pursuit...pilot."

Chapter Twenty Three

"How can the damned weather people always get it so wrong?"

Dicky Thompson knew Wing Commander Toms question was rhetorical, simply reflecting the normal frustration when encountered weather bore little resemblance to that predicted by the weather briefer.

The weather system had blown through the area, but left a single low layer of clouds which started just prior to the coast. While Holland was largely flat, if the weather went down to the surface near the landing site, their mission was done.

Somewhere near them, four RAF Spitfires, call sign "Cupcake" were flying a very loose combat air patrol for the mission.

"At least their wind predictions look right on the mark," Toms commented, the ugly grey water below them almost glassy smooth. The accurate update on their position as they left the English coast, combined with negligible winds made accurate navigation an easy task for the two experienced aviators.

Terry Howe sat quietly, his back against a small tree, now awake after the emergency with McGowan. He knew the longer they were on the ground the chances of discovery went up. But he also knew that trying to travel with the wounded pilot was going to be extremely difficult and there was no other alternate location pre-briefed by MI-6. His options were limited, and that concerned the normally confident commando.

The sounds of radial engines broke Howe out of his thoughts and as he looked up, he saw that Major Mahr was on his feet and running to the edge of the trees.

The roar of the engines hammered the clearing as the aircraft passed over at low altitude.

"It's a Hudson," Mahr yelled back to the group as Howe joined him.

"Bloody wonderful," Howe exclaimed, the logic of a dawn pickup now clear to him.

Hass joined them as they watched the bomber slow, clearly preparing to land.

"Time to go," Howe said, and turned back to the clearing. "Get ready to move Major McGowan, I need you two to get him out to the aircraft."

"Let's go," Mahr said to Hass.

"Doctor," Howe called to Tanna. "When I tell you, take Raymond and go out to the aircraft. Do you understand?"

She nodded and turned to Zylstra.

"John, you and I will cover them," Howe continued. "I want you out to the aircraft first and cover the door from the ground. I'll bring up the rear. Right?"

VanderRonhaar nodded and picked up his Sten.

"Let's go."

Jack Stewart jumped to the ground and quickly scanned the open field. The prop blast and noise seemed enough to wake the dead, but he saw no activity on the perimeter.

"Commander," the crew chief yelled down to Stewart. "There they are."

Coming out of the trees, he saw the group, led by the Dutchman VanderRonhaar. Stewart moved out to meet them then saw two men carrying a third. They were trailed by a woman and another civilian.

"Get to the aircraft, quickly," Stewart yelled over the sound of the engines. No one replied, their eyes showing they understood. Then he saw Howe, jogging up to him.

"Glad to see you, skipper."

"Is that it?" Stewart asked, knowing there would be no one behind Howe, who nodded yes.

The two men headed for the aircraft, seeing only the Dutchman kneeling by the rear hatch.

"In you go, John," Howe shouted over the engines.

The older man shook his head and smiled, holding up the Sten.

"I will stay. You gave me a good gun. I need to kill more Germans."

Howe nodded and climbed into the Hudson.

Rechecking his altimeter had the correct barometric setting, Rudolf began his descent into the thin layer of clouds. Taking comfort from the uniform low terrain of central Holland, he continued below one thousand feet, estimating he was about halfway between Arnhem and Groningen. At least he didn't have to worry about running into another aircraft, who else would be crazy enough to be out flying in this stuff.

"The woman's a doctor, the Dutchman's daughter," Howe told Stewart as the Hudson began its takeoff roll.

Both men sat on the floor of the center compartment, their backs against the fuselage.

"Damn glad she's here. McGowan's having trouble breathing."

"My father?" Tanna called over the roar of the engines.

"He said he had work to do," Howe said.

Tanna VanderRonhaar said nothing, she knew her father. Please God, look after him, she prayed.

Stewart looked aft to where the wounded pilot lay on the deck, held securely by the other two American officers.

"Can he make it to England?"

"Better ask the doctor, skipper."

The Hudson broke ground and began its climb toward the low lying clouds.

"We've got a badly wounded man back there," Stewart called over Toms' shoulder as the bomber broke through a thin layer of white, climbing hard.

The wing commander called back, his eyes locked on the instruments, "Well she's not a Mosquito, but I'll get you there as fast as I can."

Stewart watched Toms push the yoke forward, stopping the climb and allowing the speed to build as he left the throttles full forward.

"Christ!" Dicky Thompson yelled, his head turned toward the side window. "Jerry fighter, three o'clock."

Rolling left, Rudolf turned toward the brown and green camouflaged bomber, realizing it was a Hudson, exactly like the one reported the day before. And it was coming out of the area where Dieter thought the Americans had been hiding. My God, this could be them.

Thoughts raced through Toms' mind. His only hope would be to turn back into the cloud layer and try to lose the fighter. But the American had to get back to England.

He keyed the radio, "Cupcake, Cupcake, this is Cyclone, come in."

The tinny response came right back, "Cyclone, go ahead."

"Where the bloody hell are you? I have a FW-190 on me."

The radio was painfully silent.

"Here he comes," Dicky said, "Bandit closing, guns."

"I got 'em," came the reply on the intercom.

Toms made his decision, no fighter pilot liked flying on the deck and no one could fly lower than an old Mosquito pilot. Maybe the bloody Spits would find them after all.

"Cupcake, Cyclone is crossing the coast at the lighthouse, on the deck, get the hell on top of me."

Pushing the yoke forward hard, Toms kept the throttles two-blocked and put the bomber right on the water. They would make it home unless this German had balls of brass.

Dicky Thompson watched the water as the Hudson leveled at five feet above the flat surface. He realized he was holding his breath, mesmerized by the Channel racing by just under their propeller blade tips. His mind screamed too low, too low, but he couldn't make himself talk.

Rudolf watched with amazement as the Hudson leveled out on the water, so low that the turbulence from his propellers left two wakes in their path. He matched the bomber's speed and pulled even with the cockpit, staying well outside the range of the Brit's .303's in the aft turret. Whoever was flying that crate knew what he was doing, he thought. The only attack that he could make would be a slashing deflection shot or climb up for a diving attack. Enough, his mind told him. This plane will make it home to England. And I

268

will go home and have a good breakfast and get ready for another day. He looked up at the clear sky over the channel and realized he was closer to England than he had been since 1941. Rudolf slowly waggled his wings in farewell to the gutsy Brit and began a turn for home.

"What the hell? He's just rocking his wings," Dicky exclaimed. "There's the Spits. About time those bastards showed up."

"That's him," Randy Mahr said aloud, staring out the right cabin window at the single orange-tailed FW-190. He watched as the German pulled up, smoke coming from his engine. Two Spitfires were circling the enemy fighter as they disappeared from Mahr's line of sight.

Jack Stewart walked back in the cabin to find Mahr standing over the doctor, who was kneeling next to McGowan. Billy Hass looked up and Jack could see fear in the big man's eyes.

Doctor VanderRonhaar looked up and asked Jack, "When will we get to England?"

"I can ask," he replied.

"It has to be soon, there's nothing else I can do for him," she said, her voice urgent.

"Horsham.....Norwich," Toms said, "The closest field and they have a full hospital on station."

"I'll get on the horn and let them know," Dicky said.

Toms thought for a moment then said, "Tell them we'll be there in fifteen minutes."

"Right."

The group stood on the tarmac and watched the ambulance speed off less than five minutes after the Hudson had touched down. Dicky Thompson, who had flown out of Horsham in Blenheim bombers early in the war, had taxied the aircraft directly to the operations building using a route that surprised even longtime observers at the station.

"That should do it," Wing Commander Toms said. "We'll call for petrol and get you back to Tangmere in short order."

Billy Hass turned to Toms.

"Sir, I'm not going anywhere."

The surprised look gave way to realization when he heard Major Mahr.

"I'm staying with McGowan, at least until we find out what's up."

Toms turned to Thompson.

"Dicky, I'm assuming you know where the officer's mess is located?"

"Indeed I do, skipper."

"Haven't been to Norwich in ages," Toms said then began to walk toward the operations building. "One night shouldn't hurt, don't you agree, Jack?" He turned to look at Stewart. "Well, come along, old man."

Doctor Renni Hanson opened the door to Wing Three of the military hospital in Dortmund. He felt empty, not sad as he should feel, but empty. And he dreaded what he now had to do.

"Good afternoon, herr doctor," Karin Spengler said looking up from the patient chart on her desk. Obviously recording her notes from afternoon rounds, she looked tired but happy. "Let me finish this and I will be right with you."

Hanson sat down across from her in an upholstered chair and put his hat on the end table.

She looked up and smiled.

"It's been two weeks," she said, "I wondered if you'd been sent to the Eastern Front."

"Karin, I'm sorry to have to tell you this, but Rudi is missing."

Her eyes widened as the words registered and she raised her hand to her lips.

"What can you tell me?" she asked, her words hesitant.

Hanson shook his head.

"Not much, I'm afraid. He was over Holland, by himself. The sector controller had talked with him, but there was nothing unusual. He simply didn't return to base."

Karin had always known this could happen. It was something she lived with and had accepted. But still she asked, why now, why him? She knew there would never be an answer to her questions.

Major Sean McGowan turned his head to see a nurse enter the room. She moved to the edge of his bed and examined the inverted glass container that hung above Sean's head.

"How are you feeling, major?"

Her thick Scottish accent gave him comfort. He really was back in England. The flight from the continent remained a mixture of images and sounds. He had felt helpless and barely aware of the world around him. Now he reveled in the reality around him.

"Sore," he said, his voice raspy.

"That's to be expected."

"Where am I?"

She smiled, "An RAF Hospital near Norwich. Horsham actually."

"How long?"

"They brought you in yesterday morning." She poured a glass of water and brought it to him. "Short sip, please."

"The doctor will be here shortly. Can I get you anything?"

"I'm fine, thanks."

"Once cleared by the doctor, you'll be able to have visitors. Apparently you have a group that's been hounding Doctor Ainsworth since you arrived."

Thirty minutes later, Doctor Thomas Ainsworth, a tall distinguished looking man, came into Sean's room, a chart in his hand.

"Major, good morning."

"Hello, doc."

"Bear with me," he said, taking a stethoscope from around his neck. Over the next five minutes, the doctor conducted his examination.

After making several notes in McGowan's chart, the doctor said, "You're doing quite well, actually. I think another three or four days here and you'll be able to travel. I'm sure your medicos will want you back under their care. But really not much to do, the body is a remarkable healer of itself sometimes."

"How am I?"

"Lucky I should say. Single bullet wound, passed through the lower quadrant of your left lung, but it has finally sealed and your breathing should not be a problem. I want to make sure the wound isn't infected and continues to mend before we jostle you about. So a few days of bed rest, letting the nurses take good care of you and then off you go."

Sean realized it really was over.

"Now, I am going to allow this unruly mob that arrived with you to come in here. But you will stay in bed and not move any more than is needed. Understand?"

"Sure, doc."

Major Randy Mahr and Captain Billy Hass had taken advantage of the station laundry and now appeared no worse for wear, just another two aviators visiting a sick friend.

"You sure look better than that last time I saw you," Mahr said.

"You're right, can't say I enjoyed that flight much." Sean replied then looked at Hass, who had a white bandage wrapped around his head. "Looks like the doctors got a hold of you too."

"Tanna, I mean Doctor VanderRonhaar, had them on me as soon as we walked in here looking for you."

Sean asked, "Everything okay?"

Hass nodded.

"Billy, see what you can find out about the crew. Maybe by now they know something."

That seems like a long time ago, Hass thought, Huggie, Moore, all of them, what had happened to them?

McGowan continued, "Better try to call the base. I'm not sure who needs to know what's happening down here."

"I called into my guys yesterday. The wing was going to contact Paddington," Mahr said.

"Thanks."

"I got through to Forster too," Hass added. "He was going to call a certain young lady in London."

There was a knock on the partially closed door and it swung open to reveal Commander Jack Stewart and Terry Howe.

"Wanted to see the patient and let you know we're going back to Tangmere in about an hour. How are you feeling, major?"

"Okay, sir. Thanks for getting us out of there."

Stewart smiled and said, "I'm glad it worked out the way it did. It was a pretty close thing with that FW-190."

Mahr remembered the orange-tailed fighter trailing smoke.

"In fact, two of our MTB's were in the area and picked up the pilot. They pulled into Lowestoft last night. Apparently he was busted up pretty good, but should survive."

"He could have attacked us, but didn't," Mahr said. "I would like to meet him. Any chance?"

Stewart thought for a moment.

"I don't see why not. I'll see what I can do."

Chapter Twenty Four

"Here we are, sir, the Norfolk and Norwich Hospital," the taxi driver said, pulling the car to a stop at what appeared to be a main entrance. Mahr looked up at the grey stone and wondered if this was such a good idea after all. What the hell, in for a penny, he thought and opened the door.

Accompanying a middle-aged nurse through the dimly lit corridors of the hospital, Mahr wondered why every hospital seemed to have that same smell. Even the ones that have been here for hundreds of years, he thought, noting the turn of the century woodwork above the doors.

"We used to have quite a few German pilots here, but that was back at the beginning of the war," she said. "Many were badly burned and all we could do was stabilize them. Most were sent north for further treatment."

"Yes, ma'am."

They turned a corner and Mahr saw a British military policeman sitting at a desk outside the doors of what was identified as "Ward Three."

"Sergeant, this is the American officer they called about."

The man stood and came to attention.

"Good morning, sir."

"Hello, sergeant. I'm Major Mahr."

"Yes, sir. We've been expecting you. I do have to see your identity card."

"Here you go."

"Very good, sir," the sergeant said, handing the card back.

"If you would sign the log, I'll take you in."

The corridor was narrow and the rooms on each side seemed small to Mahr as they walked the entire length, stopping at the last door on the right. Two more men in British battle dress passed them, obviously making a security patrol.

"Here you go, sir. Just check out with me when you leave."

Mahr knocked twice and opened the door.

The room was indeed small, but with only a single bed, it appeared comfortable. On the bed, with a blanket drawn up to his chest, Oberstleutnant Rudolf Steinfeld turned and looked with curiosity at his visitor.

Mahr had been told by the intelligence officers that the German colonel spoke passable English, the result of schooling and traveling in Europe before the war.

"Colonel Steinfeld, my name is Mahr."

Steinfeld's eyes widened slightly. "Good morning, major."

"May I sit down?"

Steinfeld nodded.

The two men looked at each other, quietly appraising the other. Steinfeld's eyes moved to the wings pinned to Mahr's left breast.

"You are a pilot?"

The American nodded.

"Most of my interrogation has been by intelligence officers."

276

"Colonel, I'm not here in any official capacity and certainly not to interrogate you."

Steinfeld's eyes registered mild surprise.

"I would like to ask you some questions."

"You seem to be playing word games, major."

For the first time, Mahr smiled at his former adversary. "I assure you that is not my intent."

"Very well, what questions do you have?"

Mahr looked the German in the eye and asked, "Why didn't you attack the Hudson bomber that morning?"

Steinfeld showed no reaction, but said, "You know of that?"

"I was on the aircraft. I saw you off our right wing."

The German shrugged his head slightly and asked Mahr, "How long have you been in England?"

"Six months."

Steinfeld looked at the American.

"My war began in 1939." He paused then continued, "Germany will lose this war, of that I am certain. The survival of that bomber was not going to change anything."

Mahr hesitated, then continued. "Your aircraft's vertical stabilizer was orange."

"Yes."

"I fought against your squadron several times and I have come to believe you and I have faced each other personally."

Steinfeld smiled, thinking to himself what a strange turn of events.

"I recognized your name, Major Randy Mahr."

"My name? How?"

"From a picture taken of a P-51 that had crash landed in Holland."

The two men looked at each other, each now knowing the truth.

Continuing Steinfeld said, "I am glad you survived, major. You were a formidable opponent."

"I thought I was a pretty good fighter pilot, colonel. But I think you are a true master."

The German looked at Mahr.

"Thank you. Respect by your enemies is one of the few noble things in war."

"I want to tell you about another pilot who was on that same aircraft."

"Major McGowan?"

Mahr looked back at him, the surprise obvious.

"You knew?"

"I knew of *Jezebel* and McGowan. In a war with thousands of aircraft and sorties and flyers, our paths crossed enough that I had my people find out about this squadron commander. When I realized what was happening in Holland, it all came together. So there you have it. Just another story of this war."

"So you knew we were on that Hudson?"

Rudolf Steinfeld smiled.

The ivy covered walls of the Acton Place manor building anchored the multiple outbuildings that comprised the 136th Station Hospital. Sixty miles north of London, next to the Stour River in Sudbury, over two hundred patients were recovering from the war over and on the continent.

"Squadron Leader Forster?" John Forster turned as the American nurse called his name.

"Yes, I'm Forster."

"I'm First Lieutenant Gallagher, please come with me."

"All set?" he asked Jamie Taylor-Paige.

She nodded, her eyes apprehensive.

The two followed Lieutenant Gallagher out of the waiting area and along a gravel walkway to a single story building, passing several orderlies who were obviously in a hurry.

"Major McGowan's right in here," she said, opening the door and indicating a doorway immediately on the left.

"Major, you have two visitors."

He looked up as they walked into the room behind the nurse. Nurse Gallagher walked around the bed to pull the curtains fully open.

"A little more light wouldn't hurt," she said, then turned to Forster. "I'll be down the hall if you need anything."

Jamie stepped to one side as Gallagher left the room, then her eyes met Sean's.

He smiled at her and said, "Hello Jamie Taylor-Paige."

Tears welled in her eyes as she moved to his side.

John Forster quietly followed the nurse out the door and swung it closed.

"I do love you, Sean McGowan, with all my heart and forever."

He took her hand and raised it to his lips, lightly kissing it.

"Dear lady, there is nothing else I would ever want more."

Jamie leaned down and kissed him slowly on the lips, the tears continuing to run down her face.

"Major, welcome back."

Lieutenant Peter Allen stood up as Sean entered the 23rd Bomb Group Commander's office.

"Hey, Pete, is the old man in?"

"Yes, the old man is in," Paul Bloch called from his door.

Sean grinned at Bloch.

"Wasn't so sure you'd be here. Last time I saw you things didn't look too good for."

"Shitty day all around, but at least we got the aircraft back home." He motioned McGowan into his office.

"Coffee?"

"No, thanks, the doc told me to cut back."

"By the way, nice job taking over the formation that day. You're going to get Silver Star, and I'm glad it won't be posthumously."

McGowan sat down on the couch.

"I read the reports, only one of my guys has been reported by the krauts – Huggins, my tail gunner."

Bloch shook his head, "Doesn't mean much, the intel types tell me the whole system is screwed up, and the Red Cross is swamped. Just give it time. We're sure to hear something. What's the story on your medical?"

"Won't be flying for a long time is my take, but I'll be fine in time."

"There's plenty left to do in the Pacific, you can follow Forster out there."

Sean had seen John two weeks prior, but the Australian had said nothing.

"What's up?"

"The RAAF wants him back in Australia to command a B-24 squadron."

"When does he leave?"

The wing commander looked through several documents on his desk.

"Here it says he leaves in three days."

Sean thought about the feisty Aussie. He would miss him, but some RAAF squadron was damned lucky. He wondered if Aubrey Rose would follow him? One more life sent in a different direction. The result of so many events that could have gone so many ways. But that was the nature of war and he accepted it.

"What about me?"

"Headquarters wants you back in the operational plans section. After that, if you can get your medical clearance, you'll likely get a wing here in England or get sucked up for final push in the Pacific."

McGowan nodded.

"How about Hass?"

"They finally clipped his wings. He's going to headquarters with you in the strike planning section of op plans."

"He's not gonna like that one bit."

Bloch grinned and said, "That's why you're going to be the one to tell him."

He started to protest, but then realized it would do no good.

"Major, your paperwork appears to be in order."

Sean McGowan sat opposite a British colonel, who ran the specialized German detention center in Sudbury Park. A former boy's school, the cells, which held senior German prisoners, were wired with listening devices to help pull out any useful intelligence from recently captured enemy officers.

"But I must ask, what is your interest in Steinfeld?"

"Actually it's personal. His wing attacked my squadron on several occasions and I need to question him on numerous points that may help further prosecution of the air war against Germany."

The man, whose right arm appeared to have been lost at the shoulder, sat back, his expression one of alarm.

"Major, we can't have any problems or abuse just to satisfy personal grudges."

Sean smiled, "It's nothing like that, I assure you."

Rudolph Steinfeld looked up as Sean entered the room. Behind the German officer a British military policeman stood, his eyes giving the American the once over.

Sean sat down opposite Steinfeld and looked at his former adversary.

"I wondered if you would come," Steinfeld said.

"How could I not?"

"You survived, who am I to you now?"

McGowan looked hard at the man sitting across from him.

"Twice you could have killed me and didn't. Why not? I need to understand."

Steinfeld laughed.

"I'm sorry, I will disappoint you. I don't understand myself. Perhaps I was simply tired of war."

His tone strident, McGowan snapped back, "We were all tired of the war, but you chose not shoot me down. Why?"

Steinfeld looked at him, his expression one of sadness and resignation.

"Perhaps too many good men had already died. I couldn't stop the killing, but those two times I could make sure that brave men didn't die. That may not make sense to you, it doesn't make sense to me when I think back on it. But at that moment I just couldn't pull the trigger."

Sean McGowan looked at the man who had been his enemy. He had fought for Germany and the Nazi regime was the enemy. They must be defeated and never allowed to rise again. What they had done to the world was past criminal. But this man was not his personal enemy. He was an honorable officer and someone who had flown into that terrible battle over Europe day after day after day. He is not my enemy anymore.

"I am being ordered back to headquarters," Sean said. "It's only twenty minutes by car from here."

Rudi listened without comment.

"Perhaps I can come and see you on occasion?"

Oberstleutnant Rudolf Steinfeld nodded. "I would like that."

Epilogue

Post war investigation by the Graves Registration Bureau discovered that on 18 June, 1944, the body of an American airman identified by dog tags as Sergeant Thomas Moore was found near the small town of Huven and buried by German authorities in a local cemetery.

The body of Technical Sergeant Larry Parr was recovered from the wreckage of USAAF B-17 serial number 43-0938 by a German work detail on 16 June, 1944. He was buried in the churchyard of Osterwolde.

In 1949, the remains of Tommy Moore were moved to the Allied Cemetery near Margarten, Holland, to be joined in 1950 by Larry Parr. The final count of Allied soldiers and airmen in the cemetery was to reach 8,301.

A frequent visitor to the cemetery, Doctor Tanna Hass continues to practice medicine in Holland. Her husband of fifteen years, retired Lieutenant Colonel Billy Hass, coaches soccer for the local boy's academy.

The remaining crew members of *Jezebel* were repatriated following the surrender of Germany in 1945 and all returned to the United States for out-processing. Only one of the surviving crewmen remained in the Air Force after the war.

Master Sergeant Anthony Michael Fortino rose through the ranks to the most senior enlisted grade, holding leadership positions around the world as the Air Force moved into the jet age, through the Korean War and finally became embroiled in South East Asia.

Master Sergeant Fortino was killed during a mortar attack on Pleiku Air Base, Republic of Viet Nam on the night of 5/6 January, 1967. At the time he was the command master sergeant of the 633rd Special Operations Wing of the United States Air Force.

Aubrey Rose did not follow John Forster to Australia. However, during B-24 training in Oklahoma, he met a young American girl, Donna Reed, who did follow him down under. After a full career in the RAAF, they retired to the coast, south of Melbourne.

Neuburg Air Base
West Germany
23 August 1961

Oberst Rudolf Steinfeld stood looking out a window of the temporary office he had occupied for the last month. Neuburg was the home of one of the newest units in the Federal German Republic's new Luftwaffe, Jagdgeschwader 74. Tomorrow, he would be taking command.

Such a strange road, he thought. His time in England, the end of the war followed by the horror of postwar Germany had made him wonder if life would ever return to normal. The Soviet Union had been the driving force behind the resurgence of the German economy and the fledgling air force. Former enemies had become allies in a very short time. The Marshall Plan and the Berlin Airlift had all helped erase some of the anger and pain from the American's aerial assault on Germany during the last war. Now the Luftwaffe was growing in strength to help defend the west from the dark empire that had been spawned from the ashes of the war. It had been a long road, but now he felt that the world was on the right course, as was he.

On his desk was a single picture of Karin. They had married in 1946 and their first child, Andrew, arrived in 1950 as they both struggled to make a new life in a Germany that was trying to rebuild from the ashes of war. But the west knew that the ability to deter the Soviet Union was going to take an effort by all of the victors of the war in Europe. While the North Atlantic Treaty Organization expanded, the logic of rearming West Germany was proposed and approved.

At the senior levels of what was now the United States Air Force, key officers of the Luftwaffe were identified to provide the leadership for this new free air force. Rudolf Steinfeld had been identified early and strongly endorsed by several highly decorated senior officers to assume one of those leadership roles.

Almost thirteen years after the end of the war, he was about to reassume the command of a fighter wing, now flying the swept wing F-84.

Looking out the window across the concrete parking apron he saw the wing's aircraft lined up in readiness for the next flying day. On the fuselage of each aircraft, the Iron Cross identified the aircraft as German, with heritage of excellence from the flamboyant World War One dogfighters to the brutal savagery of the aerial battle over Europe. He thought an addition he would make on taking command would be an orange tail flash, a remembrance of those terrible days when so many young men went out to battle and never returned. The memory of Bertie and Karl would always be with him and the desperate days flying out of Dortmund.

He had never thought that he would again wear a uniform or fly a German military aircraft. But at 43, he was flying one of the best jet fighters currently in service as a colonel commanding one of the three fighter wings in the new Luftwaffe.

"Herr oberst?"

Steinfeld turned to see Leutnant Hans Schmidt at the office door, a quizzical look on his face.

"Yes?"

"The operations officer is on the telephone. An American F-94 fighter is fifteen minutes from landing and according to the flight plan there is a code 9 aboard."

"An American major general? In an all-weather interceptor? That makes no sense."

"They thought you might know what was happening. Perhaps it has something to do with the change of command tomorrow?"

"Neuburg approach control, this is Air Force 4078 passing 12,000 feet. I have the field in sight. Request a visual approach to a full stop."

"Air Force 4078, roger. Altimeter is 29.98, contact the tower on 340.2."

Major General Randolph Mahr reached down and changed the UHF radio frequency as he retarded the throttles to idle on the jet.

"Neuburg tower, this is Air Force 4078, VFR passing ten thousand, field in sight. Requesting a straight in to a full stop."

"4078, roger. You are cleared number one, visual approach to runway zero niner, report on final with gear down and locked. Winds are currently down the runway at ten knots, altimeter 29.99."

"This is 4078, copy altimeter 29.99, wilco, and I have a request."

"4078, tower, go ahead with your request."

"Roger, please contact Oberst Steinfeld and let him know the orange tails are arriving."

There was a moment of silence on the tower frequency.

"4078, would you repeat that?"

Hans Schmidt knocked twice and pushed the door open.

"Herr oberst, there is a message from that aircraft with the code nine aboard."

Rudolph Steinfeld looked up from his desk.

"And what is that?"

"The aircraft wanted you to know that the orange tails are arriving."

The next commander of Jagdgeschwader 74 looked puzzled then he smiled.

"We shall drive down to operations, Hans. It seems there may be an old friend of mine in that aircraft."

The F-94 was designed for high speed/high altitude intercepts of Soviet bombers. Rudi had not seen one in person and the roar of the two jet engines did not resemble the throaty roar of the F-84 that he had come to know so well. A sleek fuselage with thin wings turned into the parking apron, and Rudi saw the bright helmets of the pilot and back seater moving as they picked up the German aircraft director and began following his signals. Several ground crewmen waited with wheel chocks and a portable fire bottle as the director brought the fighter to a stop in front of the operations building. In a standard and practiced routine, the wheels were chocked, canopy opened and the engines began to wind down.

A dark blue sedan crossed the ramp toward the aircraft as the pilot descended the boarding ladder.

Walking toward the aircraft, Rudi watched the operations duty officer approach the pilot and salute. Both men turned as Rudi came around the vehicle. Randy Mahr quickly returned Rudi's salute. The men shook hands warmly.

"Welcome to Neuburg, herr general," Rudi said.

Mahr smiled and said, "You didn't think we would miss the big day, Colonel Steinfeld?"

For a moment Rudi looked confused, he had thought that the Chief of Staff of the Fourth Allied Tactical Air Force might attend the ceremony, but what did Mahr mean by 'we'?

"It has been a long time, my friend."

Sean McGowan extended his hand to Rudi.

"It is good to see you as well, herr general. But what brings you to Europe?" Steinfeld knew that McGowan was a major general attached to the Strategic Air Command and stationed in the United States.

"Can you believe that my inspection tour just happened to coincide with your change of command?"

Steinfeld smiled at his friends. It had been a remarkable journey.

"And your beautiful wife let you come to Europe by yourself?"

Rudolf Steinfeld and Jamie McGowan had met at the end of the war. The two had become friends and Karin had gotten to know both of the McGowans as well during Sean's tour in Frankfort as part of the occupation.

"She would have given anything to be here, but too many kids to chase around the house."

"I've always said, fighter pilots make history, bomber pilots make babies," Rudi grinned at his friend.

"Depends on your priorities, my German friend."

In the private dining room of a local inn, the three aviators sat enjoying a round of very old brandy, the remnants of a memorable meal on the table in front of them.

"Are you sure you won't be in trouble with Karin?"

Rudi shook his head 'no.' "She is fully engaged with her mother and father. We will all be together tomorrow night after the ceremony. Will you be able to stay?"

"I don't feel my inspection can be completed until at least the day after," McGowan said, taking a drink of his brandy.

The men sat without talking, the mood of friendship strong, words not necessary.

After several minutes, Rudolph Steinfeld spoke up. "Do you think there will be another war?"

Mahr shrugged his shoulders.

"My dear oberst, that is above the understanding of simple airplane drivers. All we can do is be ready to fight it, if and when the damned politicians make a decision.

"Can we stop the Soviets?"

McGowan said, "Rudi, I don't know what the army can do. There are a hell of a lot of Soviet tanks across the border. But I do know that we now have the ability to destroy their homeland with our strategic bombers. Will they think it's worth the risk, who knows?"

"Sometime it seems like we are caught in a giant web," the German observed.

Mahr raised his glass, "To the web that entangles us all."

"So are there Soviet airmen sitting across the border, good men who would fight for their homeland, drinking vodka and wondering the same thing?"

Sean laughed. "That is the way of things, my friend. We are the pawns who fight the wars and die.

It has been that way since the dawn of time. All we can do is what we think is right and honorable."

Rudi took the bottle of brandy and refilled the glasses.

"Thank you for coming. And thank you for your support. I would not be taking command tomorrow had it not been for you two. The general told me as much."

My friend, Germany needs you," Mahr said. "They have always needed you and thank God you have been there."

Oberst Rudolph Steinfeld, former commander of Jagdgeschwader 9, holder of the Knight's Cross of the Iron Cross, an aerial ace with over 100 victories in air to air combat took a deep breath and raised his glass to his friends.

"To our fallen comrades."

The three men rose to their feet and raised their glasses in silence, their thoughts on so many who paid the ultimate price in the deadly sky.

Historical fiction adventure novels by John Schork:

DESTINY IN THE PACIFIC

Set in the first desperate year of the Pacific War, "Destiny in the Pacific" tells the story of Brian Michaels, a disgraced Naval Aviator. A promising career in shambles, his time in the Navy drawing to a close, Bryan is given a second chance following the attack on Pearl harbor. Just as that day changed the course of a nation, it did the same for Bryan. Fueled by anger at the loss of friends and inspired by words of Chester Nimitz, Bryan finds his destiny in the vast Pacific.

THE FLAMES OF DELIVERANCE

Terribly burned in the air war over Europe, the wealthy son of a New York banker discovers love, friendship and redemption as he painfully struggles to recover. Eventually returning to the air battle in Europe and the Pacific, Hank Mitchell finds the strength to overcome his scars and the conviction to do what must be done regardless of the personal cost.

THE KING'S COMMANDER

Following a pact between FDR and Churchill, Jack Stewart finds himself an American in the Royal Navy, tasked with learning the secrets of MI-6. Trying desperately to beat the Nazi's technological advancements, he forms an elite team that strikes deep into occupied Europe. From the back roads of France to the windswept English Channel, the young officer takes on the most difficult challenges of the war and builds a team that can defeat the Nazi war machine.

A JOURNEY OF HONOR

A strange series of events results in two men from opposite sides of the war being thrown together. One is a Commander in the Royal Navy, the other a Colonel in the German SS. But they join forces in an attempt to cripple Adolph Hitler's ability to launch a weapon that could change the course of the war. Parachuting into war-torn Europe, the two men not only prevent a devastating attack on England, but realize they have become friends and comrades.

THE FALKENBERG RIDDLE

As the most terrible war in history
approaches its bloody conclusion, the allies
and Soviet Union are already preparing for
the next. But there are secrets within the
collapsing capital of the Third Reich that
must never become public. A senior
German at the highest level possesses
knowledge which could devastate the world.
Jack Stewart leads his strike team deep into
the cataclysmic final battle of Berlin to
ensure that information never becomes
public.

THE WINDS OF BATTLE
The Journey of James Addington

Sent to sea as a young midshipman, James Addington, is the son of a British Admiral following in his father's footsteps. Born in the colonies, he sails from New York City in 1770 aboard H.M.S. Andromeda. Over the next three years, battling pirates and slavers, the young man matures into a loyal officer of the Royal Navy. But the terrible events of 1776 drag James back to the land of his birth. As a lieutenant in the frigate Challenger, he is a witness to the bloody Battle of Breed's Hill, as the fledging rebel army takes on the pride of the British Army. Stunned by what he sees, he knows the colonies will be forever changed. What he doesn't realize is that he will change along with them.

Falling in love with a young lady from Massachusetts, Addington finds himself immersed in a tangled web of conflicting loyalties and passions. Does he help crush the rebellion or does he fall victim to the lure of independence? His journey takes him from north to south in the colonies and across the Atlantic as captain of his own ship. From the Battles of Saratoga to Yorktown, he learns the price of friendship and loyalty as the fight for America's independence builds to a thundering climax.

The author's website :
http://www.johnschork.com
Contact the author at: john@johnschork.com

Format and graphic designs by
Jupiter Pixel Publishing, Jupiter, Florida
info@jupiterpixel.com

Printed in Great Britain
by Amazon